In Day of War, *Cliff Graham issues* [illegible] *life of King David and his mighty men, th*[illegible] *just a story about swords and shields. It's about real men who struggle with more than the enemy soldier before them. You will enjoy this book on many levels. I strongly recommend it.*

—Robert Whitlow, bestselling author of *The List* and *The Trial*

If you've never read the Bible or studied Judaic history, this is a fast-paced means of exploring that time period. If you've read the tales of David and his Mighty Men, then you are in for a treat. Graham fleshes out these stories, turning them into pulse-pounding battle scenes and excursions through ancient Israel. . . . Day of War *leaves us wanting more stories about these engaging characters. The Bible comes alive through these pages, while never sugarcoating violence or the struggle of the male gender.*

—Eric Wilson, *New York Times* bestselling author of *Fireproof, Haunt of Jackals,* and *Valley of Bones*

An enthralling and captivating story that captured me from start to finish. Extremely well written. Brutal and honest, thrilling and powerful.

—Grant Curtis, producer of the *Spider-Man* movie franchise

This book about Benaiah, an ancient warrior who ranks as one of Israel's great unsung heroes, is both captivating and inspiring. Cliff Graham does more than write words—he paints pictures. He does more than tell a story—he invites readers into one of the most amazing stories in Scripture.

—Mark Batterson, author of *In a Pit with a Lion on a Snowy Day*

Finally! A gritty, intense, and real portrayal of one of the most dynamic biblical characters of all time. The images sear into your brain like you're watching an IMAX movie. Day of War *grabbed me by the throat and would not release its grip until the last page. You don't read* Day of War, *you consume it.*

—David L. Cunningham, filmmaker
and director of *To End All Wars* and *The Path to 9/11*

They call it a war of biblical proportions for a reason! Cliff Graham brings history, faith, and fighting to life, all at the same time!

—Lt. Col. (ret) James Jay Carafano, Ph.D., director of
the Douglas and Sarah Allison Center for Foreign
Policy Studies, The Heritage Foundation

The time is now for a story like Day of War *to bring the Bible to life in a way that makes you want to pick up the Word of God.*

—Loren Cunningham, Founder, Youth with a Mission

COVENANT OF WAR

LION OF WAR SERIES

BOOK 2

CLIFF GRAHAM

ZONDERVAN

Covenant of War

This title is also available as a Zondervan ebook.
Visit www.zondervan.com/ebooks.

This title is also available in a Zondervan audio edition.
Visit www.zondervan.fm.

Requests for information should be addressed to:

Zondervan, *Grand Rapids, Michigan 49530*

Library of Congress Cataloging-in-Publication Data

Graham, Cliff.
Covenant of war / Cliff Graham.
p. cm. – (Lion of war ; bk. 2)
ISBN 978-0-310-33186-5 (softcover)
1. Bible. O.T.—History of Biblical events—Fiction. I. Title.
PS3607.R337C68 2012
813'.6—dc23 2011034164

Published in association with the literary agency of Alive Communications, Inc., 7680 Goddard Street, Suite 200, Colorado Springs, CO 80920. |
www.alivecommunications.com

Cover design: GiantKiller Pictures
Cover photography: Joel Grimes
Author Photo: Alden Dobbins
Map illustration: Ruth Pettis
Interior design: Katherine Lloyd, The DESK

Printed in the United States of America

13 14 15 16 17 18 19 /DCI/ 23 22 21 20 19 18 17 16 15 14 13 12 11 10 9 8 7 6 5 4 3 2

For Cassandra, LMT

This one is for David L. Cunningham,
who has been a tireless champion
fighting to see it through,
even during
the droughts

I am for peace, but when I speak, they are for war . . .

Psalm 120:7

AUTHOR'S NOTE

This book is intended to be accurate to the time of its setting. For that reason, it is extremely violent and deals with mature themes. Please use discretion when passing along to more sensitive readers.

Several names, places, and objects have been altered for the sake of clarity for modern readers. No cultural disrespect is intended, and any errors are my own.

COVENANT OF WAR

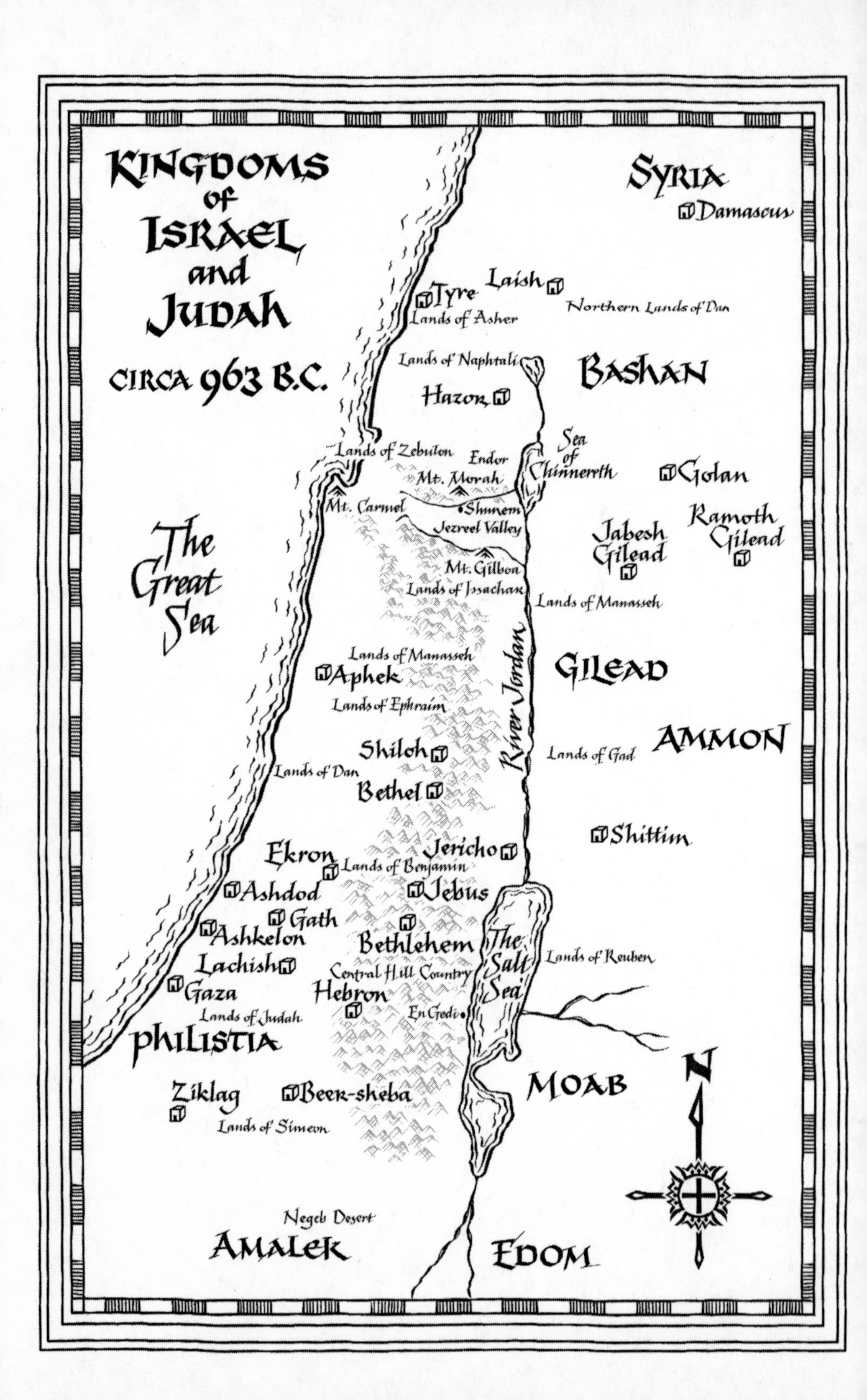
KINGDOMS of ISRAEL and JUDAH
CIRCA 963 B.C.
SYRIA
Damascus
Laish
Tyre
Northern Lands of Dan
Lands of Asher
Lands of Naphtali
BASHAN
Hazor
Sea of Chinnereth
Lands of Zebulon
Endor
Mt. Morah
Golan
Mt. Carmel
Shunem
Jezreel Valley
Ramoth Gilead
Jabesh Gilead
The Great Sea
Mt. Gilboa
Lands of Issachar
Lands of Manasseh
Lands of Manasseh
Aphek
GILEAD
Lands of Ephraim
River Jordan
AMMON
Shiloh
Lands of Gad
Lands of Dan
Bethel
Shittim
Ekron
Jericho
Lands of Benjamin
Ashdod
Jebus
Gath
Ashkelon
Bethlehem
The Salt Sea
Lands of Reuben
Lachish
Central Hill Country
Gaza
Hebron
En Gedi
Lands of Judah
PHILISTIA
N
MOAB
Ziklag
Beer-sheba
Lands of Simeon
Negeb Desert
AMALEK
EDOM

PROLOGUE

Clear, bright moonlight covered the land as four men, hiding in the trees lining the hilltop, studied the sleeping town. It was crisp and calm. The bustle of the day—merchants entering and leaving the gates, children sword fighting with branches, women chattering on their way to the washing stream—had ended an hour previously. Instead of the evening revelry common in the Hebrew villages, the people in this town were more focused, seemingly determined to get through their business and get indoors for the night.

The civil unrest must be making them cautious, David thought. He looked again at the distant roving sentries, pacing restlessly. He wondered if he would recognize any of them from better days.

One of his companions, shivering from the sudden chill, leaned close. "How many does Saul have here?"

"A thousand. Nothing we can do."

Josheb sighed. "Then why are we still here? Shouldn't we be leaving for the fortress? We aren't strong enough yet."

The leader nodded. "Just wanted to say good-bye."

"To who? The king? I didn't think you two were on good terms. Maybe that's just because he's hunting us down and trying to impale our heads on spikes."

"He wouldn't come near Bethlehem; so no, not him," David answered, then gestured toward a small clearing in the trees below them down the hill, near the city gate. "That."

"What is it?" asked one of the others.

"The purest, sweetest water in all the Lord's creation."

"I thought the well was inside the city gates."

"The main community well is. This one is the shepherd's well."

"They share it with the livestock?"

"No," the leader answered, "they keep it to themselves."

The three men next to the leader stared at the clearing, barely visible through the moonlit forest below. It was an open patch of stone-covered ground, overhung by long branches of sycamore. At the edge of the clearing were three small holes in the ground with rocks stacked around them. Dark water rippled on the surface of each. The city gate loomed close by.

"Why is it special?" said Shammah, crouched nearby.

"I used to watch sheep in these hills. While they were in the pens for the night, I would slip through the forest to that well and drink. The water was always cold and refreshing, no matter how hot the day had been. Always gave me something to look forward to. Refilled me. In many ways." He paused. "I hope it never goes dry."

His companions looked at one another, smirking.

"That is the sort of thing the men make fun of you for. Behind your back, of course," Eleazar said.

"What?"

"All the poetry, the singing, the deeper meanings."

David smiled. "As long as they stay loyal, I don't care what they laugh at."

A fifth man slowly crawled up next to them, careful to keep his profile low.

"Forest is clear of patrols. You should be able to move without being seen by the sentries if you stay in the woods."

"Thank you, Benaiah."

They listened to the night sounds a while longer. David gazed longingly at the town. His city, the roots of his youth. He could see the rocks near the gate where he'd learned to sling, and the sheep corrals, and the stump where the shepherds stood to give the shrill, unique cry that their sheep recognized.

The night was quiet and peaceful, and his thoughts wandered. David stared at the forest, thinking about when his companions first came to him.

They had approached the cave cautiously in the early morning mist, their sandals wet from the moist grasses covering the hillside. Every bead of dew glistened and twinkled as the sun rose over the distant purple mountains to the east. It was quiet, but they must have known they were being watched.

Josheb held up his hand when they reached the entrance of the cave. He carried a small pack over his shoulder, as did the other two. Each of the three fought with multiple weapons, and now they held them patiently as Josheb stepped forward.

"If an arrow flies out of that cave at me, I will catch it in mid-flight and kill the man who shot it," Josheb said.

A few moments passed, then David emerged from inside, and as he did, others crawled out of various nooks and clefts scattered around the field, all holding farming tools or rusty swords cracked from overuse. The leader of the three new warriors stood his ground as David faced them from the cave entrance.

"Peace to you, old friends. Tell these men who you are."

"Josheb-basshebeth, chief of the Three. This is Eleazar the son of Dodai, and this is Shammah the son of Agee the Hararite."

There was murmuring among the men emerging from the woods and caves. A few pointed. Others watched warily. Some had been in Saul's armies and had heard of the feats of these men, but the foreigners were staring skeptically.

"They have heard of you and your fathers," David said.

Josheb bowed his head at the compliment. "We have come to join you, David son of Jesse."

David glanced around at everyone on the hillside, then walked out of the cave to stand in front of Josheb. He spoke so that only the three could hear. "We have been here for a week. These men all came and found me."

"Your brothers?" Eleazar asked.

"They're out scouting the hills. My father is on his way." David paused. "The Three? That's what you are calling yourselves now?"

"I wanted to call us something like 'Yahweh's Blade' or 'Yahweh's Fury,' but Shammah thought that might offend Yahweh if we were to presume to use his name. You can name us whatever you like so long as you keep Shammah's feelings in mind," Josheb said. Shammah scowled at him.

David suppressed a grin. "Other than my brothers, none of these men has ever fought as armies are supposed to fight, with discipline and order. But they are dangerous and violent men and won't shy away when it comes time to spill blood. Thieves, criminals, outcasts, foreigners. I need good leaders to help me train them."

"I know. That's why we came," Josheb replied. "Saul hunts us now just as he hunts you. The three of us refused to say that you were a traitor and deserving of death. Saul ordered us killed. We didn't agree, so we left. We assumed you would need an army."

David nodded, wishing he could embrace them immediately at this act of loyalty. He looked at Eleazar. Loud enough for the men on the hillside around them to hear, he said, "Your father is a man of war and a mighty leader. Are you?"

"Yes, lord."

He looked at Shammah.

"Your father followed Yahweh, the God of Jacob, better than any

I have known besides the seer Samuel. Do you follow him the same as your father?"

"By Yahweh's great mercy, I do, lord."

David nodded. Then, quietly again, "Your wives?"

"Eleazar and I have them in a nearby village awaiting our word. Shammah, as you remember, still has no woman because his manhood shrivels when they come near."

David had to hide his smile as Shammah swung at Josheb.

"These men won't respect me if you say things like that," Shammah said.

"They'll respect your ability," Josheb said. "And half of them are probably uncircumcised, so why would you care?"

"They will need to see a demonstration or they will not follow you," David said.

"Show us some Philistines, and we will give a demonstration," said Josheb.

"One day—but not yet. We still need them."

"*Need* the Philistines? For what?" Eleazar asked.

"Just for a while. I will explain later. But first you need to show these men something that will demonstrate that you deserve my trust and their loyalty, something that will make them love you and be willing to follow you into Sheol."

"What could we possibly do that would gain that kind of trust?"

"They are simple men. Do something amazing and they will follow you."

Josheb nodded. "Then we need your best javelin throwers, slingers, and archers."

David studied him. "Many men can avoid a javelin thrown at them by a skilled thrower when they know it is coming. Same with a stone or an arrow."

"All at one time?" Josheb asked, grinning.

David looked at Eleazar and Shammah to see if this was a joke, but they only smiled. He ran his hand through his auburn hair. "If you die, the blame is on your head before Yahweh."

"Agreed. You are absolved of guilt, lord."

David shook his head, but inwardly he was eager to see what would happen. He gestured to a group of men standing nearby.

"Three will throw the javelins. Three archers from the tribe of Benjamin will draw arrows. Two more will sling with me."

The Three and their attackers all took their positions. The men gathered on the hillside called out taunts and whistled at the three warriors, who now stood side by side several lengths apart. David organized the attackers.

"If Yahweh has willed that these men should join us, perhaps they will withstand our assault," he said to all present.

Josheb, Eleazar, and Shammah crouched low and each raised his sword in a protective posture. Then David shouted the signal, and instantly arrows flew, javelins were thrown, and stones spun toward the three men.

And everyone present saw two things happen at once: the flash of blades against the morning sun and the splintering of arrows and javelins.

Then Eleazar and Shammah were standing in front of Josheb with swords drawn, panting from exertion, while Josheb was holding the three stones that had been slung at them. David was the first to understand, and he shouted a war whoop.

Eleazar and Shammah had destroyed the arrows and javelins in midflight while Josheb caught the stones with his bare hands.

Now there were cheers, and David embraced each of them. The others at the cave chanted their names. But as David leaned close, he whispered into their ears, "Sleep with one eye open, because they will slit your throat if they get the chance."

The weeks passed, then the months, and David remembered the endless days of training and drilling and weaponry, and how the three warriors never lost heart. Just like in the old days when he led Saul's armies, he put himself and them through everything a man could bear, and they withstood it, encouraging those in their command to go the full distance with them. The new members of the army and the foreigners had never experienced anything like it. Running up hills for endless hours, leaping over logs rolled down the mountainside toward them, the times around the campfires trying to sort out who had offended whom with what remark. And the breaking of the laws of Yahweh by some Hebrews, and the mocking of it by the foreigners.

Eventually David had to move his father and brothers away from the cave to keep them safe from the ever-increasing patrols of Saul. His band's families were hidden in the villages and visited at night. Some of the original band deserted, but the Three and those loyal to them remained, and David's army grew in size and skill, preparing for the day they would be used. David had embraced them one by one as they streamed in, often angry or hopeless, but he did not ask their full story unless they were prepared to share it. Each man came in his own way.

Later that night as his companions dozed, David stood and walked down the hill, moving noiselessly and leaving no trace. His thick hair swirled with the night breeze as he walked, his wool cloak hanging loosely over his shoulders, disguising the unusually large iron blade strapped across his back with leather belts. His sandals were new, a gift from his men purchased from a merchant and made of the finest leather, so their slight squeaking as they broke in was the only mark of his movement. He would not have worn them on such a journey, but the eager and proud faces of his warriors had weakened his resolve.

An owl went quiet as he walked beneath it, humming softly to himself. He was close enough to the city garrison now that he could see the flicker of campfires and the Hebrew soldiers sitting around them. There was occasional laughter. Every army is the same, he thought. He wondered if he had ever commanded any of the men in the Bethlehem garrison.

At the edge of the clearing, David remained in the shadows of the trees and watched the moonlit grass near the water. There was no movement; no sentries guarded this place, and he praised his God that it was still unknown to outsiders, as though divinely shielded.

He stepped forward again, pulling the great Philistine sword out from under his cloak, and as he approached the edge of the small well, he laid the weapon next to it. The blade was chipped, scuffed, and in need of reforging, but he would never give it up.

The dark water reflected his face as he leaned over it, its surface as smooth as a burnished silver plate. David touched it with his lips, and as he drank the water, his throat prickled in cool refreshment. He would know the taste of this water anywhere, a taste no other well could match—the taste of his home. As boys, he and his friends had lain around it talking of becoming great warriors.

His father had been the one to show it to him when he was small. It was one of the few memories David had of spending time alone with his father.

David cupped the water and splashed his face, relishing it as it ran through his hands into his hair and beard.

David lowered his head back to the water, closed his eyes, and immediately he was back in the cave again, and Saul was there, only paces away. All he had to do was strike him and kill him on the spot. The Three urged him, Abishai and the others urged him. It would be fast and the kingdom would be his.

But it was not yet time. He couldn't betray Jonathan like that, couldn't rush Yahweh.

While Saul's army continued to hunt them, David's band raided Amalekite villages for the Philistine king and stayed away from Saul, who was slowly ruining their land. There was battle, and death, and murder, and betrayal. David had many chances to take the throne.

But it was not yet time.

David breathed slowly between drinks. He kept his lips on the surface to savor it. The night was still and calm. Not even a breeze stirred across the heavy boughs of cypress and pine. He shivered.

Something was close.

You do not have what it takes to lead them.

The voice was nothing more than a whisper in his soul. His skin prickled. He raised his head from the water of the pool and looked across the well.

The dark figure was there, towering over him and blocking the moon.

David took several breaths. He knew this figure. It was the one he had seen in the mountains as a boy, the one that had sent the bear and the lion, the one that told him to slay the king in the shadows of the cave, the one that brought despair like a storm.

It hunted him like the king hunted him.

David spoke, his voice shaking. "In the name of my God, the commander of the armies of heaven and the source of the covering, be gone."

You do not have what it takes to lead them.

David felt his knees weaken. He closed his eyes, concentrating. "Adversary, in the name of the Lord my God, Yahweh, who rules from the heavens and rests his feet upon the earth, be gone from here!"

You do not have what it takes to lead them.

David tried to speak. His voice was lost, hidden somewhere.

Then he felt a hand on his shoulder. A strong, firm hand that had seen the centuries and knew the secrets of the presence of Yahweh, and David wanted to cry out in gratitude.

The Lord of Heaven, the God of your salvation, will cover you in the day of war.

This voice was quiet like a whisper as well, but it held pure and clear in his spirit, more powerful than the shadow facing him. Then the hand left his shoulder, and David looked across the well once more.

He saw nothing.

He turned his head to find the voice behind him, but his helper was gone as well.

Lord, God of my salvation, you have covered me in the day of war.

David's heart was weak. The melody of the song was too soft to come through his lips, but he sung the lyrics in his soul.

Lord, God of my salvation, you have covered my head in the day of battle.
I will not fear the arrow by day, or the terror of night.
I am weary with moaning, my bed covered with tears,
but the Lord has heard my cries and my prayer.

After a moment of worship, feeling his courage come back to him, David poured another handful of water over his head and watched the silver trickle flow down his cloak. He adored this well and savored every precious drop from it. He lowered his lips to the surface as though to kiss it again. The water was pure and sweet, filtered by the black depths of the earth. The well of his youth.

He stood, turned, and walked away, back to his men, his heart heavy but his path clear before him.

In the distance came a sound like thunder, but as he listened, he realized that no storm was coming.

Predators.

The roar of a lion echoed up the mountainside and across the dark lands, as though calling to him.

PROLOGUE

▲▲▲

It has been two years since the battle of Mount Gilboa.

The land is divided. The tribes in the north are loyal to Saul's son Ishbosheth. The tribe of Judah has recently acclaimed the warlord David as its ruler.

Ishbosheth is a weak man, and General Abner, a Gilboa survivor and commander of the dead king Saul's forces, rules the north. He has managed to drive out the Philistine armies from most of the tribal lands.

It is the first month of the campaign season.

Part One

ONE

Eleazar wiped sweat from his forehead and studied the line of men streaming toward the bank of the pool. This pool, over which much blood was about to be shed, was the water source for the town of Gibeon nearby, and also for much of the region. It was wide, and in the spring it filled to the brim. It was the most strategically important water site in the central hill country of the lands of the Israelites, and that is why men armed for battle were now gathered there.

There were hundreds of men. Eleazar had difficulty counting them because they constantly shifted position. This, he knew, was being done deliberately because their commander wanted to disguise their size. This could only mean that their commander was experienced and competent. Moving troops without standard formations was a good way to hide the size of the force.

Eleazar clenched his jaw. Surely the commander for whom he scanned the enemy forces would not be leading a simple border-scouting company. His presence there was both dangerous and unnecessary—unless he knew he could not trust his own men, just as David did not trust Joab, currently standing on Eleazar's left.

"See him?" asked Shammah quietly, sliding a pouch from his side to his front.

"No," said Joab.

"He might not be there," Eleazar said.

"Abner would not miss a chance to take new ground. He is there," Joab replied, his eyes darting up toward the stone-covered ridge near the pool. "He might be scouting from higher up, but that would be unlike him. He will want to be in the middle of this."

Eleazar wiped his forehead, irritated. He was not a tall man, but he had a powerful chest and arms that were tightly knotted with muscle and twitched with nervous energy. Like the other warriors, his hair and beard were cut shorter than most men for freedom of movement in close fighting. His tunic was light and short, reaching only to his thighs. His back was crisscrossed with weapon scabbards.

His two companions in battle, Josheb and Shammah, were as different from one another as an olive from an ox. Josheb was the leader, slender and calm, quick with his wit and his blades. He possessed both blazing passion and calm contemplation, depending on the need. Despite his unassuming and ordinary physical appearance, his feats on battlefields and training arenas were so legendary that scribes had approached him about recording them. Josheb frequently sparred with entire companies—by himself. He moved so fast and had such endless reserves of physical stamina that to contain him was akin to containing a stampeding herd.

But he was best known among the fighting men for his laugh. Josheb knew well the value of humor to keep men moving when all hope seemed lost. If there was a laugh to be had at the expense of someone else, Josheb never failed to exploit it, and his most frequent target was Shammah.

Shammah was the largest and most physically imposing man in their ranks. His weapons were so heavy that only he could carry them. Somber, devoted to the Law of the God of Jacob, he was awkward and ill at ease when speaking to others—especially women. Even when presented daughters as war prizes he shied away and refused to marry them, offending many patriarchs in the process, much to David's annoyance and Josheb's endless ridicule.

The men considered him odd. He prayed much like David did, out loud and with everyone watching. He fell asleep at random hours of the day, sometimes even while standing up. His demeanor made it easy to overlook his extraordinary strength, both physical and spiritual.

They were known as the Three—the deadliest of all of the Lion of Judah's fighters.

"Maybe Abner will listen," said Josheb.

Eleazar nodded. The bloodshed must stop. Not even the most savage of tribal men, men such as Joab, wanted war between the house of Saul and the house of David to last forever. The bond of kinship that bound the tribes was nearly gone as it was. Early in Saul's reign there had been a brief period of eased tensions among the twelve tribes, but since the old king's death, the country had fractured between those northern tribes loyal to Saul and his line and the southern tribe of Judah with its new ruler, David. Neither liked the other, but all knew that disunity would eventually mean certain defeat at the hands of their mutual enemies.

The troops across the pool began to sit in ranks along the bank of the water, demonstrating a semblance of order for the first time as section leaders began to organize their men. There appeared to be about six hundred men with weapons, not counting their supply and logistics troops unseen at the rear.

Eleazar looked at their own force. Forty-seven of them. Good men, most of them. Joab was commanding the small force, but

Eleazar, Shammah, and Josheb had been sent by David to keep watch over his nephew.

Three sons of David's sister Zeruiah were here—Joab, Abishai, and Asahel. Joab was a capable leader—a brilliant strategist and brave warrior. But he was also vain and easily angered. Abishai, however, was respected by the Three. He was silent, brave, and humble, a stark contradiction to his brother Joab. Eleazar liked him almost as much as Josheb and Shammah.

But Asahel, Zeruiah's youngest, had every poor quality of Joab's and none of Abishai's admirable ones. He was foolish, pushed to heights of arrogance by his exceptional physical abilities. Asahel was the fastest runner Eleazar had ever seen, and his capacity for endurance during training sessions was seemingly endless.

The soldiers across the pool crouched together along the bank in a mass of wool cloaks and weapons. Even from this distance, it was clear that there were no men of Gilead, nor men of Ashur. Ephraimites, the largest of the northern tribes and the one most likely to participate in a maneuver such as this, were nowhere to be seen.

There was, in fact, only one tribe present, and this concerned Eleazar so much that he wondered if they should withdraw before anything tragic happened.

The men facing them were Benjamites.

Benjamin, the smallest tribe, was also the lineage of the dead king Saul. It had been hoped by those in Judah that the Benjamites would defect to David. If the tribe of the former king changed its alliances because Saul's son Ishbosheth was an ineffective and weak ruler, then the other northern tribes might follow suit.

This had not yet happened.

Eleazar and the rest of David's force were crouched among the rocks and spread out to give the appearance of size, hoping to fool the Benjamites into believing that they were just the scouting party of a larger force.

"Why hasn't he stepped out yet?" asked Eleazar.

"He's looking for David," replied Josheb. "He will come out soon enough when he realizes it's only us."

"David stopped coming on scouting missions last year. Abner knows that."

Eleazar blinked. He watched Joab from the corner of his eye. *Wish David were here now.*

The pool became quiet. Insects chirped. A few men cleared their throats. There were no taunts, none of the usual jeering or clanking as fighting men readied themselves. Neither side wanted to be standing opposite other Hebrews. And yet here they were.

"Who else do you see?" asked Joab.

"Baanah the Benjamite is to the right. Behind the archers. If he is here, then Rechab is here as well. Seems like an awful lot of archers," said Shammah, squinting.

"They're all archers. They are Benjamites."

"It looks like they have other weapons as well. Abner has been training them."

"None of those men look like they have seen battle," said Josheb.

Eleazar nodded. While David's warriors were gazing calmly and awaiting orders, the men from the north were clearly nervous. They were quiet, but hands were shifting and throats clearing, revealing anxiety. Commanders, still standing while their troops sat, gripped bows and sword hilts tight.

"They do look green," Eleazar said.

"Most of Abner's army was destroyed at Gilboa. Of course they're green," said Joab.

"But Abner's army has been fighting Philistine armies all season. Surely some of these men fought in those battles. And they must know how much they outnumber us," said Shammah.

Eleazar replied, "You're too humble. Didn't you see the look on that boy's face as we were coming into Gibeon when he heard who we were? If people in the villages have heard the 'mighty deeds of the Lion's men,' how much more so the army?"

"Abner's veterans might still be patrolling the valleys in case of a Philistine invasion. These might be all he has," Joab said.

Eleazar closed his eyes and let the sun's warmth calm him. Gibeon was disputed territory, strategically important because of its well on the trading route. He shook his head, raked his fingers through his beard. Joab would not relinquish the ground. Neither would Abner.

Hebrew sons would die this day.

TWO

Across the pool, among the ranks of fighters holding slings and bows and covered by cloaks to disguise the armor that would give away their rank, two men were staring through the flies and hot afternoon haze. The soldiers around them, following their orders, sat along the bank as the officers debated their next move.

"Do you see him yet?" Abner asked under his breath. His thick beard flowed down from his collar, tucked under the cloak. That would give away who he was as well, for all knew his beard. He did not trim it for the war season as others did. It would have shamed the memory of his father, a great and respected man.

The aide shook his head. "I see Joab and Abishai and their younger brother Asahel. Zeruiah's sons never disguise themselves. And neither does the son of Jesse. If he were there, we would see him."

Abner cursed. He did not want to negotiate with Joab.

"A scouting party," Abner said. "Fifty of his men. Yahweh be with us."

"You are nervous, lord?"

Abner did not answer.

"We have six hundred men who draw weapons with us. We could overrun them in moments," the aide said.

"Not these men," Abner said. He rubbed his temples. The other warriors might be with David. They would not need many to crush us, he thought.

He shook his head and chuckled. One day he would need to leave this sort of thing for younger men.

"Come. Negotiations," Abner said, standing up. The bewildered aide stood as well.

"Negotiations, lord? Shouldn't we be able to dictate terms to them?"

Abner pulled off the wool cloak that had been disguising his armor—no need to hide anymore. He stepped through the ranks of his men, who scrambled to get out of his way, bowing their heads slightly in respect as he passed. He knew that he was an intimidating presence—larger than any of his men, with a huge chest and heavy arms from years of combat and a vast beard spilling over his royal armor.

When Abner arrived at the edge of the pool, the aide raised his arm. Across the water, the man they recognized as Joab raised his own arm. The truce finalized, Abner moved around the pool, his aide following.

One of the Israelite troops spoke up, his voice thin with anxiety. "Will we have to fight them, lord?"

Abner stopped and turned to him. "How would you perform if we did?" he asked, grinning. "Who is your father?"

The soldier, a young man with wiry hair and a frightened face, said, "Besha of Shechem."

Abner nodded. "You will do fine. I know your father. Hard man. The sons from his loins would be hard men as well."

"But these are the Lion's men, lord. They say that merely one of them could destroy an entire army."

"They are Hebrews just like you," said Abner patiently. He knew his aide would be wondering why he was taking the time to engage this lowly soldier while the commander of their enemy's army was making his way toward them. The aide, though, knew nothing about leading men.

The eyes of the troops around Abner kept darting toward Joab as he approached. They were frightened, he could tell. As well they should be.

"We are going to negotiate the control of the route near the pool with them. I do not want to fight my Hebrew brethren any more than you do, even if they are those smelly Judah rats who never bathe and shriek like women." Everyone laughed. "But we will do what we have to do. Be strong," Abner said.

Abner left the group and walked toward the approaching figures of Joab and his aide. He did not recognize the aide but saw that he carried a pike, a sickle sword, a war club, and a small iron-studded shield.

More than one weapon. So this was no mere aide.

Joab halted a few paces away. The other warrior nodded in greeting. Abner nodded back, then reached across and clasped Joab by the shoulders. He placed two kisses on the sides of Joab's face. It was a gesture of truce, but more importantly, it demonstrated to all of the carefully observing soldiers on both sides that peace was the objective.

Joab consented to the gesture, but his manner was stiff. Abner smiled.

"How is your family, Joab?"

"Well. How is yours, Abner?"

Abner sighed but remained smiling. "Fairly well. My nephew was cursed by Yahweh as king and killed by uncircumcised pagans, and his remaining son is a weak fool, but other than that things are fine. How are we going to avoid slaughtering one another?"

He saw Joab glance past him toward the Israelite soldiers.

"Your men are green," said Joab.

"My veterans are on the frontier holding off the Philistines ... alone." He had measured the insult to David carefully before speaking it. Better to not make Joab angry, but he needed to communicate how urgent it was that they put aside differences and repel the pagans.

The warrior standing next to Joab spoke for the first time. "I'm certain you've trained these well. I look forward to killing Philistines with them one day."

Abner tipped his head slightly at the compliment. "I apologize for not knowing your name, warrior. I know I will have heard of your deeds as soon as I learn it, though."

"Eleazar son of Dodai," the man replied graciously. "I served in Saul's armies under David when you were also a commander. You may have known my father. Your own deeds need no introduction. It is an honor to be in your presence."

Abner felt a catch in the back of his throat. He knew the name very well, but he did not intend to show it. "Indeed, Eleazar. I look forward to hearing the tales of your spear and killing Philistines with you as well."

Eleazar held out his arm, which Abner clasped.

Joab frowned. "You know he will come for the throne, Abner. He would welcome you and your men if you joined us."

"Saul's line still exists. They are my family as well. David will butcher them," Abner said.

Eleazar shook his head. "He made a covenant with Jonathan to allow his line to survive. We could end this today. No blood."

Abner had considered it. David and Jonathan had been closer than brothers for many years. But he also knew that the more contentious tribes would never allow David on the throne, and they would refuse to believe that his intent toward them was not hostile. The dispute between Judah and the northern tribes was too old and too deep. Eventually one side would have to defeat the other. Only then could they turn their attention to crushing Philistia; something that Abner wanted desperately. Ever since Gilboa, he had dreamed of annihilating more of their armies and capturing their women.

But above all, he did not want to fight Eleazar son of Dodai and the other two undoubtedly nearby.

Abner shook his head. "You and I both know that these men will not believe that. David has broken his word before, and I have no reason to believe he won't do it again. All of these men—" he gestured toward his army—"might accept him, as they are Benjamites. But they are pawns, Joab. They are terrified of what would happen if Judah were to control them. Ephraim, Manasseh, and the other tribes will not tolerate Judah on the throne, and they would view Benjamin as the traitor. Why don't you persuade your chief to acknowledge Ishbosheth? I would convince the king to allow David to rule the south as his governor, and you have my word that you will not be interfered with."

He glanced at Eleazar. The man's muscles were hard and covered with battle scars. His campaign cloak was extremely dirty, as if he had been scouting for many days. Abner wondered where the other two were. Eleazar of the Three. *Yahweh help us.*

No compromise would come, Abner knew. But he could tell that Joab and Eleazar also wanted to delay the inevitable a while longer. Perhaps they would all look back on this and joke about it one day while sitting around a campfire, the blood of dead Philistines staining their garments.

Eleazar said, "Unfortunately, general, that will not happen. David will not be ruled anymore. When Saul died, there was nothing left for him to wait for. Yahweh has willed it. Please, for the sake of your men, accept our offer."

For a moment, Abner thought it odd that Eleazar had taken over the negotiating instead of Joab. Who was in charge? This could be a valuable insight into David's command structure. He would ponder it later. Then he thought again about the tremendous danger he and his men were in.

"There might be a way to settle this without spilling too much Israelite blood," Abner said.

"Say it," replied Eleazar eagerly.

"Twelve of mine, twelve of yours. Our best men. No weapons, only sparring. The winner will take the pool."

Joab turned toward Eleazar and gave a slight jerk of his head, indicating that he wanted to confer. They stepped a short distance away, their backs to him.

Abner's own aide leaned close. "Odd, isn't it, lord? That Joab allows the man to speak to him in that manner."

"The man is not his subordinate. That's one of the Three."

The aide paled. "I had hoped those were only rumors."

"As did I."

"But do you believe Joab would allow anyone else to rival his authority on the field?"

"Only if David ordered it. David is the only one Joab fears. Although if any of the stories about the Three are true, he might consider fearing this Eleazar as well. I knew his father. Good man." Abner paused to take a drink from his water skin. "Joab would want to stay in David's favor, but spies claim that Joab is gathering his own following in Judah. They need each other."

"His own following?"

"David has been trying to befriend all of the tribal leaders. The tribe of Judah is uncomfortable with this because they want their prized son to rule over all of the northern tribes with a strong hand.

I hear Joab has been encouraging this and has many followers," Abner said.

Joab and Eleazar had apparently reached an agreement, because both were now facing Abner.

"Twelve against twelve it is, then," said Joab.

"The winner takes the pool?" asked Abner.

"The winner takes the pool."

Abner nodded, grateful for the compromise. "Before we part, could you at least tell me why David himself did not come?" he asked.

Eleazar answered, "Join us and you will know all of his purposes."

Abner turned on his heels and gestured for the aide to follow him. As they walked back to their troops in silence, he wondered what it would be like to wage war if his army contained men like Eleazar. He wished David would stop his rebellion—and wished his own king were not so weak. A strong leader like David attracted men like Eleazar, men who could turn the tide of battle by themselves.

He wanted to feel hopeful that open war would not begin on this day. If it did, he and his troops would be crushed despite their numbers.

THREE

Eleazar followed Joab back toward David's men. It took all of his patience not to lose his temper. He did his best to show Joab respect in front of the other soldiers, since it was important for the troops to respect their leader.

But when the two of them had been discussing Abner's proposal for the twelve-on-twelve match, Eleazar had spoken bluntly. Joab had not wanted to agree to the contest, preferring to seize the initiative and force the attack, but Eleazar had convinced him otherwise. It was necessary, Eleazar had argued, to keep good relations with as many of the Israelites as possible, since they did not want to be fighting rebellions year after year when David became king over the entire country. The match would be a good way to win the field, spare Hebrew blood, and encourage many of the young Benjamite troops across the pool to join them later.

When he reached Josheb and Shammah at the water's edge, he said to Josheb, "You should have been with him. You're our leader."

"I don't trust my mouth around Joab. Might say something that would make him attack me, and then I'd have to kill him in front of the northerners. And Shammah doesn't know how to talk."

Shammah scowled as he leaned on his longbow. He opened his mouth to reply, then exhaled and scowled again.

Eleazar had not noticed the bow before. Shammah had a way of producing weapons out of nowhere, but this one looked Assyrian, built by a master from a blend of wood and horn. Most bows in the ranks of the Hebrews were simply a spry piece of wood with sheep's gut strung from end to end. The Thirty, David's elite company of fighters, had Philistine bows, but none as beautiful as this one.

Josheb noticed him gazing. "I was just telling Shammah that it must be nice not having a wife. You can get expensive weapons. What did Abner say?"

"Single contest, twelve against twelve. Sparring. Joab doesn't want us involved because their men need to feel they have a chance."

"Sparring?" said Josheb, surprised. "How did Joab allow that?"

"Joab doesn't want the ritual killing of his brethren any more than we do," said Shammah.

"In any event," Eleazar said, "I don't trust him."

"Agreed," Josheb said. "I want the three of us down there to make sure it doesn't turn into something more serious."

Shammah tugged at his beard. "It would be bad for those troops in battle," he said.

Eleazar nodded. "Abner didn't say it, but I think he recognized my name. They don't wish to fight."

They stood quietly, watching Abner and Joab confer with their troops. The Benjamites across the pool were talking and pointing again. Eleazar realized they were pointing at them.

"Must have figured out who we were."

"We're the only three standing apart from the others. We need to think of a better name. Something more terrifying than 'the Three,'" Josheb said.

"I like our name," Shammah said.

Eleazar rubbed the back of his stiff neck. During the night his head had slipped off the bedroll and he'd slept with it bent at an awkward angle. "I would love to know Benaiah's thoughts about all this."

"As would I," Josheb said. "But if he were here, Joab would be even more irrational than he already is."

"Where is Benaiah?" asked Eleazar.

"In Philistia with Keth. Making the kings feel comfortable."

"Do you think he gets tired of the traveling? Hard to be David's bodyguard when he's always gone."

"No choice. He and Keth are the best with foreigners. Benaiah spent time with the Egyptians, and Keth was a Philistine mercenary."

Shammah turned. "I never knew Keth was with the Philistines."

"I didn't either until Benaiah mentioned it not long ago. Easy to understand why he kept it a secret. Walking into David's camp with tales of being paid in Philistine gold to kill Hebrews would tend to make one unpopular."

"Good man. Beautiful wife. Did her father ever make his peace with her marrying a foreigner?"

"It's hard not to like Keth. Although I think her father would prefer that he go by Uriah rather than his pagan Hittite name."

"I think he feels as though he is still unworthy to have a Hebrew name," Shammah said.

"Hopefully we'll see them soon." Eleazar said. It was understood by all of David's elite troops that the less they knew about one another's movements the better. Each would be sent here or there for purposes known only to their leader. If one of them was captured, he would be unable to give the complete overview of David's movements. The Thirty were rarely ever in one place together; their appearances all over the kingdom kept the population uneasy.

Across the pool, twelve Benjamite fighters had been selected and were standing in the clearing awaiting their opponents. They had stripped to the waist and wrapped their tunics around their hips. These were obviously the choice warriors among the Israelite ranks, their bodies shaped by well-defined muscles and marked by scars from previous battles. They stretched their arms and legs, jumping up and down.

"Joab is untrustworthy," Shammah said, cracking his knuckles.

"Nevertheless, we have to wet-nurse him for David's sake," Josheb said.

Joab had been conferring with his brothers, but now he walked through their troops, his head sweeping back and forth, searching for the fighters who would represent them. One by one, he pointed, calling them out.

"He's picking the new men. Do you know them?" Eleazar asked Josheb.

"Just what I've gathered since we have been out on patrol. They keep to themselves. They paid close attention to their *abir* instruction, though, so this should be easy for them."

The *abir* was the ancient fighting method of the Hebrew tribes that the Thirty had mastered, instructed by the Three. Josheb had studied it as a boy from the old scrolls his father had kept; then he taught it to the other two. It was based on the movements of the animals in their lands: the lion, the bear, the eagle, and others.

Joab had appointed twelve men, and now they were assembling at the front of their lines and preparing themselves.

Joab strode toward the Three's position. He spoke under his breath so the troops could not hear him.

"You three need to be available in case something goes wrong."

"Nothing will go wrong unless your troops stir up trouble," Eleazar said.

"You trust Abner to keep his word?" Joab asked.

"Tell me the real reason you don't want us in there, Joab," Josheb said calmly. Their troops were watching this conversation. Things were tense enough as they were, with multiple tribes of Hebrews, foreigners, and mercenaries patched together in their ranks.

Joab said, "Trust me."

Eleazar studied Joab. But his face betrayed nothing.

"Fine, Joab," Josheb said. "Use your men. But don't change the arrangement again without telling me."

Joab left.

Eleazar walked to his pack, exasperated. He pulled out a lump of hard bread and ate it, then began to rub handfuls of dust onto the handle of his pike. It had been wrapped tight with strips of wool to prevent slippage from perspiration, but like other warriors, he frequently powdered his weapons with dust, an extra precaution.

Shammah, watching him quietly, said, "You don't expect this to go as planned."

"No, I don't."

FOUR

Abner held his weapon, a sickle sword with a long, hooked curve, against his chest. He could never watch a battle unfold without something to grip. The iron sword was old and had needed multiple forgings just to remain intact—not ideal for any soldier, especially those of his rank, but necessary in these times of iron scarcity. The sword was the only weapon he had used since the Gilboa battle, and he liked it, wise or not. Now that he was getting older, he was more content to let Yahweh determine if he were to die on the field of battle and less inclined to fret over weapons.

The warriors he'd chosen for the contest were good men, some of his few remaining battle veterans. Seeing Eleazar among David's men had caused Abner to conclude that the pool, although it was an important strategic water point, was not worth the risk of a great many more deaths. His troops would not prevail in open battle against David's men. And he did not want to risk a debilitating decline in morale if his men should lose confidence in him as their leader.

A circle had been carved into the dirt by the edge of the pool bank. The troops who would be fighting were gathered inside its perimeter, stretching arms and torsos. Each man from either side had stripped off his tunic and wrapped it around his waist, muscles gleaming with sweat in the hot midday sun. They spat nervously. Flies swarmed their exposed flesh.

Crowding the outside of the circle were the designated twenty troops from each army who would serve as encouragers and sparring guides. A foul move from any warrior would be shouted aloud by a sparring guide for the benefit of his side, warning of treachery and giving a warning of any group mass maneuvers that might be coming. Farther out from the circle were the hundreds of Benjamite soldiers from Abner's force.

Abner had seen many such displays. Kingdoms had been won and lost in many lands on the outcomes of these competitions. Traders from Greece told stories of games played by warriors that also included hurling rocks for distance or the two fastest warriors sprinting head-to-head for a predetermined distance. Such contests seemed odd to Abner—the fate of nations decided through athletics? Better to fight as men and let Yahweh determine it.

But watching his countrymen prepare for their match, Hebrew tribesman against Hebrew tribesman, he wondered if athletics would not have spared the grief of countless mothers the past few years. Well—he shook his head. There was no way to know what would unite them all against the Philistine threat. Until then, he would lead as best he could.

He noticed, to his surprise, that the sun had slipped in the sky. He had not realized how much time had passed since they'd all arrived at the pool.

Each man in the circle lined up directly across from a warrior from the opposing army. They glared at one another, each of them veterans of many desperate fights, issuing taunts and yelling curses. The Benjamites shouted how despicable it was that some of their own tribesmen had become traitors and joined the rebel from Judah. Those loyal to David demanded that the Benjamites quit resisting and accept that Yahweh had willed David to take the throne. Benjamites retorted that the rebels should not presume to speak for Yahweh, and David's fighters shouted that at least they were fighting for a man as king.

Abner glanced at his troops in the ranks farthest back. These were the greenest soldiers, those too nervous to taunt the Lion's warriors. They stared wide-eyed.

He squeezed the sickle sword tighter.

FIVE

Eleazar saw a foot lashed out and withdrawn, then a hand, then the first pair started fighting. Joab's warrior pivoted his hips, using the force from his charging attacker to hurl the man head over heels. As soon as Abner's man landed, the other eleven pairs tore into one another.

Billowing clouds of sand and dust obscured them after only a few moments. As the shouting of the spectators rose to a roar, Eleazar strained his eyes, trying to catch a glimpse inside the fray. But dust rose with every kick. He could not discern what was going on.

Then, through a break in the dust cloud, one of Abner's fighters leaped outside the circle and snatched the short sword handed to him. It happened so quickly that none of Joab's sparring guides had the chance to shout a warning. The man with the sword then wrapped his arm around the neck of his nearest opponent and plunged the tip of the sword through his back until it burst out of the front of the ribcage in a crimson spray. Joab's fighter slumped forward, shock on his face.

Eleazar was so angry that he charged down the rocky slope to kill the man himself, but he found himself watching events unfold too quickly. Every sparring guide from each side of the circle suddenly produced a blade from under their tunics and tossed them to the fighters in the middle. The warriors caught them, as though previously rehearsed, and yelled angry war cries as they rushed toward their nearest opponent.

"Stop!" Eleazar yelled. It was Abner's man who had started it, but he was sure that Joab had prepared his fighters beforehand to do the same. Before he could reach the circle, the duel erupted in blood. Each of the remaining fighters attacked his opponent with such hate that none controlled his aim. Men seized the hair of their opponent in one hand and stabbed with the other.

All twelve pairs slumped against each other on the sand, writhing in pain. Some vomited blood and bile; others pawed agonizingly at the hot metal buried in their midsection. Screams, gagging, spattering of urine and blood, all of it reached Eleazar's senses as he arrived at the edge of the dueling circle.

Shammah and Josheb arrived next to him. Around them rose the shouts of soldiers grieving the loss of their brothers.

There was but a moment of hesitation, and then Eleazar saw the first ranks of sparring guides from Abner's army run forward, driven by vengeance. Behind them up the slope came the line of soldiers from the main force.

It was impossible to stop it now. Josheb shouted at Eleazar and Shammah to fall into their wedge. Open war had begun, and as distraught as he was at the treachery and needless death, they could spare lives by taking some.

Abner was moving as soon as his soldier struck the first blow to begin the slaughter. Furious, desperate to save his men from the coming massacre, he ordered his archers forward to provide defensive fire, then directed the aide to "get the guides out of there!"

The ranks of Joab's men charged, and Abner yelled, "Archers! Hit them now!"

The Benjamite bowmen and slingers planted their front feet on a line of small boulders and prepared to shoot.

Before they could release their weapons, however, Eleazar and the two fighters with him broke through Abner's lines with a yell and a crash of metal. They each had pikes, which they swung with such accuracy and speed that, before Abner could shout orders, all thirteen of his bowmen and slingers lay dead.

Abner's young army panicked. Screaming, "The Lion's men, the Lion's men!" they clambered over one another trying to escape—all but a few of the brave ones, who yelled their own war cries and charged out to meet Joab's onrushing troops.

Abner bellowed, "Fall back to the rally point!" Before the battle, he had chosen a distant hilltop as the place to set up a defensive position, if the battle went against them.

The Benjamites who had been holding back came out of their shocked stupor and began snatching up weapons and packs.

"Leave the packs, they will slow you down!" Abner shouted, but in their panic, none listened.

Four hundred Benjamite warriors in the forward ranks ignored Abner's command to fall back; they poured across the field into the first ranks of their enemy. Abner screamed at their officers to organize the retreat. A few hesitated, desperate to stay in the fight, then gathered their troops and followed his orders.

Abner was distraught at his lack of control over these green troops—or *any* of his troops, for that matter. He wanted to stay and command the field now that the fighting had begun, but he knew that Joab's men would prevail, and he was the only remaining capable general. If he did not organize the remnant, all would die when the Philistines attacked again. Exactly like Gilboa, he thought bitterly. We have to run away again. That is all we do now.

He waved over an officer named Mica, a great warrior. If anyone could hold the ground, he could.

"Take command of Hawk and Scorpion companies and hold off Joab's men as long as possible. Retreat to the rally point if they get overrun."

"Retreat? We outnumber them five to one!"

Abner pointed out the three warriors who had slain his archers with such savage efficiency.

"Those are the Mighty Men, David's greatest champions. You will need to throw everything you have at them, do you understand? That's your only chance."

Mica nodded, understanding, the lust for battle dimming a bit.

"I need to pull back and organize at the rally point. We can't lose this army," Abner said.

They embraced, then Abner turned and sprinted to the head of the retreating troops, his aide following behind.

Eleazar's pike cut through the neck of a stout warrior, sending a spray of warm blood down his arm. The soldier gurgled and collapsed. Eleazar prepared himself to spin again, checked his distance from Shammah and Josheb, then lashed the iron tip low across the tendons of two men running past him. They flopped, muscles no longer supporting them, and Eleazar thought they resembled fish in a net. He shook his head furiously. *Focus!* He buried the tip into their chests one by one.

The Hebrew soldiers he killed stared at him as their lives ebbed away. Something caught at the back of Eleazar's throat, but he shook his head again and searched for the next target. *They are targets, not Hebrews, they are targets . . .*

Shammah appeared next to him, blocking a swipe from a soldier who had run up unnoticed. The near miss startled Eleazar.

The three of them regrouped. Blood was filling the muddy footprints left by the struggling warriors and seeping into the pool itself, splashing over the stones that lined the water. The flies swarmed in greater numbers, drawn by the exposed entrails and excrement of dead soldiers. The late afternoon light gave the scene an unearthly orange brilliance, like the depths of Sheol itself.

Joab's men were drawing the less orderly ranks of Abner's green troops away from the remaining mass of their force, taking away their advantage in numbers. Eleazar knew they could fight all day in this manner.

Dozens of corpses lined the bank. Eleazar sprinted toward the pool to assault the rear of the scattered Benjamite ranks on his right. He could see many of Abner's troops in retreat, disappearing over the hill to his left.

Behind him, Shammah, who had dropped his bow when the fighting started, was praying aloud to Yahweh. "Forgive us for killing your people, great God of my fathers, forgive us for killing ..."

Eleazar winced. *Battle first, regret later.*

Shifting his pike to his left hand, he pulled out his sword with his right and slashed across the back of a Benjamite's arm. The man dropped his weapon and turned in surprise, only to catch Josheb's spear in the belly. As the man fell, Josheb threw himself close against Shammah and Eleazar.

Eleazar and Shammah linked arms and struck another soldier in the back. The Benjamites were so intent on swarming the ranks of Joab's regulars that they barely noticed the Three tearing through their lines from behind.

Those who did fled in terror.

SIX

Abner darted to the head of the column of retreating soldiers and ordered them to drop unnecessary equipment. Even the soldiers who had been left in the forest to guard the supplies abandoned their posts and fled with the rest of the Israelites.

After an hour of running, he directed his gasping troops toward a ravine nearby. They filed through it, grateful to be away from the noise of the battle. He ignored the pleas of some of the men to go back and help their comrades. Any who did, Abner feared, would die.

At the first bend in the ravine, he climbed to the top of a pile of rocks to see if any of David's men pursued.

In the distance, a man was chasing them.

As he was always aware, Asahel was the youngest son. Not a day went by that he did not resent the overpowering shadow cast by his older brothers, Joab and Abishai. For a while he thought he could maneuver his way into prominence by growing close to his uncle, David, but that had never happened.

He had earned his place among the Thirty by his will alone. He had trained himself to the same degree of skill as Joab and Abishai, and was superior to them in physical stamina and speed ... but he was the youngest. As the youngest, he was always last by birth. He would have to perform some great exploit to win respect.

Which was why he had not wasted time killing Benjamites.

He had only one objective: to win wealth and fame by capturing or killing the great general Abner. So when the twelve fighters had slaughtered one another, Asahel had followed the Three into the battle initially, but he had slipped past the fighting to get to Abner.

When he saw Abner retreating with a section of his men, Asahel decided to chase him on foot, hoping to catch him before any of the other men from Judah—especially his brothers. Asahel was the brother who always got the last of the spoils, and he was weary of it. Never again.

That would not matter today.

He sprinted past the piles of corpses, avoided a slashing blade, intent on not getting caught up in the fighting with the foot soldiers from Benjamin. That was beneath him; he would not labor away on the field without notice anymore.

He would capture Abner when no one else could, and then his brothers would be forced to respect him. He searched for them in the fighting, did not see them, but it would not matter, because when he had Abner's head mounted on his weapon they would pay attention.

Abner took several more steps and leaned against a tree to catch his breath.

"The rest of you keep moving up to the hilltop!" he yelled.

"Lord, we'll wait with you. What if he defeats you?"

Abner laughed. "I have a few moves left in me. I will be fine. You need every moment you can to escape." He looked up at the sky, took a deep breath. "But if I do fall, build your positions on that hilltop and wait for the other division of our army to arrive."

"Who is it, sir?"

"Asahel, Joab's brother. I have to be the one to kill him. I don't want that on any of you."

They left. He forced himself to move again, cutting through a stand of trees and climbing a small rise. He could see the pursuing soldier slow down before entering the woods, staring at the ground and looking for their sign.

Abner waved and shouted. The soldier's head snapped up. Even from this distance, Abner recognized him.

Eleazar killed one more. The old man, who shouldn't have been in the ranks, stared at him in anger as he died. Eleazar backed up and released his grip on his sword. The weapon clattered to the ground, as did the pike.

Eleazar knelt next to the dying old man. He put his hands on the sides of his face. The man had lived many years, had seen hope come to Israel at last—only to be killed by his own kinsman.

"Forgive me," Eleazar mouthed. The old man's eyes dimmed. He looked confused. Eleazar whispered again: "Forgive me."

The old man died.

Nearby, Josheb and Shammah had struck down their last opponents. The vengeance-driven courage of the Benjamites broke at last, and what remained of their army turned and fled in the direction of Abner's retreat.

The other two knelt in the mud near Eleazar to catch their breath. Joab trotted across the field to them and knelt as well. Abishai traversed the field, counting casualties.

"We need to chase them," Joab said.

"Give them time to withdraw," Eleazar said.

"They will regroup."

"Let them escape!"

"They are northerners!" Joab shouted.

"Benjamites, and men of Abraham just like us," Josheb corrected.

"Fine. All of you stay here, and I will cut them down myself. Where is Asahel?"

"I haven't seen him," said Josheb.

They looked around for a moment. Then they all stood to see better, but after searching, they saw that he wasn't among the corpses.

Eleazar squinted in the direction of the fleeing Benjamites. Dusk was falling; they had about an hour of light left.

"He must be chasing Abner."

Abner was not a young man anymore—not nearly young enough to outrun Asahel. But he was wise in the ways of war, and he used his knowledge of the terrain to his advantage as he listened to the young soldier chasing him through the brush.

Abner had guessed correctly. As soon as he saw him, Asahel had ignored the pursuit of the others and come straight in his direction. So he is after glory, Abner thought as he jumped over a fallen tree.

There was a ravine ahead in the forest, and Abner headed for it, seeking the advantage.

▲▲▲

Asahel readied his weapons as he ran. He would ram the javelin into Abner's back, knocking him down, then finish him with a stroke to the neck.

Ahead, he saw Abner glance over his shoulder. The general was losing two steps for every step Asahel took.

"Asahel, is that you?" Abner cried out.

"It is I!" Asahel shouted.

The voice carried firm and strong despite the struggle of the chase and the density of the forest.

"Turn aside! Take the spoil from one of the young warriors!"

Asahel chuckled as he ran. *Begging for his life now.*

Another look told Abner that Asahel had closed the gap further; clearly, he had no intention of turning back. Abner would have to stand and fight the foolish young man, the last thing he wanted to do. Enough blood had been spilled today.

"Stop following me! Why should I kill you? How could I look at your brother Joab again?"

The plea was unanswered. Abner reached the ravine and leaped to the bottom. As he crashed through the undergrowth, he heard Asahel make the leap behind him—directly into a thorny tree that Abner, knowing it was there, had avoided. Asahel screamed a curse.

Abner scrambled up the opposite slope, holding his spear in one hand and pulling himself up with the other. He looked back—Asahel was cutting himself loose from the bramble, his body covered in scrapes. The maneuver was costing the younger man a few moments, and Abner used them.

He turned and ran back toward where he and his men had first entered the forest. Asahel was going to catch him eventually, and if Abner had to kill him, he would do so where his brother could find him.

He pushed his aching legs forward. Behind him, Asahel shouted as he escaped the ravine. Abner clenched his teeth and ran as fast as he could, but Asahel was closing in, his famous speed bringing him back within attack distance.

Asahel hated Abner more with every step. He readied his javelin, his legs gliding over the terrain as though he were flying, his speed carrying him close for the kill. He would be the most famous warrior in Israel. David would give him wealth and status; Joab would finally respect him—

Abner felt the rush of air around the body behind him and then jumped forward with a last effort, planting the head of his spear into the ground. At the same instant, Asahel slammed into the butt end of the spear. The shaft slid under the front of his armor.

Abner rolled out of the way as Asahel, impaled on the spear, vaulted headfirst and crumpled to the ground.

Abner knelt, staring at the dying man. Asahel was facing away from him, clutching at the head of the spear protruding out of his belly. The butt end had torn away his intestines and they hung like ropes on the shaft of the spear, sticking out of his back.

Asahel made a gurgling noise before finally shuddering. He lay still.

Abner's eyes burned with tears. He crawled to Asahel's body

and pressed his face into the man's bloody tunic. He wiped his eyes on the cloth. Another waste, another waste, another Hebrew killed needlessly by a Hebrew . . .

He grabbed a handful of dirt, tossed it into his hair, and cried aloud. He tore away at the front of his tunic, reaching under his armor and ripping a seam in mourning.

SEVEN

After leaving a detachment of soldiers and the priest from the village to purify the corpses and give aid to the wounded, Eleazar and the others in Joab's force took up the pursuit of Abner. Eleazar wished to allow the Benjamites to escape, but Joab was in command. They dutifully followed.

The setting sun forced them to move urgently before nightfall. Back at the pool, Josheb had seen a promontory on the horizon that he guessed would make a good rally point for Abner's men, and as he suspected, the tracks of the fleeing troops led into the woods in that direction.

Eleazar pointed out where footprints led into the forest away from the main force, but they did not follow that trail, choosing instead to chase the main group. He tried to concentrate, but his mind was full of images of his dead kinsmen, fellow sons of Abraham who had wanted only to fight for their homeland and their ruler but were now descending into Sheol and its depths, killed by his own hand.

Joab ran in front of him, alongside Abishai. Eleazar saw them crest a slight ridge on the trail and disappear from sight. Then he heard them screaming. Eleazar sprinted faster and reached the ridge.

Below him on the trail, Joab and Abishai were crouched near the twisted body of their brother Asahel. Blood covered the rocks nearby. A spear shaft protruded from Asahel's back, with the tip of the spear lodged in the top of his chest.

Eleazar saw what had happened. Asahel had been chasing Abner, foolish and eager to capture him as a war prize, when Abner had planted the spear into the ground as Asahel got close. Unable to stop his momentum, Asahel had run into the shaft.

Joab grabbed Asahel by the beard, crying out. Abishai knelt by his dead brother, weeping softly.

Then Joab stood, a murderous scream bursting from his throat. He bolted down the trail. Abishai cursed aloud and followed him.

"Joab!" Eleazar shouted. "He was defending himself! Let them go! Enough!"

Abner pushed the men hard until darkness. He managed to put the death of Asahel out of his mind for now. He hoped he could make peace with Joab one day.

At the top of the rally hill, known as Ammah, he directed the men to build fighting positions around the peak. They were too exhausted to keep running, and if they tried they would only be cut down in the open field by Joab's troops. They would take up their positions here, and he would attempt to negotiate a truce. If Joab's troops decided to attack up the hill, they would have to climb over a rock wall with defenders crouched behind it.

The soldiers trembled as they stacked rocks next to trees to make fighting positions. Abner watched one soldier vomit as he bent to pick up a rock. The man coughed and spat. Then he knelt and put his head between his legs, vomiting again.

Abner trudged over to him and sat down. He placed his hand on the man's back.

"Apologies, lord," the soldier said.

"No need. At least you didn't wet yourself like the first time I saw battle."

The man glanced at him, surprised. Then he nodded.

"You all did well today," Abner said aloud to the group now spreading across the hilltop.

"Lord, why did you order our retreat? Our brothers are back there," someone called from the edge.

"We would all be dead if we had stayed. It wasn't worth everyone dying over a well."

"But our brothers are back there! We left them!"

"All of your life you will wish you had stayed on a battlefield where your brothers died. I have wanted to stay many times. But we are all that is left. Dying needlessly does not get your wife pregnant or bring your crops out of the ground."

"I would rather my wife be a whore to the Philistines and my crops burn than run away!"

Abner nodded. He knew the feeling and did not have the heart to argue with the soldier.

The breeze was dying for the night. The soil in this part of the land was a mixture of purples and reds. The moon made dull the colors that shone so vibrantly during the day, and now it looked as though someone had dipped a finger in blood and swirled the ground.

EIGHT

Joab and Abishai were crouched on a boulder at the base of the hill of Ammah, each one pointing to a different attack route.

Eleazar jogged up next to them. "Joab, we need to pull back."

"We are attacking."

"We will be slaughtered if we go up that hill in the dark. Even though Abner's men are green, if we attack now we will be cut down by swords and spears behind every bush. It's not worth losing your men over. I grieve for your brother—"

"You grieve nothing for my brother! We are attacking!"

Josheb joined in as he walked up beside Eleazar. "If you order these men up that hill, I will kill you during the attack and tell David you fell at their hands."

His tone was calm and steady. Eleazar tensed for the fight that had been a long time coming.

"Joab!"

The voice boomed down the hillside through the trees. They

turned and saw Abner, sword raised, silhouetted against the luminous stars at the top of the hill.

"Will the sword destroy us forever? Don't you know that the end will be bitter for all of us? How long before you tell your men to turn from the pursuit of their brothers?"

They looked at one another. Joab was about to shout a reply when Eleazar pulled at his elbow.

"Joab, listen to him. These are *Hebrews*. How many more need to die tonight?"

Joab was about to lash out at Eleazar again when Abishai stepped between them. He took his brother Joab's face between his hands and cupped his ears.

"Let's go bury our brother. The sun has set."

"But Abner!"

Abishai nodded. "Abner will suffer for this. But Eleazar is right. Enough mother's sons have died today. Let's go bury our brother."

Joab winced. He lowered his face into Abishai's chest. The two men held each other a moment. Abishai whispered a few words the others could not hear. Joab finally nodded with resignation.

Wiping his eyes with his wrist, Joab turned back toward the hill. The anger in his eyes had diminished, and now Eleazar saw a tired, grieving brother.

Joab called to Abner, "As Yahweh lives, if you had not spoken, the men would have not given up the pursuit of their brothers until morning."

His voice trailed off as he reached for the ram's horn at his side. Taking a deep breath, he blew the battle signal long and loud, the mournful noise resonating through the deep woods. The sound of the pursuing fighters of Judah making their way up the trail ceased. It was the signal to stop what they were doing and await orders.

Josheb shouted for the troops to return to the pool and then disappeared into the night. The sound of complaints rose, but Josheb could be heard angrily quieting them. Some of the soldiers were upset that they would not be able to plunder their enemies. Eleazar watched as Joab and Abishai staggered away together.

When they were all gone, Eleazar leaned against Shammah for support. The big man put his arm around his shoulders and they stood in the quiet darkness, weary with grief.

"When will Yahweh just kill us all and be done with it?" Eleazar whispered.

There was no moon, only starlight, as Joab's force filtered out of sight in the direction of Gibeon, but Abner sensed that they were gone, returning to the site of the battle to collect their dead and assist their wounded. Now he had to find a way to break it to his own troops that they would not be able to do the same.

"Gather your things. We are leaving."

"Lord, the bodies need to be purified. We need—"

"Our kinsmen will bury them and perform the ceremonies," Abner said.

"The same kinsmen who slaughtered us today?"

"Our men were treacherous as well."

"Will we have the chance to fight them again one day?"

"Unfortunately, yes," Abner replied. He wished he could tell the young troops around him that this would never happen again, that all of Israel would be reconciled one day soon. But he knew otherwise. The heaviness in his words brought silence to the group. He heard weeping in the darkness. His own eyes burned.

They moved sluggishly, muscles cramped and sore from the exertions of the day. Abner felt the bones in his knees grinding against each other. This was common, but the pain was always worse when he had to run. He was old, far too old to be a warrior.

One by one, the troops filed off the hill into the valley, heading east. His plan was to cross the Jordan that night and reach Mahanaim, the capital city of the north, by midmorning.

"Lord, will there be anyone sent to retrieve our dead?"

Abner looked at the young soldier standing next to him. The man was holding his tears back bravely. Abner touched his ear and leaned forward, kissing the soldier on the forehead. He seemed to understand and nodded, then walked back to his unit.

Abner waited until the last soldier had moved from the hilltop, then trotted to the front to lead the way.

They marched all night. The river had ebbed from its high and the crossing was not difficult. Abner moved among them as they marched and made it a point to hug and kiss each of them on the cheek. He did not know how many hundreds of their troops had fallen. They would all receive mourning rites in the villages. All of the women would wail; the men would wear sackcloth and carry ashes to dust their heads with. Even their miserable king would mourn. Of that, Abner would make sure.

When they reached the city, it did not take long for the wailing to begin. Wives rushed out of the gates, looking for their husbands. Abner always hated this moment. Some of the women were ecstatic that their men had survived and wept with joy, while a hand's breadth away another wife was finding out she was a widow and was now the property of the village elders until they decided what to do with her, usually giving her to the fallen soldier's brother.

His own wife did not come to the gates anymore. That was for the young and the foolish. She was prepared for his death at any time, and to wait for him eagerly would only serve to increase her sorrow needlessly when the end came.

Instead of going home, Abner walked down the street lining the city walls. He would wait for the full report at the barracks. His men used to laugh behind his back at how he still kept a room in their barracks. His wife had kicked him out again, they would say. Mighty general Abner, able to spear enemies by the dozen, unable to keep a woman happy. But he knew they loved him for it. They loved that he loved them and wanted to spend time with them. He treated them as his own sons. He was stern but loyal. Willing to face the teeth of battle with them, willing to stay in front of them at all times.

Until Gilboa—and now again yesterday—when he had been forced to flee.

He would eventually have to go into the throne room and stare at the soft, sniveling boy in his extended family to whom he had sworn allegiance. Ishbosheth would demand to know what Abner had done, and Abner would give the report. He could see it all now, in detail, as though it were a stage play like the ones the foreigners brought to the markets. The king would shriek hysterically, Abner would calm him—and then go across the countryside finding more sons to be butchered by Philistines in the east and David in the south.

Abner entered his room and sat on the limestone floor near the blankets. The cold stones felt good on the backs of his knees. He stretched his legs out.

Somewhere in the distance he heard women screaming.

Somewhere in the distance he heard weeping.

Twenty of Joab's men had fallen. He and Abishai oversaw the purification of their brother's body by a priest, and they watched silently as the ashes of the red heifer were sprinkled over the corpse and the prayers spoken. No one really cared about the ceremonies in the Law anymore, but today, with their kinsmen, it seemed appropriate. Only Shammah knew what to do to purify oneself after battles, when a man was considered unclean, and he was patiently instructing the troops.

Eleazar agreed to supervise the rest of the cleanup while Joab and Abishai slipped away to Bethlehem in the night to bury Asahel in their father's tomb. The Philistine garrison that held the city would ask too many questions if they went during the day. David and his troops were still thought to be vassals of the Philistine rulers who held the lands of Judah, something David had been careful to keep them believing.

Eleazar found the elderly Benjamite who had died in his arms earlier. His face was frozen in the terror mask of death. His body had expelled the urine inside him and the front of his tunic was damp and smelled musky. Eleazar had smelled the blood and urine of the battlefield many times, but this time it nauseated him. He sat next to the old man and watched as Shammah paced around ensuring that the rituals were completed correctly. The priests from Gibeon had never presided over a scene of mass death before, and they lacked enough red heifer ashes to purify this many corpses. Some of the men would be ceremonially unclean for days. Most of them did not care.

They have not cared for centuries, Eleazar thought. Yahweh should have destroyed them long before now.

Eleazar motioned for a priest, who doused the old Benjamite's body with the ash. Some of it splattered across the wrinkled face and gray beard.

Eleazar sighed. A man this old should not be fighting. He should be sitting next to a fire and giving council to stupid young fools trying to kill each other.

In another hour, the men were ready to leave. They carried the purified bodies of their brothers between them. The bodies of the

Benjamites—over three hundred of them—were left for the people of the town to bury.

The troops marched hard all night, barely slowed by the burdens they carried, anxious to get home. As they reached the point near Bethlehem where the trade road bends before descending into the lower hill country near Hebron, Joab and Abishai appeared silently out of the night. Eleazar did not exchange a word with them, and they continued marching.

Eleazar did not go into Hebron with the rest of the men. In the forest, he pulled out of the column unnoticed and made his way to the merchant camps. These were the foreigners from the caravans traveling the King's Highway and other trading routes between Egypt in the south and the nations of the north. They brought many wares with them, including the unclean pleasures.

The city walls of Hebron loomed against the starry sky. Careful to avoid the sentries, he stumbled through the dark forest on the outside of the wall, shoving aside branches, his head aching from the tears he had shed that day.

He dropped his weapons next to a large tree whose roots had been undermined by a flash flood, leaving a deep cleft. He ran his finger along the edge of the sickle-sword blade. It was still dark with blood. Hebrew blood. He stuffed the sword under the cleft. He would never use the sword again. Surely it was cursed by Yahweh.

Eleazar continued his trek through the forest, intent on his destination but feeling his heart resist him. Thoughts of his nearby home came, and he hated himself. He was only a Sabbath day's walk away, but he could not do it, could not go into the city where his home and his bed were. His wife, his children. Their faces were dark to him, wrapped in mist.

He kept moving, drawn by the call that so many men heeded. He wanted to release the violence of the day. He paused for a drink at a still pool. The warm water was foul to his taste, but he managed several gulps before he spat out the remnant. Images. The old man dying.

Eleazar glimpsed the camp of the Syrian nomads ahead in the clearing. For a moment, the tents and laughter repelled him, and he trotted away, shaking his head. He made his way back to the Hebron city wall. The night was cool and dark, and Eleazar felt his strength deserting him. He pressed his hand against the stone wall, then his face. He rubbed his face against the cold stone.

Eleazar stared down the city wall, his heart racing, his mind screaming black hatred at himself. Inside the city, he could hear shouts of reunion and of grief. Men had been lost, but others had returned. All would be looking to him for leadership and comfort—to him and Josheb and Shammah, the Mighty Three.

He turned his head toward the Syrian camp. They were the enemies of his people—one of a thousand enemies. He was too far away to hear the sounds of their camp now, and the forest was thick and dark. But it was there.

Go home, Eleazar.

He heard it in the covering. His spirit melted. *I want to.*

Then go.

He began to run, then ran faster, the branches cutting his arms and face. His chafed thighs burned, dirty and slick with sweat. He clawed at his eyes to clean the grime, but it was not good enough. Though he had cleaned away the dust and grit, they felt rancid and foul, and they were dry from the loss of tears.

Men of Abraham killing men of Abraham. Sons of Isaac and Jacob butchering one another.

He burst out of the woods into the Syrian camp. There was a large fire, and an unclean animal roasted over it. A split-hoofed animal. A pig. David had forbidden such animals within the city; the foreign traders kept them outside in their camps. Three men prodded the meat with roasting sticks. The fat boiled and drizzled out of the flesh. A circle of tents surrounded the roasting animal, and in front of each tent were a rug and cushions where the women lay waiting for men such as him and times such as this. *Like desert vipers.*

The three men roasting the animal leered at him through the night, obscured by drafts of smoke, the flicker of the fire dancing across their features and making them look like fetid creatures from Sheol. One of them had a soiled bandage over his eye, caked with yellow pus from an infected wound. He had missing teeth and a twisted smile. He held out his hand.

Eleazar withdrew his money pouch and fumbled for several coins. He threw them at the ugly man, who laughed and pointed at the circle of tents.

Eleazar had never been here before; he had only heard of these places. Camps of pleasure. He caught the scent of cooking and olive oil. The smell of the roasting meat and the oil made his stomach growl and his heart pump faster in his chest. There was a tent in the back, away from the rest of the tents. He could not be seen there.

No one must know.

He staggered toward the tent opening. From inside came the gentle glow of a lamp. The woman would be in there, waiting. Other men would come after him. Soldiers always did after battles; wives could not meet the needs that these women could.

He tried to say something to stop himself, to at least think something, but there was only heartache, and the sound of men laughing as the animal roasted, and the smell of the oil.

Four Years Later

Part Two

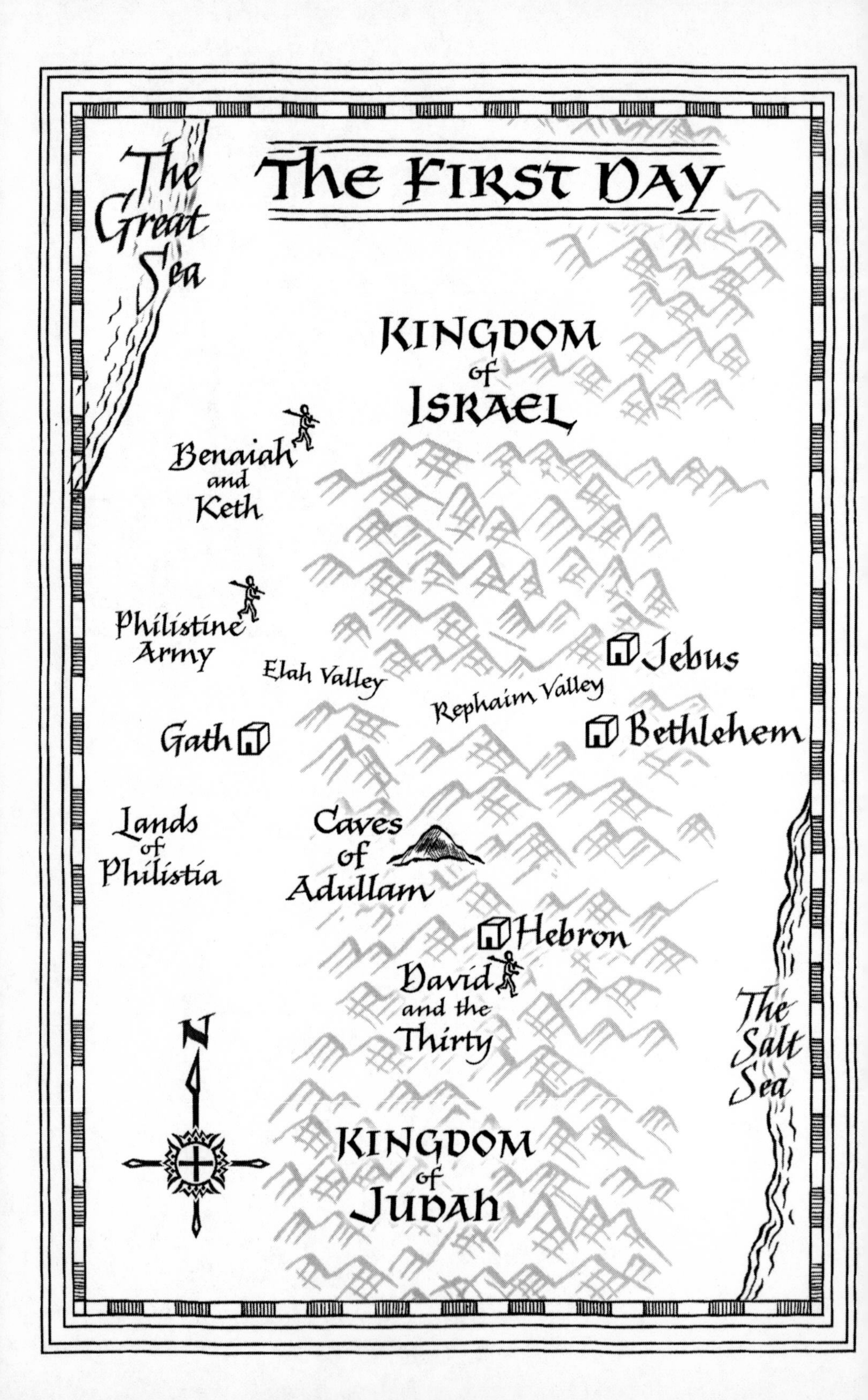
The First Day
The Great Sea
Kingdom of Israel
Benaiah and Keth
Philistine Army
Elah Valley
Jebus
Rephaim Valley
Gath
Bethlehem
Lands of Philistia
Caves of Adullam
Hebron
David and the Thirty
N
The Salt Sea
Kingdom of Judah

NINE

The snake warmed itself in the sunlight, basking in the heat of the stones next to the watering hole. It slithered out each day at the same time, always regular in its habits, always sensing a new lair that would provide the best chance of surprising a desert mouse or one of the larger animals that were frequently herded near the water.

It glided through the cool shadows and hot gaps in the stones. Reaching a clearing, it raised its head and froze. Sensing something new, it flicked its tongue rapidly. It retreated back into the rocks to wait.

A boy was standing next to the pool. He was short for his age, with a dusty tunic and sleeping garment of dull cloth wrapped around his torso. A small flint dagger hung on a belt around his waist, and a sling was tucked into the belt behind his back. A leather water pouch was draped over his shoulders. He held a gnarled, splintered wooden staff that had been passed down to him from an older brother. He leaned on the staff casually, his mind wandering.

On this day the flies were swarming. The heat of midday allowed clouds of them to thicken along the bank and cover the mud along the water's edge. With the south still in the grip of drought, the muddy water hole was the only water source for livestock within a two day's walk, and with each passing month of drought it seemed the number of flies increased tenfold. Normally sheep were not watered in the heat of the day—they were herded into the shadow of a tree canopy or overhanging cliff. But the boy preferred coming at this time because he knew he would be alone, with no one to harass him.

It was the time of year when many shepherds led their flocks out of the rough terrain of the desert mountains into this basin for this pool's water. The flies were the only real trouble for the shepherds under normal circumstances, far as it was from the contested areas of the kingdom. The flies were annoying to the boy, but they were less annoying than listening to his mother lecture him about how poorly he did in everything. He did not spend much time with his father; as the youngest, he was shooed away often.

This season had been especially tough. While the war between the northern and southern tribes had strung out for years, here on the northern frontier people were mostly concerned with which ruler would be able to help prevent raids and encroachment from the Philistines or other foreigners or bandit warlords. The elders had a difficult time deciding who to support. Some said Ishbosheth and his general Abner were the future of their land; others claimed it was David, the king in the south.

The boy knew the argument for David well because his father had influenced many in the community not to oppose him outright. True, David was from Judah, and their size and power were intimidating, but at least they were Hebrews, and if David was the best chance at preventing rape and pillage from unclean outsiders, making him king might be the will of Yahweh.

Yet those meetings of the elders were endless and usually went nowhere. They preferred to sit in the shade of their gates and eat figs and dates and wait for events to unfold. The centuries had turned his people into survivors, not blindly stepping out for any one side until they were certain the other would not rise up. The boy's brothers told him that they had been a proud race once. That Yahweh had singled them out as his people and that this land was theirs, but that they had turned their backs on their loving God and his ways, only to suffer great punishment for their rebellion.

They were divided, they bickered, they turned and ran from fights. The men were soft and the women resented them for it, afraid that their rolls of fat and docile attitudes would not stop a lustful, battle-mad Philistine soldier. Their enemies mocked them. Perhaps it was time to bring the sword back into their land, his father argued, and the sword most worthy of it was David's.

David's actions and his motives were shadowy. No one ever seemed to know where he fully stood. They had heard terrifying rumors about his alliances with Philistines, but here and there they had also heard about inexplicably courageous acts for the sake of his kinsmen.

The boy's father made it a point to tell his family about political events, even the girls. He wanted them to know about their lands, but he was careful to remind his daughters that their opinion only really mattered if their future husbands asked for it.

When news came that Abner was going to turn over the northern kingdom to David after four long years of tribal war, his father had been thrilled and had rushed into the family home to tell them. At last, it was time for unification!

The news had ignited the debate anew in his village. Would David remain under the thumb of the Philistines? Would he be able to broker peace within the tribes? Would he take blood vengeance against those who had been loyal to Saul's son Ishbosheth?

Such intrigues were above and beyond the boy, though. It was his fate to languish in the heat and misery of muddy sheep pools. Part of him thought he would never have to encounter the war. That was the business of warriors and kings, and he was neither.

The boy swatted at a fly. What did he care? All he knew was that the day was very hot. Flies crowded around his ears, trying to force their way in. The sheep, twenty-five of them, the prize of his father's flock he was told, mewed and bawled in misery as they picked their way toward the water. The flies were relentless. The boy rubbed his face. He shouted at the sheep to keep moving, swatting the hind leg of the nearest with the tip of his staff. The sheep bleated at him. Irritated, he swatted it once more.

He was getting tired of the heat and the sheep and the flies—and the endless arguments about which king would be better. Something would need to change soon. The boy leaned his staff against a sycamore and sprawled in the tree's shade. His legs ached. He rubbed them a few times.

The pool was several cubits deep at its center and fed by a trickle of water from a spring deep in the mountain canyons. Two cliffs surrounded it, casting shadows over the muddy water most hours of the day. Since millennia before the young shepherd was born, it had served as a crossroads for the nomadic wanderers in the great deserts of the east. As the only strategic water point in the region to support the livestock of an army, it had been contested in ages gone by. But now, the pool sat in silent peace at the base of the cliffs, the only sound usually being the trickle of water down the stones and into the basin.

Nearby, just out of sight, was the village of Detheren. A day's walk beyond that, near the sea, was Dor and its fortress. The same mountain spring that fed this desert pool also rolled through the ravines into those towns and filled their pools.

He froze. Very close to him, only cubits away, a cobra raised its head.

The snake held still for a moment, tongue slipping in and out of its mouth. Dust rose. The sound of bleating grew louder. The serpent bobbed its head slightly.

The boy rolled away instantly. The snake lashed out for him, missing. The boy dropped a stone in his sling and snapped it around once before releasing.

The snake's head burst open in a spray of crimson, showering the dull rocks nearby with a coating of bright blood. The body coiled and snapped. It thrashed in circles, spraying blood from the stump where its head had been. The sheep bawled, scampering over one another to flee.

The shepherd boy, who had seen the deadly thing lying still in the sand, held it up on the end of his staff. He looked closely at the crushed head. Amber liquid draining from the head mingled with the blood coursing out. It was the poison that had felled so many of his father's sheep. It would have felled him this day had he not seen the scaly hide.

He tossed it aside in disgust, shaken. Serpents were cursed and unclean. The lazy afternoon heat had made him careless and he had nearly paid with his life. He looked over the herd. The sheep were still bleating and jostling one another with great anxiety, but they did not appear to be on the verge of scattering. He was grateful. This day had been eventful enough without having to chase them all back into the corner of the cliff.

The sheep calming down, the sun warming the rocks, and the haze of the pool conspired to make him drowsy again, and before long his eyes began to droop and his shoulders sagged. The staff propped in the crook of his arm slid down and he dropped his sling.

A hand touched his shoulder, and he started violently.

"What have you seen since you have been here?"

The boy looked up, trembling. A large man stood over him.

"N–nothing."

His lips parted to speak again but no words came out. He felt foolish and scared.

The large man's face was dirty and calloused, with a short, well-trimmed beard. He had a noble demeanor, as one who had been under authority and who held it now. He was a warrior, judging by the weapons he carried.

What caught the boy's attention even more than the warrior's size and weapons was the tangled mess of scars that covered his neck and top of his head, visible even through thick black hair. There were also scars on the warrior's arm above the leather greaves—vicious, disfiguring scars, like what a desert demon would have—raised, jagged mounds of light flesh on dark flesh.

Next to the large, scarred warrior was a foreigner—the boy could tell by the man's dress and skin tone, much lighter than Hebrews'. His long hair was braided. Both had similar armor and weaponry, but the foreigner also carried a bow. They appeared to have been out on the frontier for a long time. Their fierce eyes made him lower his.

"Where are your brothers?" the first man said.

"The younger work for my father. The elder are away. War," was all the boy could reply.

"What tribe is your father?"

Now the boy was worried. If these men were from the south and the lands of Judah, he was in great danger of losing his father's flock, even though his family was sympathetic to David. Hebrews had been fighting for generations amongst themselves, sometimes treating fellow tribes worse than even the Philistines.

The foreign warrior must have sensed that the boy was afraid of the question, so he said, "That was good aim on that cobra. You sling like you've done it more than your years."

"My brothers fight with the Lion of Judah," the boy said. "They sling for his army. They taught me well." He was suddenly afraid that he had given away too much in his outburst of pride.

The scarred one lowered his head. "Their names?"

"Shethra and Bothra, sons of Banaa. My grandfather has disowned them, but my father is proud.

"Makes sense. You come by your lazy ways naturally. They sleep all the time like you do."

"You weren't laughing when they saved you at the boundary," said the foreigner.

The scarred man frowned. "Well, everyone hits something once in a while," he said, then winked at the shepherd boy.

These were the Lion's men? Men who fought with his two oldest brothers? Shethra and Bothra were the only ones he did not know well, for they had left his father's home when he was young because they were deeply in debt. They found the man David in a cave, and he gave them a place in his army. Only in recent years had he seen them, since their lord allowed only brief liberty from his armies, but in the time the boy had had with them, they'd told him stories of slaughtering Amalekites and battling Philistines, and he listened wide-eyed to them, taking their instructions with the sling as though it was the Law of Yahweh.

The boy wanted to ask these men many questions. Questions about the war against the north, about his brothers—but most of all, he wanted to hear about the Lion himself. His legend had grown. The Lion and his Mighty Men. The Three and their slain thousands, Benaiah and his battles with beasts, captures of hidden fortresses and witches. He suddenly wanted to hear all of it. These were *David's* men! How the other boys would be jealous of him when they heard who he'd seen this day!

"It's not all that, boy," said the one with the scars, as though reading his thoughts. The boy could not hold back his words.

"Is it true that Benaiah son of Jehoiada fought fifty lions in a pit with only his hands? Did he kill an army of Egyptian giants and was given ten women as a prize?"

The foreign warrior smiled broadly. "You want to answer that one? Seems it is up to fifty."

The scarred one scowled. The foreigner chuckled again.

Unable to stop himself, the shepherd boy asked, "Does the Lion of Judah really call down fire from Yahweh upon his enemies?"

"Haven't seen that yet, but I'm sure he could do it. Probably with a song," said the scarred one. "Did you see any Philistines recently? Any other foreign filth wandering around?"

The boy nodded. "A troop of thirty-four yesterday. Light weapons. They were heading in the direction of the coast, across those hills."

"You have a trained eye."

"Like I said, my brothers."

"We should keep moving. I will tell your brothers when I see them that their little cub slings like a man now." The foreigner winked at the boy and started to leave.

The scarred one nodded. He grabbed the boy by the chin and tugged him playfully.

"Keep up your slinging and grow your beard. You can have a place among the Mighty Men one day with those skills. Might even put you in the bodyguard."

As the two of them walked away, the boy called out, "I will! Mention me to Benaiah!"

The scarred one said over his shoulder, "It was only two lions. One was in the pit. But that was enough, trust me."

He watched them disappear around a bend. He reluctantly went back to the tedium of watching the sheep, ecstatic over his encounter with them. No one would believe him—none of his friends, none of the girls he wanted to impress. His thoughts drifted to the scarred warrior, and he wondered what had caused those scars.

And he finally realized who it had been.

TEN

The tent of meeting was in a desolate place.

Benaiah, noticing from the look on his closest friend's face that he felt the same, rolled his head in a circle to loosen the muscles in his neck. They had been traveling for several days and were feeling the effects of marching again. But they loved it. In recent years they had been spending less time on the march and more days in Hebron. They trained hard and frequently, but life in cities softened their backs and legs. Both wished for campfires and sleeping among stones, exposed to the frigid night wind of the desert and the comforting depths of the stars. This mission met that need.

Moving in obscurity was impossible in the towns. Everyone knew who Benaiah was by reputation, and although very few of the Israelite people had seen his face, it would not have taken them long to deduce who he was: Benaiah the Lion Killer, son of Jehoiada, chief of the guard that protected the King of Judah. His neck, the top of his head, and his hairline were covered with old scar tissue from when claws had torn through much of his scalp. Though leather greaves covered up most of his arms, scars were visible there as well.

Benaiah did not revel in such notoriety. He had a quiet manner, and although he was not averse to laughing hard when the occasion merited it, he preferred to keep to himself and his closest friends. He knew people trod cautiously around him, and while he did not wish to be avoided out of fear, he had to admit he liked the peace of being left alone. There were only a handful of people he felt comfortable around—the warriors he lived and fought with, including the man walking next to him.

Keth, or Uriah, as he had come to be known since David had bestowed the name, was a mercenary from the Hittite lands of the north. He had come to their camp seven years previously, just in time for them to discover that their town had been raided and destroyed by Amalekite soldiers.

Keth had proven himself during the resulting battle to reclaim their families from the raiders, working furiously to keep their brittle weapons replaced and their water resupplied. In a successful new strategy, they had designated special armorers to run new weapons to the lines as warriors lost them or they shattered. It had demonstrated to David that he had commanders who could think on their feet, and Keth was foremost among them.

Hittites knew how to forge iron, and Keth had been appointed to lead the new company of armorers. David's goal was for all of his weapons to be produced in his own ranks, using the new iron-forging methods. David no longer wanted to rely upon the weapons captured from Philistines, and with Keth's help, most of his troops now had the coveted weapons.

David had given his bodyguard and chief armorer this mission: to meet secretly in the eastern and northern lands with tribal elders to see where they stood. The nomadic groups were a mixture of the tribes of Manasseh, Zebulun, Asher, and Naphtali. Despite the ancient allegiances, times were different than when the land had first been settled. Many clans were breaking off and living in the best manner they could, away from the wars in the heart of the country.

These missions had occurred often since the beginning of the tribal war. The information provided by these tribes was almost as reliable as the Issachar tribal scouts in David's army. Any shifting of political alliances or invasions of their lands would first be known by the nomadic warlords on the frontier. Benaiah believed that was a legitimate reason for meeting with them, but he also suspected that David simply liked them. He had been one of them, after all.

It was important to send envoys to the tribal warlords to offer them payment for military commitments and service. It would benefit them all in the long view, since the land they would be conscripted to defend would be given to them as payment for their efforts, and any man fighting on his own land is a fearsome opponent.

Benaiah and Keth had set out on this mission after Abner had arrived to inform David that he was turning over the northern army. The tribal war was finally over. Benaiah thought it would finally give him time to devote to his wife, Sherizah, as he had been promising. There was talk of a unity banquet to heal old wounds. He imagined that he could be with Sherizah there.

But it was not to be. David had pulled him and Keth aside and dispatched them to the northern borderlands with the news. The warlords would be needed to keep Abner honest about his commitment. And so once more, Benaiah had held his wife close their last night together, whispered more hollow promises that this would be the last time he would need to leave for a long while, and slipped out into the darkness.

As they approached the ragged goatskin-tent camp, Benaiah's eyes flicked back and forth continuously. This was the last desert warlord they would visit on this mission. Benaiah and Keth were alone, demonstrating the purity of their intent, assuming that any treachery that might befall them would come from a rogue.

"Do you think there are other Philistines around besides the troop the boy mentioned?" Keth asked.

"I haven't seen any sign. But possible."

"Hope they haven't been here before us."

The desert warlords and their tent camps were a small part of the Israelite population, but they were important. They rigorously trained their young men in combat discipline to fend off nomadic raiders like the Amalekites in the south or Syrian bandits in the north.

What was most important to them was their livestock and their water; anything that threatened either was violently resisted. Unlike other warlords, they did not care about hoarding vast wealth or obtaining tracts of land. Such wealth would have been meaningless to them. Better to have a hundred head of cattle, fertile women, and a deep well than a bag of gold. They would have been a useful ally to the dead king Saul if he had stopped hunting David long enough to cultivate a relationship with them.

They passed a line of tents and corrals, forming a small village. There were few people around—mostly women and children. Just before they reached the tattered flap that served as the entrance to the largest tent, which they assumed would be the council tent, Keth stopped. Benaiah turned to ask what was wrong, but Keth held up his hand.

"They would have come out to us before now."

Benaiah felt his heart flutter, a sign of danger. Keth was right. Their fatigue from the long march had dulled their judgment.

Keth stared at the tent flap hard. Benaiah, sharply alert now, searched the desolate surroundings nearby. The other tents of the warlord's clan were a short distance away. Camels bayed their guttural noises, dogs yapped occasionally.

Visitors to these camps were normally a great event worthy of everyone's attention, for good or ill. The desert breeze stirred up swirls of dust and sand. Nothing seemed terribly amiss. All looked normal. Yet Keth did not move.

"We should go," he said quietly.

Benaiah nodded. If Keth said it was not right, then it was not right. Benaiah started to turn away, reaching over his back to secure the strap he had begun to shrug off his shoulder in anticipation of dropping his weapons outside the tent. As he did, an arrow whistled through the air and slammed into his chest. He pitched backward from the force and thudded into the sand.

Keth did not hesitate. He threw the javelin he had been carrying. It sailed through the opening of the tent.

Benaiah gasped for breath, convinced that he had only moments to live. He snapped the shaft protruding from his chest. Pain finally registered, severe enough that he yelped like a wounded animal.

"Philistines," Keth grunted, grabbing Benaiah by the collar and dragging him across the sand. Benaiah lurched to his side and shoved Keth's hand away. He prodded the arrow a moment; it had not gone deep into his flesh, slowed by the leather armor before striking his collar bone, but the hooked barbs were excruciating.

"I'm good," Benaiah coughed. The two warriors crouched behind a boulder just as another flurry of arrows thumped around them. Benaiah counted the number of arrow strikes as Keth readied his own bow.

"Three archers. From the tent. They're shooting together," Keth said.

"Why are they attacking us? They're supposed to be our allies!"

"I don't know!"

"Can you tell how many?"

"No."

"Flank?"

Benaiah glanced to his right, then his left, then watched as a helmet emerged from the narrow ravine between the tents that served as a waste dump. Another helmet popped up next to it, and two soldiers rushed across the sand toward them.

"Left flank! Two!"

Keth fixed the arrow, spun, and fired it in the same motion. The iron head pierced the leg of the closest man, who tripped and fell, screaming. His partner in the ambush, not expecting the warriors to be carrying a bow as well as heavy weaponry, leaped back into the ditch.

Benaiah, angry about the arrow in his chest and angry at himself for missing the warning signs of the ambush, frantically searched for other assaults. Keth shot another arrow into the tent and at the waste ditch to hold whoever else was in there at bay.

Benaiah sat up, looked quickly at the tent and the hillside beyond it, saw no other attackers, and finally pulled out the weapon he preferred for these types of fights—in his right hand, a hardwood war club with a stone fixed at the tip, and in his left, a small iron-studded shield. It was light and could be wielded by his powerful arm for a lengthy amount of time, and in close quarters he did not risk cutting himself. It also made death very agonizing for his opponent.

"We need to assault our way out of this," Benaiah said, wiping sweat out of his eyes. "If we just escape they'll run us down. They'll have fresh water and we don't."

"Hit the tent first. We need to conserve arrows, so give me clear shots," Keth said, his arms a blur as he fixed another arrow. "They can't be very experienced or they would have waited until we entered the tent. One of them got anxious."

Benaiah nodded. He allowed himself a few seconds to think about it. They wouldn't be able to see him if he came at them from the side, buried as they were inside the dark interior and unwilling to step outside in the face of Keth's arrows. But they would probably try to escape and attack out of the side openings.

"I'm going to wait for them to slip out the side of the tent. When I draw them out and you have a shot, hit them."

"Why can't I attack the other side?"

"If we're both fighting we won't be able to see if more of them arrive. I need your eyes here."

Keth nodded. "Yahweh be with you, my friend."

Benaiah rolled to his side and sprinted forward while Keth shot another arrow toward the ravine. Benaiah felt a Philistine arrow whistle past his head from the tent opening. After a few more strides he knew he was out of the angle of fire for the archers in the tent. Crouching behind his shield as he ran, searching for any sign of other assaults, Benaiah reached the edge of the main tent.

He hurdled a rope fastened to a tent stake and crouched on the side of the tent, waiting, his shield in his left hand, club in his right.

As expected, a tent flap was briskly pushed open. Benaiah swung the club toward the arm holding the flap open. Bone snapped, and as the Philistine screamed in agony, Benaiah's club crushed the man's throat.

Benaiah darted along the side of the tent toward the rear, the pain from the arrowhead in his chest agonizing. He decided not to rush inside because his eyesight would not adjust to the dark interior fast enough.

Keth called out "Shot!"—a warning to him that an arrow was in flight and to watch out for it. Reaching the backside of the tent, Benaiah saw just in time another man peering through another flap.

He swung the club and it crashed against an unseen helmet. The man cried out. Benaiah swung another hard strike.

He spun on his heels, running back the way he had come. As he turned the corner, the first flap was opening again.

Benaiah lowered his shoulder and ran into the body on the other side of it. They fell through the flap together into the dark interior of the tent. Benaiah drove his elbow into the throat of the man.

Something smacked against his leg. Benaiah whirled. Darkness. He had to get back outside where he could see. A shout. The arrow tip in his chest burned like a coal.

There!

A Philistine was swinging at him. Benaiah avoided the swing and dove back outside the tent. The Philistine chased him outside. Benaiah was just about to turn and face him when he heard an arrow thump into flesh. He stopped running and spun.

The Philistine chasing him, now on his knees, groped at the arrow shaft protruding from his torso. He glared at Benaiah, cursing in the Philistine tongue. Keth came running. "Have you seen any more?" Benaiah asked.

"No, these were all I saw."

Benaiah knelt next to the Philistine and locked eyes with him.

"How many of you are there?"

"Many. We are coming to put our seed in your women and kill all of your men."

"Invasion?"

The Philistine spat out blood and looked back and forth between Keth and Benaiah. "Your wives will become screaming whores, and Baal will rub your god's face in his—"

Benaiah punched him as hard as he could, relishing the crunch of several bones. The man fell onto his back.

"Once more, then I break the other side of your face."

The Philistine was holding the arrow shaft with one hand and pawing at his face with the other. Benaiah let him curse a moment, then nudged him again.

The Philistine lowered his hand and glared at him . . . then, unexpectedly, a grin.

"More are coming than the waves of the sea, more than the sand of the Negeb. Your new king has become lazy, his army is scattered, we will—" He suddenly reached into his waist belt, withdrew a dagger, and slashed at Benaiah. Benaiah, reacting from instinct, caught his wrist and drove the dagger back into the Philistine's neck.

Benaiah watched him bleed until he was dead. Then he stood up.

"Are you all right?" Keth asked.

"Sore, nothing bad. Not very deep. We need to move."

Keth nodded. "Do you think he was telling the truth?"

"It's wise to assume so. Made the mistake of doubting the Amalekite about Ziklag."

"Why this small group?"

"They must have been expecting emissaries and politicians from David's court, not warriors, else they would have had more men on our flanks. Maybe they thought we would go into the tent unaware," Benaiah said.

"But where are the rest of the men around here? Surely a warlord would not have simply packed them up and left all of his women and children," said Keth.

"We could ask the women here where their men went."

"They knew who we were and that we were coming."

"The warlord might have sold his allegiance to Philistia in exchange for peace. He would not strike his fellow Hebrews himself, but he might have been persuaded to turn a blind eye."

"I'm not a Hebrew, but that does not seem possible. They hate Philistines the same as us. Perhaps they were lured away by a larger Philistine force, and while they were gone these assassins snuck in," said Keth.

Benaiah nodded, wiping sweat from his eyes. "Better get back to David," he said.

"I will retrieve my arrows."

Benaiah trotted to the side of the tent where he had left his shield. Keth ran to the fallen archers and pulled fresh arrows out of their quivers; he did not have time to inspect his own and they would likely be broken anyway.

Benaiah and Keth trotted away from the tent in the direction of the nearest hillside, wanting to get out of sight as quickly as possible. Other tents in the village were showing signs of life. When Keth and Benaiah had been ambushed, all of the Hebrew women and children in the tent village had disappeared. Now, a few women looked out from under tent flaps with children hovering underneath them in the opening.

Several men emerged from the tent village and watched them. Keth held his bow higher, showing them his warning. Benaiah reached up and pulled out the javelin Keth was carrying and waved it menacingly, along with his club. Only the most elite warriors carried multiple weapons, and from the looks on the faces of the men, this was sufficient deterrent.

As they moved out of the area, Benaiah could not help but be angry with these Hebrews. Were they now in league with the heathen Philistines? Had it become so wretched in their lands that his own kinsmen were willingly submitting to their enemies?

As they were about to crest the ridge, Benaiah heard the yelling of several men behind him. Tense, he stole a glance backward, but to his shock, the people were cheering them on.

Lines of Hebrews, mostly women but a few men as well, emerged from the shadows and were whistling and yelling at them. Women spun in circles, the men tossed dust into the air and called out blessings. Children picked up rocks and threw them at the dead bodies of the Philistine soldiers.

Confused, Benaiah and Keth stopped running.

"Maybe they weren't allied with them after all. They might have been under threat from the larger force to keep quiet," Keth said.

"Then where are their warriors? I see only older men and boys."

"Probably lured away, like you said."

The people in the warlord's clan started chanting. The sound reached Benaiah's ears.

"Giborrim! Giborrim! Giborrim!"

Benaiah grinned in spite of himself. They knew who they were.

Giborrim.

Mighty Men.

Waving, the two warriors disappeared over the ridge.

ELEVEN

In the council room at David's palace in Hebron, Eleazar son of Dodai was doing his best to hold his tongue.

He listened, twitching when the remarks irritated him, unable to hide behind a stoic face, as Josheb and Shammah could. His feet were tucked under his legs. He, like the other warriors, sat on a dull rug that had become brown with the dirt clinging to the cloaks and tunics of the fighting men who always rested on it during councils such as these. They always refused clean rugs; only the campaign rugs that traveled with them on the frontier were acceptable.

Across from him in the room, well lit from the high windows in the walls, David himself reclined on a clean rug with a bowl of figs. Eleazar glanced at him occasionally during the meeting. During the winter season, stuck inside the palace, David had allowed his perfectly toned and muscular figure to become soft. His auburn hair and beard were well groomed, but his eyes were strained, his features displaying stress and weariness beyond his years. His words were dull when he spoke, lacking their usual poetry and passion.

To Eleazar, it appeared that David was simply existing and nothing more, unable to decide whether he wanted to be alert and engaged or aloof and lazy. Eleazar held in a sigh as another commander gave his lengthy description of what his own spies were telling him about the movements of foreign armies. There was an endless stream of them, all maneuvering themselves into the favor of the new king, all with their sights set on acquiring ample holdings of the newly acquired northern kingdom.

Listening to the man ramble on, Eleazar looked over at the royal historian busily transcribing the notes from the council chamber. The historians and scribes had had much to write about recently. In the past weeks, several events had taken place that led to this meeting of the commanders and elders of Israel.

The war between the tribes was over. Abner had finally decided that David was the future of Israel and intended to turn over the northern kingdom to him, ripping it away from Saul's heir and the current king, Ishbosheth, a weak puppet. David demanded that, as a sign of good faith, Abner bring along Saul's daughter Michal, to whom David had once been married. Abner had fulfilled his end of the arrangement, and it looked like there might be a peaceable transfer of power. Perhaps Abner had finally realized that David was the only way Israel could be unified. On the other hand, one rumor said that Abner had taken one of Ishbosheth's concubines and laid claim to the throne himself. But Eleazar doubted that rumor. Why would Abner then turn it over to David?

Regardless, the truth would never be known. Joab and Abishai had seen to that. Eleazar exhaled, fighting the sorrow rising up in his spirit. Such a good man. Such a waste.

Eleazar looked away from the historian. The man speaking to the council now was the newly appointed general and liaison of the conscripts from the northern tribes, and he looked untrustworthy in every way. His charm was ample, as were his words. He had earned renown on the battlefield under Abner and was the one appointed in his place to negotiate the structure of the new Israelite standing army, but like other war leaders, his vain ambition was limitless. Eleazar hoped that David saw through such men, but life in the royal court might have softened him up to those with sweet words of admiration.

"Majesty, the army of the people must be divided into two distinct corps," the general, named Korah, continued. "If we integrate the men from the north too quickly, the officers will lose control. Men will fight over who insulted who and who looked at who's woman—all of it."

"Your argument is valid, but they will never integrate at all if we keep them entirely separate," David said.

"But the Israelites will not want to be a part of Judah's forces for many months, perhaps not until the next campaign season."

"We are all Israelites. The circumcised sons of Abraham, Isaac, and Jacob. There is Judah and Simeon and Ephraim—but there is also Israel, and Israel is *all* of us now. When the Philistines and the Arameans and everyone else who wishes to destroy us are defeated, then we can get back to squabbling over who can farm on what hill."

Now everyone, northerner and southerner, chuckled in disbelief. Saul had tried to create one nation out of all the tribes, but a long history of infighting was against him. It was also against David.

"Laugh now, but you will see. We shall all be one people soon."

"Lord, I know you mean well—"

"I do mean well. Just as Abner meant well." The council went quiet at this. David looked around. "I grieve him. I do. As much as any of you. How I wish he would be here for this. But he is gone, and now you must follow me. We have many common enemies."

David's tone was diplomatic, and Korah nodded and sat down. Eleazar looked for signs of the man's displeasure. It had not gone the way Korah had planned—he had no doubt hoped to be appointed chief of a powerful, independent, and ethnically united group that could rebel at any time.

Eleazar shifted visibly again. David smiled at him and said, "Eleazar, bring your wisdom to the group."

Eleazar leaped up almost before David was finished. "We need to keep it as you have designed it, lord." He picked up the staff that served as their pointer and aimed the tip at a cluster of large squares drawn into the box of sand in the middle of the group.

"The army of the people needs to be fully integrated with men of all tribes from the beginning and given their own identity. Make them form a new history. Let them create their own standards and set up competitions between them for the right to boast. Let the best warriors from each unit spar and be given prime places on battlefields so that they can win renown for their units. They will bond quickly. We can even have athletic competitions like the merchants describe from their travels."

"You can't remove generations of hate with a foot race, Eleazar," Korah scoffed.

"You certainly can't if you are serving as a Philistine slave and your wives and daughters are being whored out to a barracks of soldiers. We do not have the luxury of keeping all of the men isolated into their own groups. What if you have a traitor in your officer ranks? He could turn the tide of battle with a single defection."

Korah visibly bristled at the insult. "What about my lord the king's personal army? You have them divided between men of Israel and foreigners."

"You said the difference yourself. Foreigners. We are all descendants of Abraham, Isaac, and Jacob here. It is one thing to separate foreign mercenaries and another to separate our own kin."

"Let's ask the foreigners what they think of this," David said. He gestured toward another corner of the room. A fearsome man with thick braids of black hair and straps of iron-linked armor stood up and bowed low. His name was Makat, and he served in Benaiah's bodyguard.

"We serve you, lord king. Whether you are a Philistine or a Hebrew."

David nodded at him and the man bowed. Eleazar saw that this must have been an uncomfortable piece of information for the elders gathered from the northern tribes, and they shifted uneasily.

"Eleazar, Josheb, and Shammah stay behind. The rest of you are dismissed, we will continue after the midday meal," David said.

As men murmured and bustled out of the room, Eleazar sat back down on his rug. He felt as though he could continue pacing for hours, the restless energy in his body never finding enough outlets to satisfy him. He was a man who thought quickly, acted quickly, lived quickly. Such endless councils and meetings vexed him. He knew their purpose, but his place was outside among the troops. Life in Hebron at the royal court had been hard on him these past years.

He looked at David again and tried not to be disappointed by what he was seeing the king become. So many days spent in the court, so many women coming and going from the harem. David was plagued by endless headaches from his numerous wives, all chattering and competing for primacy in his chamber, each eyeing their own child to be the successor when the day eventually came that the Lion could no longer rule. It was sad to Eleazar that a man still so young, only thirty years, already had to worry about his own death and succession. David had been king over Judah for seven years, but only days into his reign over the whole kingdom, the trappings of rule were already weakening him.

We need to get him back out on the frontier, Eleazar thought. Out in the wild, where the desert and the enemy's arrows would sharpen him once more.

The door shut. Now only the Three and their king were left in the council chamber. The light from the window dimmed momentarily as a cloud passed outside. It seemed to rouse David from his trance. He stood and stretched his legs. He wore a royal robe with fine linen and expensive dyes of purple, but now that he was alone with the Three, he pulled it from around his shoulders, exposing a simple tunic and leather weapon belt. He carried a dagger with him at all hours—even, it was rumored, in his bedchamber when the women came to him. Women made dangerous assassins, and everyone knew of the king's amorous passions. But despite his nightly visitor from the harem, David was especially harsh to women. He spoke to them even more dismissively than other Israelite men and often ordered them out of his bed the moment he was through with them.

But of course, this could all be the silly scuttlebutt of women that frequently wasted everyone's time. Eleazar's wife had been whispering these things in his ear, but Eleazar had been quick to dismiss them. He did not know. All he knew was that the sooner they marched out against their enemies, the better for everyone.

David raised his hands over his head and stretched his shoulders, then jumped up and down a few times. "Still feeling that stiffness in my arm, Josheb," he said.

"You should have listened to me and soaked it for three days in that oil bath," Josheb answered. Josheb usually voiced the concerns of the others. It fell to him to be David's right hand and to ensure that not only were the Giborrim ready at all times, but also their king.

"You speak like Abigail," David said.

"I don't care if I sound like that cackling hen married to the palace baker. You need to be ready to fight, and you are not. It would be excusable if you were copying a scroll of the Law to read every day, as Yahweh commands his king to do. But you're not."

David ignored him and looked at Shammah. "What do you think about this new alliance?"

"I have not been here long, but from what I have seen, the Gibor-rim and the mercenaries are fine with the idea of a new people's army. They just don't want to have to fight with them," Shammah said in his low, rumbling tone. He had returned from a scouting mission on the Ammonite border the day before and missed most of the activity going on in Hebron since the coronation.

David sighed. "From what I can tell, the people cannot wait to fight their king's battles. You three will have them ready soon. No one will move against us yet; we have some time. Anything else from the kings of Ammon and Moab?"

Josheb shook his head. "Not yet. But I suggest you consolidate your power inside of Israel first before looking at foreign alliances. Again, as Yahweh *wants* his king to do. Philistines are crawling over our lands like ants, and they will not accept that you are going to remain a loyal vassal."

"I like your idea about forming new regiments, Eleazar," David said.

"A necessary precaution. The northern elders support you because you are the only man with the means to defeat the Philistines. It is either submission to you or rape and murder from the Philistines. They probably don't fully trust you, nor the highly paid army that is loyal only to you. Especially since you have surrounded yourself with foreigners and not Hebrews. The northerners are somewhat appeased by how you handled Abner's murder, but it will take a while for them to forget the last few years of seeing their sons butchered at the hands of your warriors."

"We never killed that many. All of you at the pool of Gibeon spilled the most blood, and I was nowhere near there."

"Yes, you were nowhere near there—and therefore your nephew instigated that battle," said Josheb.

"Abner killed Asahel; Joab was not entirely in the wrong."

"*After* the battle began, and *after* Asahel chased him down to kill him," Josheb corrected.

David nudged a pillow with his foot impatiently and rubbed his eyes. "This has nothing to do with what concerns us right now. Our people have been a barbaric nation of petty tribal alliances for too long. We need to join the civilized nations and create stronger rule from the throne. The Egyptians have an efficient means of ruling their people—"

"The men have not seen you in a while," said Josheb.

"I have been busy," David replied, irritated.

"Not that busy," Josheb held firm.

That was all it took.

"Stay in your fighting position, Josheb, and leave governing to me," David said, his voice quaking with anger. He walked to the window and looked out over his city.

Eleazar knew that Josheb was the only one who could get away with such insubordination.

Josheb waited a moment before responding. "Your arm was injured during basic sparring. Never, for as long as I have known you, have you ever injured yourself in simple training. Only weak, out-of-shape new recruits injure themselves during training. You find every excuse to delay your battle drills with me—"

"I said stay in your area!"

"—and you will keep injuring yourself and finding more excuses not to train, and the men will continue to grow fat and lazy—"

David whirled and glared at him. "It is your job to make sure they are *not* fat and lazy! Whom do you serve? You all sound like you have forgotten who you are. I have too many pressing matters around here—"

"None more pressing than the welfare of your men! Jonathan is gone! He lies in Sheol, and he will fight with you no more. Stop dishonoring his memory!"

Josheb had shouted the rebuke so loudly that the council door broke open and two members of the bodyguard entered with bows drawn. David waved them off. Warily, they retreated and shut the door behind them.

David glared at Josheb, and Josheb glared back at him. David had only to say the word and Josheb would be put to death for this affront. Eleazar waited for another outburst.

But none came.

Instead, David's features softened. He rubbed his eyes and sat back down on his rug. He reclined, then curled into a position a child might take if they had been scolded by a parent.

That response shocked Eleazar. Josheb's face registered the same response. He cleared his throat. "Lord, I want—"

"You are right, of course." David's voice was muffled by the pillow his head rested on.

"But I had no right to bring up Jonathan. I know how that hurt you. Forgive me."

Eleazar waited. The room was silent. Outside the door he could hear the continued murmur of the other members of the war council as they discussed their politics and alliances and interests, all bringing ambition to the table, all focused on something other than the kingdom's best interests. All bringing a request to the king, or a complaint, all wanting power and position. And though they all heard this, there was nothing but silence in the room.

Keth eased his head up just enough to see down the canyon and count the Philistine force approaching. The morning skirmish had left him and Benaiah wary and watchful, and as they crossed a second ridge of the desert hills after fleeing the tent village of the tribal warlord, the first company of Philistine troops emerged from hiding a short distance from the trade road and pursued them.

This confirmed to Keth that they had not expected only two men to come on such an envoy. Their commander would not have prepared a counterattack for a failed ambush if he was facing only two men. Instead, he'd have assumed that the ambush squad in the tent would be sufficient.

Clearly, he had not expected David's Giborrim.

Keth counted the squads, organized by tens as the Philistines occasionally preferred. There were eighty men in the company moving up a small draw—away from Benaiah and Keth. The false trail he and Benaiah had lain was working; either the Philistine commander was new to this type of warfare or he was unskilled as a tracker and had not supplemented his force with men who were.

Keth sat back down. It was probable that the Philistine commander would eventually return and slaughter the Hebrews remaining in the village. There was nothing he and Benaiah could do about it. Keth held his breath for a few seconds, then exhaled deeply to calm his nerves. Next to him, Benaiah was rubbing dust onto the handles of his weapons for grip.

"Where should we go?" he whispered.

Benaiah replied, "Hebron. We have to get back and warn David. This country is probably covered with Philistines. If the Levite garrisons have been as neglected as our spies reported last month, Philistia could slip thousands of troops into the Rephaim or Jezreel valleys without being contested. The northern kingdom would be cut off from Judah."

"Levites are supposed to be priests, not garrison commanders."

"That's why I tell people I am of Judah."

"David has not been crowned more than a fortnight. How could they muster so quickly?"

"A spy in the court could have tipped them off that it was coming weeks ago. Maybe even among the Thirty. That last Philistine we killed knew much about what's been happening at court, and about our level of military readiness. Josheb and the others have been suspecting a spy."

"Joab or Abishai?" Keth asked.

"Possible, but unlikely. Joab schemes to stay in David's favor, and Abishai would never support treason. The real problem is that we have no idea how organized the northern armies are anymore. We have all of this new territory but are not prepared to defend it."

"Then I think we need to assume that war has already broken out and go straight to the caves. David may already be there. How else can he stop the Philistines from invading Judah?"

"He won't mobilize until he knows what he is facing."

Keth heard Benaiah sigh, likely frustrated anew that David kept sending him away for these missions. Why even have a bodyguard?

Finished with his weapons, Benaiah wrapped them back up in the leather and tied it around his shoulders securely. The exertions of the previous hour had left the grips slick with sweat, and Keth knew how paranoid Benaiah was about a slick grip. It had been thus since the time he had slain a man-eating lion in an old hunter's pit trap. Benaiah had told him that the handle of the spear he was using was so slick from the blood and sweat of their fight that he was unable to hold the weapon firmly.

Keth looked at the jagged flesh at the edge of Benaiah's dark hair, briefly wondering what it would have been like in the pit with a monster like that. He shook his head. "We should go to the caves," he said, patiently prodding Benaiah.

"He might remain at Hebron," answered Benaiah.

"He will need to defend the passes. We can't let Philistia isolate us from the north."

"You go to the passes or the caves or wherever you feel is best. I am going straight back to Hebron," Benaiah snapped.

Keth lowered his eyes. "I know your wife is in Hebron, but that is not Ziklag. Brave men guard the city. Trust them. The caves are between us and Hebron. If David and his army are not there, we can continue to the city."

Benaiah inhaled sharply, then apparently thought better of lashing out at his friend again. Keth knew that after several disasters while Benaiah was away, including a long-ago raid where Amalekites killed his daughters and raped his wife, Benaiah would not leave her alone when there was a threat.

"Is she well?" Keth ventured.

Benaiah shrugged his shoulders and nodded.

"Your sons?"

Benaiah nodded again. "They looked a lot more like her than me before we left."

"Praise Yahweh for that."

Benaiah looked away to hide his grin. "Hopefully they still do. I am worried that they will look like me. No woman will take them."

"Eleazar mentioned that he wanted to betroth two of his daughters to them," Keth said as he shifted his back against the rock. He held out a piece of dried goat meat, which Benaiah took and promptly bit off a piece.

"Good. Maybe then I will get the money he owes me."

"I think we should go to the caves first, brother, and then return to Hebron from there if nothing is happening. It is not too far out of the way. But I am with you in whatever you decide."

Benaiah leaned over and looked down the valley. It was clear of Philistines at last. "There are far too many soldiers out here just to assassinate tribal leaders. I think troops are converging from the Philistine outposts."

"To where?" asked Keth.

"If they are invading, it will be Pas Dammim, in the Elah Valley."

"Decide, my friend. We are going to run out of water soon. None of the streams are flowing, and we don't have time to dig."

Benaiah nodded. Keth watched him scratch his head thoughtfully.

Then he was up and moving. "The caves," he said, and Keth followed him.

David rolled over and faced the three of them again. He fumbled with a fig in the bowl and tossed it into his mouth. Eleazar saw such age and weariness in his countenance that he thought once more how remarkable it was that David was only thirty years old. Each man present and nearly all of the senior commanders of his army were at least seven years older than him.

"What else?" he continued.

It was as though the confrontation had never happened. Eleazar glanced at Josheb, who seemed content. At least the necessary words had been spoken. Whether they were heeded was between the king and Yahweh.

"Your men in the towns of Judah are setting about preparing their own units for the next campaign season," Josheb answered, extending a peace offering to his king, which David accepted with a gentle nod of his head.

The *gedud*, some of David's old outlaw companions, had been placed throughout the land of Judah as the administrators and landowners of sizeable populations. This rewarded them for their service and was also a clever way for David to protect his interests, since they would be battling over the fate of their homes if an invasion ever took place. The lands of Judah had become a mixing bowl of different nations and tribes who had been aligned under the service of David; the actual tribe of Judah was proud of their native son but wary about the influence of so many foreigners as their leaders.

"The drought is destroying all the crops in the land. Only a handful of towns where the wells have not dried up yet have clean drinking water. Philistine garrisons are everywhere in the north and have taken over many of those wells," Shammah said.

"Has it really become that bad?"

"The worst I have ever seen. The water that does run is bitter and foul. It would poison any man or cow who drank from it. Yahweh has cursed the land."

Shammah was not given to exaggeration, so if he said it was bad, Eleazar knew it was dire.

"The farmers?"

"Unable to irrigate. No streams are flowing. The Philistines ..." Shammah hesitated. "The Philistines have reinforced their garrison at Bethlehem."

At the mention of his hometown, David closed his eyes. It was a while before he spoke again.

"How long have Benaiah and Keth been gone?"

"Over a week," said Josheb. "They don't know about Abner. Benaiah won't take the news well. Especially since it was Joab."

"I pray they can convince the *apiru* leaders to join us. We need them. Warlords are more trustworthy than those scoundrels," David said, gesturing with his head toward the hallway, where the tribal elders and leaders from the north were still talking.

"What do you plan on doing about Joab and Abishai? The northerners won't fight under them," Eleazar asked, only a little hesitant to bring it up again.

"I am working on that. Give me time."

"Killing Abner was inexcusable. Joab should be executed," Eleazar said plainly.

"I told you—he is too powerful now. I can't just kill him. Too many men of Judah are loyal to him. There are many powerful commanders who approved of what Joab did. Tribal fighting. Yahweh forgive us, it will be our undoing."

"We still need to do something about them," Josheb said.

"There will be an opportunity."

David paced, thinking. The other three waited.

"The new army will be composed of two corps. One corps will be drawn from the people, north and south. We will set it up as Eleazar has recommended. The other corps will have the mercenaries and the Giborrim. I will think about what to do with Joab and Abishai. Go get your midday meal."

The Three left the chamber.

TWELVE

On the edge of the Israelite hill country, a Philistine named Ittai was daydreaming.

In his dream he saw a dark sky and a darker ocean, with waves that roared around his head like a predator chasing prey. The waves grew higher and higher, and he was clinging to something, a stray piece of wood perhaps, but it kept sliding out of his grasp before turning into a serpent. He swam as hard as he could, pulling his hands frantically through the growing waves, trying to outswim the serpent and the monster that lurked beneath the waves—the monster his father had warned him of, the one who would pursue him always.

And then the daydream ended the same way his dreams at night ended, with the waves fading to blackness; a long quiet, the cool of the dark, and then he would awaken.

Shaking his head to clear his thoughts, he watched the large, solid clouds billowing upward over the Great Sea and wondered if the drought over the land of the Israelites was finally going to break. If it did, it would make their task of moving an army into the mountains that much more difficult.

Ittai made his way to the edge of the camp, nodding at a couple of guards who snapped their feet together as he walked past. When he came to the clearing where they kept prisoners, he saw two Hebrew women lying on their backs with their ankles and wrists fastened to stakes. Their garments had been torn apart and their bodies exposed. Blood pooled beneath them. It was obvious that a number of soldiers had been taking turns with them.

"How many went through before it was stopped?" he asked the nearest guard.

"A dozen or so, lord. These aren't lasting as long as the others."

Ittai nodded. The only way to prevent men from abandoning an attack on a town in order to rape captives was to get it out of the way early. Depending on how long these two stayed alive, most of a regiment could take their turn and be satiated. After every platoon of soldiers had raped them, the women were given a rest so that they didn't pass out from shock or, worse, die. Then they'd have to find more, and he had other things to worry about.

They looked at him now. Empty expressions. All tears had been cried.

Ittai was nearly thirty-five and had strong, broad shoulders from years of drawing the long bow. His beard was short and neatly trimmed, an indication of his willingness to adopt the methods of other nations when it came to keeping himself fit for war. He wore a full set of armor custom forged to his body by the best smith in the land. His eyes searched the surrounding countryside constantly. His only physical flaw was the fragment of his ear that had been removed by a poorly aimed Ammonite war axe.

He was standing at the entrance of the valley the Hebrews referred to as *Elah*, a wide field leading into the hill country, traversed by a trade road following a dry creek bed. The army encamped here was vast. Not the largest force he had seen, but much larger than the typical hastily mustered gathering of battalions that usually preceded invasions into Hebrew lands. The garrisons at the seaports had been notified. Regional kings were sending what they could in the way of military support with promises of even more once it had been proven that the Hebrew vassal David was trying to break his yoke.

Ittai hated rumors, especially when they came from his commanders. The troops knew nothing; they were here because they were paid well and would be able to use that money on whores and wine when they returned home. Their loyalty to Philistine kings was bought.

They did, however, hate the Hebrews. They hated them as only men who had been instructed from an early age could hate. For generations, Ittai's people had been told the stories of the filthy Hebrew tribes and their warlike god Yahweh who destroyed his enemies. There was a firm belief among many that this god was simply a magic trick. The Hebrews were known to have sorcerers, old men who carried staffs and wore tattered garments, wandering the countryside proclaiming curses and warnings. There were legends of great champions who ripped apart creatures with their bare hands and killed his countrymen by the thousand with devious tricks. Dagon, he knew, was a pure god, one who commanded strict obedience and was ruthless with his enemies, not content to let his deeds be done by old wizards.

Ittai had joined the Philistine forces when he came of age following his swim in the Great Sea. The swim was required of all youths who aspired to command troops one day. They were dropped far away from shore in the tossing, vicious waves of a storm and told not to come back to land until the sun rose and set a complete cycle.

He was only fifteen years old when he was tested, but he remembered it now as he watched the thunderheads over the western horizon gathering. The lightning had relentlessly shattered the air around him, causing his scalp to flood with heat as the storm gods threw their worst at him. He swallowed more of the grimy dark sea than he could fathom and wretched repeatedly, slipping beneath the surface countless times, only to sense Dagon and his scaly hide shoving him back to the surface. More than once Ittai was convinced that he saw the bearded face of the half-man, half-fish monster he worshiped staring at him from the deep.

The storm had calmed the following morning, but then the thirst came. Salt filled his eyelids and nostrils; his mouth burned with the desire to take deep gulps of the water all around him. But he remembered what his father had told him during preparations. The sea was foul—it was to be tamed, not drunk. "The body dies after drinking the sea!" his father had warned him the evening before.

Ittai had lasted all that day and into the evening, barely clinging to life. When the signal fires on the beach were lit that indicated it was all right to return to land, he lacked the simple strength to pull his body through the waves to land. After a few dizzy attempts at swimming, he rolled to his back and passed into oblivion.

There was the cold shadow of the sea, and he occasionally felt movement, and then arms were pulling on his hair and shoulders. A violent heave came from his gut as he wretched the last of the sea water and opened his eyes. There were blurry faces, shouts, the smell of blood. A goat had been brought to the beach and sacrificed in his honor. The more he came to, he recognized his mother and father in the crowd, and his brothers.

Of the twenty young men in his town selected for the swim, five had returned alive. Accomplishing this most sacred of feats gave him a profound sense of awe that Dagon had chosen him from beneath the waves, pushing him toward the surface whenever he was drowning, rescuing him to one day be a conqueror in his name.

Ittai was grateful for the chance to conquer in the name of

his god. His father and mother were proud of him, were prouder still when he made the rank of chariot platoon commander much younger than most due to his extraordinary skill. He distinguished himself in action against the enemies from the north who would attempt to seize valuable crop and herding lands.

He ascended through the ranks fast. His heroism at the battle of the Brook of Egypt against the better-trained and better-equipped Egyptian charioteers and bowmen, with their devastatingly effective recurve bows, made him famous. When all others were running under the withering assault of the chariots, Ittai snuck behind the lines and captured the Egyptian commander's chariot, then sawed through his throat and mounted the head on a pike, which he waved to his men to rally them. It had worked. The Egyptians retreated back across the brook. Ittai was given three days with the temple prostitutes for this feat. In the steam and mist of the lodges of Dagon's temple at Gaza, he had been pleasured by these women, the snarling face of his god leering from the wall and commending him for his bravery.

His first battle with Israelites had come at the place called Gilboa. Despite his inbred dislike for the Hebrews and his tendency to ignore the more ludicrous superstitions of his people about the Hebrew god, he was wary. Word reached him that the defecting Hebrew warlord, David, would be joining them on the campaign, and Ittai was one of the most prominent of the voices calling for this madness to stop.

David and his mercenary army were highly feared by the veterans who had met them on past occasions. Ittai knew of a commander who had lost his entire company when David had butchered them and cut off their foreskins, an act that sent those brave warriors into the afterlife without the ability to seed women, a horrendous insult. If David were to turn against them in the fray, it would be disastrous.

In the end, David was sent away, and Ittai believed along with the rest of the assembled army that he would go back to being the private force of King Achish, gathering riches into the king's storehouse for a commission.

Personal glory on the Gilboa slopes eluded Ittai, for at the time, he was a chariot commander, and chariots were quickly rendered useless on the steep slopes where the Hebrews gathered. He waited out the battle on the valley floor, watching the lines of his countrymen advance up the mountain until they finally chased the Israelites to the gentle slope that allowed the Philistine chariots to attack them. But Ittai's chariot had broken an axle, and he had watched in humiliation as other commanders stole his glory.

The Hebrews had been crushed at Gilboa, their best commanders killed or frightened off, David banished to the southern wastelands, and the celebrations and sacrifices went on for days. Ittai took part in a sacrifice on the third day after the battle. Several priests from the temple of Dagon, wearing shimmering fishlike scales on their colorful robes and head wraps, had slit the throat of a young Hebrew girl over a rock. As she gagged, priests pried open her mouth and studied the signs. Blood drained out of her throat when she coughed. The priests took turns studying the pattern of the blood on her neck, arguing with each other about the meaning of the pattern. Ittai had watched the girl struggle weakly before her lifeless body was thrown to the waiting soldiers who lustfully tore into her.

Declaring the god's favor, the priests gave their blessing for the invasion, and celebrations were delayed until the northern part of the Israelite kingdom had been captured. They went from village to village, enslaving and destroying, stealing everything valuable and burning the livestock and crops dear to the residents of the nearby towns. On the fifth day, the priests sacrificed another girl, but this time the omen frightened them, and they ordered an immediate withdrawal back to the plains. And so the army had left the mysterious mountains of the Hebrews, and Ittai's first campaign against them drew to a close.

But Ittai never forgot what he had seen on that campaign. The Hebrews were proud, defiant, and would not submit to any foreign master without a vicious fight. Even with all of their army dead or missing, they believed they would eventually be saved. When salvation did not come, they met death stoically, even the children. It had bothered him. He had thought about it for months and then years afterward.

Ittai turned away from the Hebrew women and made his way back to his tent. He saw his armor bearer, a grizzled veteran who had been with him for years. Most armor bearers were younger, but Ittai loved the man's companionship.

"Tell me, old man. Let me hear your thoughts."

"May Ashtoreth hide her skirts from our kings."

"That's what I assumed you would say. But it doesn't help me."

"Chariots into the valleys. Ridiculous. You would think we'd learned nothing from previous invasions here. It's a good thing that the Hebrews are holed up with their king in Hebron."

Ittai nodded, then looked back up the pass. "We'll be at Jebus, cutting them off from their northern lands, before the end of the week."

THIRTEEN

The walk from the royal residence to his home usually took Eleazar less than a Sabbath day's walk--the distance a man could travel and not violate the Sabbath. He intended to use every moment along the way to think about what he had seen in the council chamber. Josheb had stood his ground, had told David what only he could tell him. So now the king knew what his men were thinking.

The old David would be horrified at this king. *Yahweh, open his eyes. Do what it takes.*

The heat was suffocating as Eleazar walked down the entrance steps of the spacious palace. He saw numerous courtiers and tribal leaders waiting in line to have an audience with their new ruler. They sat on cushions in the shade provided by servants holding broad, purple-dyed wool blankets on the ends of poles, an extravagance meant to impress upon visitors and emissaries that David was wealthy and powerful.

Along the courtyard wall, casually nibbling on dates and enjoying the stares they were getting from the men, were concubines from Ammon, sent as tribute to persuade the Hebrew Lion that it was not worth his time to attack their kingdom. Eleazar gave them one more glance, then shifted his gaze away.

A woman ran up to him with a roasted piece of lamb in one hand and her other palm open. It smelled wonderful, but he shook his head and pushed past her.

Councils of minor elders, those who had less influence than the men who had been in the chamber that morning, waited impatiently at the far end of the courtyard for word of decisions made within. They eyed him expectantly, and when he shook his head, they lost interest in him and concentrated on the entertainment provided for those waiting.

On this day it was a troop of acrobats, tossing one another high into the air and performing feats of swordsmanship.

"Three flips or four? Three flips or four?" a man was crying out to the crowd, waiting for them to shout their guesses. The crowd chanted four, and the acrobat launched into the air, performed four flips, then landed on his feet with a wave. A roar of approval rose up.

The displays reminded Eleazar of the courts of the Egyptians that Benaiah had once described and seemed dramatically out of place among the tribesmen with roots in shepherding and farming. Much had changed in recent years, though. He shook his head.

Turning left onto the main street, he looked at the quiet religious quarter of the city, where the Levites and the priests had established a formal system of sacrifices and observances according to the Law of Moses for the first time in centuries. As opposed to the public courtyard near the palace, the corridors were silent with contemplation. Scholars of the Law came from all parts of the land, from Dan in the north to Beersheba in the south, because David had offered them sanctuary. They spent all of their waking hours hunched over scrolls. The people had not been observant of the ways of Yahweh, and David was determined to change that.

The Feast of Unleavened Bread would be the first official nation-wide observance of Yahweh's ordinances in generations. It was set to begin on the fifteenth day of the following month of Nisan and was to remind the people how Yahweh had delivered them out of the pharaoh's slave camps generations ago. The *korban pesach* lamb had been bought from the most expensive herd in the land and was being kept in a secret place to keep it from blemishes.

It was an ancient tradition, one that Eleazar's heart yearned to see among his people again. Only pockets of tribal villages had celebrated it in the past centuries. Eleazar mused at how David could be so contradictory—adamantly demanding that the observances of Yahweh be restored while still allowing the pagans to pitch camps just outside his walls and their performers to soil his courts.

He passed the single soldier barracks after leaving the holy quarter. It was the part of the city where the regiments of the newly formed standing army lived. David had conscripted three corps of troops to rotate full-time duty as the main fighting force of Judah. After all the years of raiding, they finally had the wealth to pay for a standing force, and the men no longer had to serve only between the planting and harvesting seasons. This standing force and its steady wages were an immense boost to the trading and merchant activity in the city, and the city had flourished as a result.

There were five thousand of them living in the barracks quarter, sharing rooms and facilities, living, eating, sleeping, sparring, and laughing together, developing the camaraderie that would lead them to ever higher feats of bravery and courage as they fought for their fellow warriors. There would be a mass reorganization of the military now that David was the king of a united Israel, so the troops knew that soon everything would change. The soldiers were given leave to celebrate the coronation of the king and told to report back in two weeks. That had been a week ago.

He saw that some of the men who had remained were gathered

around a private well in their courtyard, dug to keep them away from the women at the main city wells. Every precaution needed to be taken, especially with the unmarried troops. There had been numerous stonings following the discovery of a married woman and an unmarried soldier over the past year as discipline had begun to slacken. The war had officially ended only the week before, but the fighting had eased since that day at the pool of Gibeon. It was a day no one spoke of anymore, a day that had died and was buried under the sands of the harsh desert sun with all the rest of the Hebrew blood spilled by Hebrews.

Eleazar deliberately changed his thoughts and smiled to himself as Gareb came to mind. Gareb had arrived among them after the loss at Gilboa seven years before, coming as many did when he had nowhere else to go in the face of the Philistine threat. He had been the armor bearer of prince Jonathan once. Better days, Eleazar thought. Gareb was now the member of the Thirty in charge of discipline and order, and had endless headaches rounding up the troops who let their licentious nature get the best of them.

Which was odd, of course, as it was well known that a large number of women came to David's bed on a regular basis. The old David would never have taken pleasures forbidden to his men. As their army had grown, it became necessary for the leaders to make periodic visits to the darkened corners of the city to pull out soldiers trapped within. It was Gareb's grumbling and complaints that had caught the ear of Josheb, and it was agreed before council that Josheb would be the one to confront David about the problem. The army was lazy because its leader was lazy.

The troops sparred in the courtyard of the barracks so that the citizens of Hebron could watch them. They were trained by the Giborrim. Unmarried members of the Giborrim, including the mercenaries, were given their own barracks. Occasionally a member of the Thirty, the most elite unit of the Giborrim, would step in and challenge all comers, and the result, without fail, was a platoon of bruised and cut warriors and a laughing champion.

Josheb was a particular lover of this exercise. He had the record for the most appearances in the sparring arena. He would vary his method of challenging himself. Sometimes he arranged for one of his arms to be fastened to a smelting anvil as he fought, other times he was armed with only his fists while his dozens of attackers carried heavy weapons. The troops adored him even as they were pummeled, as they adored all of the famous Thirty and the Three who led them. Eleazar, Josheb, and Shammah cultivated the image of the Thirty very carefully. The people needed their heroes, needed the hope that valiant men gave an oppressed nation.

Eleazar came to the end of the barracks quarter and walked down the street where the married members of the Giborrim lived. In addition to the estates they had along the borderlands, which David had cleverly given them as both a reward for their service and as additional incentive to fight for him, many members of the Giborrim kept homes in the city of Hebron itself. Women liked to socialize, men loved competing for power and prestige in the royal court, and children loved the company of others their age to get into mischief with.

None of the homes could be considered large; the dependence on few things of material value was ingrained into the culture of his people and in the fighting men in particular. But as Eleazar approached the dwellings where the Thirty lived, there was a noticeable growth in the size of the homes. This was largely due to the sizes of the families. The men frequently teased each other about, as Josheb put it, the "lack of warrior spirit in their loins" if they did not have at least six or seven children.

Competition was of the utmost importance to the Thirty. They had no equal when fighting, so they were forced to look inward. Every social gathering (and many of the ceremonies, when the priests were not watching) eventually became a wrestling contest or a foot race. Not even the older and supposedly more mature members of the Giborrim could resist the temptation of besting one of their fellow warriors. When it happened, wives would roll their eyes and call the children to watch, since the men had made it a standing order in their homes that boys should watch and learn from their fathers, and girls should learn to tolerate these displays.

Eleazar ascended the short hill where the homes of the Thirty perched near the walls of Hebron. It was just enough of a rise that he could see over the rooftops of all the buildings he had passed on his way from the palace.

He paused a moment to watch the city as it bustled. The unobstructed sun beat down witheringly on the sand of the street. He wiped sweat from his eyes, then glanced at a building standing near the end of the street, near his own home. It was David's private residence, the one he'd ordered built so that he could escape the trappings of the royal house and live among his brother warriors whenever he sought solace in their company.

He had not been there in months.

Eleazar sighed and was about to continue his walk when he noticed that he was being watched.

A woman stood in the doorway of a nearby house. Her hair spilled out of her head wrappings in an unruly manner, and she held a basket of clothing. She looked away as soon as she saw him looking at her and disappeared into the house. It was Sherizah, Benaiah's wife.

Women did not make eye contact with men who were not their husbands, but the wives of the warriors closest to David had forged a strong bond and were permitted to socialize in a more informal manner.

Eleazar continued walking. Sherizah and Eleazar's wife, Rizpah, had become close over the years. Both had been captured in the

Amalekite destruction of Ziklag, their previous home, then rescued when Benaiah, Eleazar, and Josheb had tracked them down. The two women shared the same gentle temperament, but Sherizah seemed to carry far darker secrets.

Rizpah had told him once that Benaiah and Sherizah had lost several children during an Amalekite raid years ago, before they came to David. She and Benaiah had always struggled since, although things had been better between them since the births of two sons. Sons always brought happiness and long life to a household. But tension remained, and Eleazar knew that the strain of Benaiah's constant absence from home took its toll. Many men did not care about their domestic affairs, but the Giborrim did.

Eleazar found himself at the gate at the back of his own house, having wandered there through a side alley littered with carpentry tools and work benches that signified yet another project that Josheb's wife was demanding of him. Deborah was proud and talkative, and her endless nagging of Josheb had been the subject of countless jokes around campfires in the woods. Since Josheb lived next door to Eleazar, he could frequently hear them arguing in the courtyard of their four-room house, something other women did not have the courage to do with their husbands. He assumed it was this fiery personality that had attracted Josheb, the man who never backed away from challenges, to her in the first place. She too had been captured in the Ziklag raid, and there had been such poignant joy when they were reunited that it convinced Eleazar that no matter how much they might fight, they would always make up.

Eleazar was proud of his dwelling. The stones had been expertly cut and sealed. The beams were of fine wood, carefully chosen—not from the Lebanon cedars that some of the others in the Thirty had purchased for their homes, but equally strong and beautiful.

Eleazar did not like to spend much of his large bounty, collected during his raiding years, on frivolous things like fancy furnishings.

Cushions and thick bedding made him uncomfortable. It was not uncommon that his wife found him curled up on the roof in the middle of the night, having shoved aside his blankets to seek the refuge of the cold stone and night breeze. Many years of desert fighting did not easily leave a man.

Yet he liked the home, even if he was never fully comfortable in it. He had allowed his father-in-law, a man of trade, to build this home to his wife's wishes. Eleazar had built the bridegroom house himself, according to custom, but he'd vowed to never do it again. When they moved from Hebron with the king to a new capital, as was certain to happen one day, they would repeat the process. Eleazar would enjoy his wife's satisfaction with planning yet another new home.

He paused after entering the gate, the sunlight warm on his face. No breeze stirred the dust in the streets, no sound of warning. But inexplicably, his neck began to prickle with the feeling that he was being watched.

He looked left and right casually, avoiding warning whoever was watching him. He pretended to be examining the gate that a local carpenter had recently replaced. The wood creaked a little as he pushed it back and forth, his eyes discreetly sweeping the area around him and covering the city walls that towered nearby.

Nothing he could see. Nothing he could smell. But he felt alert and wary, felt danger as real as if he were staring at the tip of a javelin slicing toward his face.

He felt cold, shivering even in the broad light of day. His eyes lifted from the gate.

A figure was standing against the alley wall.

Eleazar's mind clouded, and he felt it coming, the sense of darkness and despair, as if the sunlight itself were being swallowed. He remembered the tent and its dark opening, the smell of perfumes and fine oils. The women knew how to prepare their bodies to please men. This one had been captured in the north, the Ammonites said, where skin was pale and eyes the color of honey. She was waiting for him inside. The night breeze was cool across his face; warmth flowed from the tent. It would never be known, never be seen . . .

Eleazar blinked. He was breathing hard. Sweat crowned his forehead. He pulled his shawl over his eyes and dabbed the cloth against his skin. He could not bring his eyes to stare at the figure again, but he felt it standing there, condemning him. Depression, the worst he'd ever felt, came as it only came when he remembered that afternoon at Gibeon and the following night at the Ammonite tents.

The cloth of his shawl was thin enough to see through. He could see the house and the inner courtyard and the accumulation of all that made him happy in this life, stricken with the gray night of his heart as he watched it.

Cover me in the day of war, God of Abraham.

Suddenly, he heard screaming and shouting inside. There was crashing. But where other men might rush forward to find out what was wrong, Eleazar knew the sound well enough. Like spring rain, he felt his soul revived. The night withdrew, the sun shone, and he knew that the figure was gone.

He felt the quivering in his jaw that came before tears. He whispered thanks.

He unwrapped the shawl covering his head to see a small boy emerge from the doorway into the entryway of the house with a long wooden stick. The boy took careful aim and launched his weapon into the yard. It flew true, and Eleazar had to duck to his left to avoid being hit by it. Right behind him was a little girl, her head wrapped in a pale gray shawl, elbowing her way past him into the yard.

"Father, Jacob has been throwing that spear at us all day!"

"It's not a spear, it's a javelin. You don't throw spears if you can help it," the boy retorted.

Eleazar looked down at his daughter. "If I was outnumbered seven to one by women, I would start throwing javelins too."

Jacob retrieved the javelin and held it up menacingly to his sister. Eleazar turned his head aside to avoid letting them see him laugh.

They darted back through the entrance screaming at each other. The street was quiet once more. Eleazar saw small heads bobbing across the rooftop, another group of his children playing one of their games. The occasional rock was tossed over the side, the occasional shout and laugh. The sound of a frustrated woman yelling.

They were good sounds. Clean sounds. The sounds of hope. The sounds that kept away the storm.

A woman appeared in the doorway as the two children raced past. She had a delicate face with a short nose, kind features, and the sort of beauty that lingered with men even if it did not stop them in their paces. Eleazar gazed at her.

She smiled with a curious expression. "What happened?"

"Nothing. Just looking at you," he answered.

"Well come in and look at your food. And tell your son to stop throwing spears at the girls."

"Javelins. You don't normally throw spears."

"The only spear that you should be concerned with is your own. We don't have enough sons, and I am not getting any younger."

She gave him a mischievous smile and disappeared back into the house. The sounds of his family playing continued unabated. Girls squealing, his son bellowing his war cry.

Eleazar knelt down behind the wall of his yard so that he could not be seen. He let himself take several deep breaths.

He lifted his head and glanced around the alley. No one.

He raised his hands in that quiet place and looked at the heavens, holding very still. He listened to the sounds. Undeserved mercy was in them. He thanked Him of the Mountains for sending the sounds when he needed them and asked for the covering to come whenever the storm came again.

FOURTEEN

Benaiah dropped out of the tree. Keth reached out and steadied him as he tottered on a loose stone.

"You need to see it. Don't go above the second branch because they have scouts in the woods."

Keth leaped and caught hold of the lowest branch of the oak tree and swung his feet sideways to brace himself as he climbed. He reached the second branch.

They were in the forest near the top of a mountain. From where he perched on the branch, he had a clear view of the vast western slope of the central hill country all the way to the Great Sea. In the valley below were several thousand Philistine troops gathered near the pass of Elah, leading up to the passageways that bisected all of Israel. They had been encamped only a short while, because none of the usual traveling merchants and prostitutes that followed armies on campaign were present. He was still too far away to get an accurate count, but as he squinted against the late afternoon sun, he knew that there were too many. Far too many for their fledgling new army of bickering tribes.

He spotted the scouts Benaiah had mentioned—a squad of five soldiers making its way through the trees toward his position. Which made sense—this was the best vantage point for miles, and they would want to be able to scout the valleys to the left that led deep into the hill country to see if any of the small farming villages were crowded with Israelite troops.

It was the same invasion route that had been used through the generations; it had been the site of countless skirmishes, precisely because it was the most strategically important place in the land. Keth had sat through many councils over the past several years about what to do if the Philistines were to make such an invasion when David came to power. And here it was. Precisely when they least needed it.

He saw an advance column preparing to march into the Elah pass. He and Benaiah were going to have to hurry if they were to cross the valley before the Philistines swarmed it and blocked their way to Adullam.

He dropped down next to Benaiah.

"We will need to be fast," Benaiah said, picking up his equipment.

"What about the scouting team?"

"Kill them. When the Philistine commander finds out his troops were killed on a simple reconnaissance, he will assume there are a lot of us waiting for him and proceed more cautiously, giving us time to rally the army."

"I agree," said Keth. "Your wound is good? Ready to fight again?"

But Benaiah was disappearing into the woods, and Keth ducked low under the branches to keep up with him. They darted in and out of crevices and notches covered with bramble along the side of the hill. After a few moments, they crawled on their bellies until they could peer over the edge of a rocky outcropping below the summit of the mountain where they had just been.

Below them, about twenty paces away, the Philistine squad had paused for a water break. The leader had the sense to order them to keep their position secure, and each man was sitting behind a rock or tree in the shadows of the canopy, but the arduous climb had made them thirsty and they were lazily failing to keep watch.

Keth waited for Benaiah to give the hand signals that would direct their attack. Benaiah was studying their position. He crawled another few paces until he was near the trail they had taken themselves. He gestured to Keth.

"When they file out of the trees and see this path, they will come one at a time. I will take them out and you can cover me. Remember to let one of them escape."

Keth nodded. It was better to let one escape and spread rumors of Hebrew demons among the ranks of the enemy. The two of them clasped arms and spoke a blessing to each other, their ritual.

Then they waited for the Philistines to finish their water break. It was very hot, even in the shade, and Keth's thoughts became drowsy and erratic. He and Benaiah had been traveling for a week and had not rested since their morning battle at the tent. Their water was limited; no streams flowed in the land and every well was bitter.

He began to daydream as he waited, staring vacantly at a flat stone that glinted in the sunlight. He saw Benaiah shift, stirring up dust, which shimmered and rose a handbreadth from the earth. Keth felt extremely tired, and thirsty, and was eager to be able to move freely again. He never cared much for the work of the infantry, slogging through the forest. He was an armorer, a fighter of single combat, and the one who assisted Benaiah, his friend. Those were his missions.

He loved his new wife as well. She was younger and more beautiful, by far, than any other woman in the city. Her hand had been hotly contested, and her father had protested marrying her to a foreigner, but David and the others had deferred to Keth when they saw his fervor for her. He had also paid an enormous dowry, and that had quieted her father's objections.

Footfalls on the trail nearby roused him. His senses prickled, alert and ready. He clenched the bow.

Keth blinked, focused, frustrated that his mind kept wandering.

A leg appeared around the rock, and Benaiah waited for the soldier to round the corner before he thrust his dagger into the man's throat and slashed with a single vicious cut. The cut was so deep that the Philistine could not make a sound. Benaiah pulled him down and waited for the next man, who rounded the corner not long after his partner and received a similar slash across the throat.

But this man was able to yelp before he died.

Benaiah jumped out from behind the outcropping, Keth following him. The other four men froze when they saw them, and Benaiah yelled his war cry and charged, swinging the club. The Philistines looked unable to move out of fright, as though they saw a demon.

Benaiah clubbed the first man across the face without stopping, then rammed the blade of the sword that suddenly appeared in his shield hand into the belly of the next one. Keth shot an arrow at the next man, but he had seen it coming and dove into the undergrowth. The last man, bringing up the rear of the squad, ran screaming down the mountain.

Keth shot another arrow into the brush where the soldier had jumped. Benaiah dove into the brush, and Keth heard a dull thump as Benaiah's club found flesh, but the man cursed aloud in his tongue and managed to crawl out of the brush onto the open trail, his face partially caved in from Benaiah's club.

Keth shot an arrow and struck the Philistine's neck. The man clawed at it, snapping the shaft in half and opening the wound, sending gouts of blood pouring over his chest, which terrified him even more.

Benaiah clubbed his head again, finally killing him.

"Tough," Benaiah panted.

Keth nodded. "More like that one and they won't need such a large army."

"How is your water?"

"With their supply we should be fine until we reach the cave."

"If there's none there, then we'll have to go into Adullam. There's a Philistine garrison there, but a small one."

Without another word they slipped into the woods, hoping to beat the Philistine army into the Valley of Elah.

Ittai had noticed the ravines to the left of the pass as soon as he arrived at the encampment. A smart king would lead his troops through unfamiliar terrain by using those ravines, he thought. Instead of prancing about in the open for all to see and count, the Philistine army should be sneaking its advance parties into the hill country through those hidden routes. Hebrews might be expecting them there, but at least they would have a harder time guessing their numbers. Once they were certain no army waited for them in the woods, then they could march the remainder into the valley. But they were led by fools, overconfident in their numbers and previous success.

He swept his eyes across the tops of the ridges that lined the ravines and thought about how he would be moving his elite troops across them if he were commanding. Not in the bottom of the cut, where Hebrews could throw stones down on their heads or barrage them with arrows, but along the ridge itself, hidden in the branches, disguised by the brush and gnarled stumps that were so thick.

Thinking about what he *could* be doing made him anxious to reunite with his company.

They were called the Sword of Dagon. Ittai had overseen their selection and training during the previous years. The elite Sword of Dagon had a purpose: the Philistine kings could send them out against other nations and win the field with few losses. Best company against best company, much like how champion fought champion for control of nations. The king of Gaza had once arranged a combat between the Sword and the elite company of Egypt, the Red Nile. The Sword had crushed them, and as a reward received their women as slaves.

"I'm ready to get back to the Sword," Ittai said, for what may have been the fifth time that week.

"Me too. Do you think they will match with the Thirty?" his armor bearer asked.

"If they exist. There's probably more than thirty of them anyway. Probably just a name to scare young troops."

"I overhear the men talk about David's Thirty. They're terrified."

"More than you hear them talk about the Sword?"

The armor bearer nodded. "Why are you surprised? You've kept quiet about them."

"Politics in Gath and Gaza. Kings needing to be wet nursed. When I'm back with them, we'll make our name among our own men."

"They've heard about it, of course. Only one hundred, the best of our warriors. Named for our chief god so he would fight with them against the Hebrew god. But they've heard more about David's Thirty, and even more about their god."

The Hebrew god was a concern, Ittai thought. Worse was the possibility that there were other friendly gods in Canaanite country giving support to David when they saw that the Hebrew god favored him.

Ittai was eager to put the Sword into battle against Hebrews. If the Sword could destroy the Thirty in combat, should such a unit exist, it would paralyze the Israelites with fear and put the country into a terrible uproar of panic and flight. As frustrating as Philistine political maneuvering could be, it was nothing compared to the tribal bickering and warring that occurred in Israelite country. David was now the king of the most fractured nation in the world.

"Have you heard how it has been for them hiding in Bethlehem?" the armor bearer asked.

"Got a dispatch last week. They're tired of pretending to be regulars along with the rest of the garrison. They've loved defiling the Hebrew king's home village, but they're eager to meet up with us in the valley to push south. We need to isolate Jebus, pass through Bethlehem, and then hit Hebron before David can muster an army. But our kings want Jebus to be taken first," Ittai said.

"But the fortress in Jebus will take weeks to conquer, if not months. And that will give David time to come for us."

"I carry out orders, and so do you."

Ittai tried to take solace in the sheer numbers of their force. Hebrews would not likely assault so many troops in the open. In another day he would be back with his beloved company, and they would finally be released to accomplish the tasks they were created for.

A messenger appeared next to them. "The king wants you to lead a unit up those ravines ahead of us to cover our flanks. The scouting party has not signaled from the hilltop. Might be a Hebrew force waiting for us."

Ittai squinted at the boy in the sunlight. The youth lowered his face and gave the required salutation. Ittai shook his head. Courtesy infractions were tolerated in the Sword, but these lowly regulars needed to watch their tone around him. But the news was good, so he quickly forgot it.

"I am moving men into place," he replied curtly. The boy ran away.

Ittai glanced at the section leader assigned to him, who then nodded and darted ahead to organize a group to travel through the woods. This order was a rare decision of common sense and battle awareness, and it gave Ittai a flicker of hope.

Perhaps the kings were going to treat their generals less arrogantly after all.

FIFTEEN

They were too late.

Benaiah stared, frustrated, through the leaves of the bush he was hiding in. He spat. Keth punched him lightly on the arm.

"We will get around it. Keep thinking."

Keth and his annoyingly calm demeanor. Benaiah nodded.

The Philistines were already in the valley. They had encamped at the mouth of the Elah, and there were advance troops meandering up the pass toward the Hebrew village of Adullam, having crossed in a place not visible from the mountain lookout Benaiah and Keth had just come down from. Another group was picking its way along a ridge that would eventually lead to the place where they currently stood. Which might mean that they had a commander who had experience fighting in the mountains.

Benaiah still did not understand why they kept invading the same valley, but this time, with Israel completely unprepared, it made sense. Normally the Philistine corps used the trade roads along the dry summer riverbeds and meandered into the hill country like a great bloated ox, lazily and rudely crowding the small farming villages and outposts that lined the route to Jebus and the rest of the interior tribal lands. This was where the suffering of the Hebrews was most acute. There were rapes and thefts and endless killings. With this he was well acquainted.

Keth pointed. "There's a screening company moving along that ridge."

Benaiah saw it. The invasion was still marked by arrogance, however, with the forcing of so many quickly assembled men into the same route they had always used.

"I hope this ends like the last time they sent so many men into the Elah."

"I would love to have been there for it. A sling against their champion," Keth said.

"But there are too many of them now. We won't be able to stop them."

The Philistines could not have been more different than the ragged-looking Israelite warriors in their layers of shawls and robes and head wraps covering a simple cloth battle tunic. Only a few Hebrew soldiers were fortunate enough to have any type of armor. The Philistines wore thickly stitched battle kilts covered in small iron plates that resembled fish scales.

A layer of iron plating covered their chest and back, flesh exposed bare under their arms and belly. They had helmets designed according to lot and rank, with the same basic design: metal and leather straps lined with colorful beads and iron scales, with a bushy plume of horsehair bristling at attention. Senior leaders had tall, well-hewn horsehair plumes, while more junior soldiers had mere tufts fixed onto the leather head wrap.

They worshipped the gods of the sea, and their appearance resembled horse warriors from the deep, with matching armor and weapons. Ox carts drew wagons with individual champions, laden with the idols that were always brought along to protect the massive warrior who would emerge from among the ranks to challenge opposing armies.

The champions rode in the carts to conserve their strength; lesser men were left with the monotony of marching. The Philistines had giants as their champions, enormous soldiers from Gath who stood two or three cubits taller than normal men. Only one had ever been beaten by a Hebrew in single combat. Benaiah hoped to change that if it became necessary.

Lance bearers rode in the narrow chariots near the champions' ox carts, alert and ready for any threats to the flanks, able to throw the lance with deadly accuracy up to twenty stadia away.

Archers, with their lighter armor made only of leather for better arm mobility, tramped along near the foot soldier companies they supported. They had huge chests and were the broadest and arguably the strongest soldiers in the army. The Philistines used the long recurve bow, a weapon notoriously difficult to draw, requiring much strength and many hours of conditioning. But Benaiah also knew that archers were the easiest to frighten on a battlefield since they were unaccustomed to fighting up close, preferring to launch arrows from far away and drink wine that night and brag about their fearsomeness.

Heavy-weapons soldiers trudged along in the middle. Their ranks were usually full of the criminals and outcasts of the kingdom because they were the first to die and did not need to be smart, but from their ranks occasionally came the most terrifyingly brave warriors.

And they all had water. Satchels and satchels full of it. Benaiah tired to ignore this.

"They still bring chariots into the passes. I will never understand it," said Keth.

"These kings must not have fought Abner face-to-face and are too arrogant to listen to their commanders."

"Should we go around?"

Benaiah studied the foot soldiers prodding their way through the ravines. They were keeping out of the bottom and staying on the ridgeline, a smart decision.

But something occurred to him as he watched. At its narrowest point, the column of troops would have to cross a series of fallen trees likely felled by a bad spring storm years ago. The game trail they were following was not wide enough to hold the column marching several men abreast. The tree trunks lay vertically down the mountainside, providing a rare clearing in the dense undergrowth.

The forest canopy was a dozen cubits above a man's head. One could see the area from above, where Benaiah and Keth were crouched, but at eye level, there were only leaves and tangled branches, impenetrable.

"We could hit them there and escape in the confusion," Benaiah whispered.

"That's a risk. They could wound us. Why not just go around?"

"We need to delay them."

Benaiah sketched his plan into the dirt. Keth eyed it warily, but nodded. "How long should we hold?"

"As soon as they rally for counterattack, we will disappear. We'll hit them right before their archers go through. They won't want to shoot their own men by accident."

Benaiah took several breaths, realizing all of a sudden how exhausted he was. Climbing mountain after mountain, swinging heavy blades, drawing and stringing tension-filled bowstrings, endless running and crawling, the unwelcome presence of a fresh arrow wound. He saw weariness on Keth's face as well.

"Your wound is still okay?" Keth asked.

"Fine."

Keth nodded. "It would be good to stall them a bit. Are you certain you want to go in, and not me?"

"Your bow shot is more accurate than mine. I trust your aim."

Benaiah plucked his short sickle sword out of his belt and let his shield slide down his arm into his grip. Keth unwound the bowstring from a stick he carried and began to fit the line into the notch. He pulled hard, and the other end of the line popped back into place, the bow staff now bent with tension. The constant shifting and changing of weapons made each man wish for a moment that they had brought armor bearers along.

But only for a moment.

SIXTEEN

Ittai was immensely satisfied that his chosen company was conducting itself with such discipline. He had been right; there were good men among the regulars.

His orders were to slip unnoticed along these watershed canyons leading out of the hills to scout ahead and screen the movements of the main force into the valley that the Hebrews called Elah.

Ittai was alert. The lookout team had not signaled, and there was as yet no sign of them returning. He moved to the front of his column. He held his curved scimitar ready in his hand, sheathing it only when he had to cross a stand of fallen trees. The ground reeked of ambush when he approached it, but as it was the only way to the ridgeline that he desired to be moving along, he did not want to waste the time going around it. They needed to probe deep into Hebrew lands by nightfall.

Normally this ravine would have been blocked by rushing water, but there was terrible drought in these hills, evidence of which emerged as he noticed how dusty the game trails were and how crisp the once-green forest had become. The bushes were thick and still overgrown, but leaves and grass had become brittle. Twigs snapped loudly and unavoidably as they marched. Ittai wondered if perhaps the Hebrew god was angry at his people or their king and was withholding rain from them. Dagon did not do such things; the plains always had water, meat, and wine aplenty.

After leaping over the fallen trees, Ittai positioned himself at the other end and ensured that several warriors were securing both entrances to the clearing. Despite the treacherous ground, none of his senses alerted him to an ambush. He was prepared to keep pressing along the forest trail and ascend the ridgeline when he felt something warm and wet spray him.

He startled violently as his armor bearer slammed against his waist, a broad-head arrow nearly severing the soldier's head. Red mist drenched Ittai as he ducked to avoid more arrows.

He looked down at the gruesome expression of terror on the dying man's face. The armor bearer's eyes were fixed, his head hanging only by bone, a long arrow shaft in the ground nearby. Pushing the body aside, Ittai dove to the ground under the last fallen log in the clearing, yelling for everyone to find cover.

Troops paused on the trail to his left and stared at him blankly. His ears rang with tension and his own yelling. Then the soldiers saw the blood and the corpse and dropped to the ground. The men crossing the trees in the clearing stopped, paralyzed with fear, having seen their officer die gruesomely in a torrent of his own blood.

Ittai yelled at them to get down, to tell the others in the trees to get down and be ready to counterattack, but they only stared at him. He cursed their lack of discipline. They were not veterans of battle. They had not seen the terrible wrath of the war gods when they descended upon man.

But then the ringing abated. There was no sound of warriors screaming in bloodlust, the sights and noise of an ambush, and Ittai lifted his head higher to see what had caused—

The two soldiers crossing the trees died as fast and as violently as the first, arrows piercing one's chest and the other's neck. They gagged and fell off the fallen tree trunks, disappearing into the undergrowth. There had to be a force of multiple archers assailing them. The arrows were coming too quickly for just one man to fire them.

And then he saw a warrior, a large man, leap out of the bushes near the far entrance of the clearing and impale the gasping soldier watching the carnage. The Philistine next to that man received a stab in the torso between the armor plates, a perfect strike, a strike too perfect to have been delivered by a regular man.

Ittai clutched the amulet of Dagon around his neck, staying low to avoid arrows.

SEVENTEEN

Keth had only five arrows left, but the Philistines didn't know that. He would keep the left side pinned while Benaiah assaulted the right.

A head emerged on the left side over a log. Keth was not normally an archer; he preferred to use the metal blades that his people had forged for generations, but he could shoot an arrow as well as the other Giborrim. He aimed at the head.

Ittai chanced a look across the clearing to see what was happening. It was only a glance, and then he would lower—

The arrow rang against his helmet with such velocity that it stunned him. His vision went dark, he felt like he was swimming, swimming in a vast lake of blood, and he was dragging his men by the collar of their armor, but he was sinking. He was reaching . . .

▲▲▲

Keth cursed at himself for missing the soldier's neck, reminding himself to compensate for the downward slope in his aim. *Draw until it touches the mouth*. He fixed another into the notch.

Benaiah narrowly avoided the pike thrust aimed at his chest. He slapped it away, using the shaft as an avenue to stab through to the shoulders of the man in front of him.

He had killed four and wanted six more. Anger came over him, the darkness rose again and snarled in his spirit.

Two more emerged from the path, and Benaiah waited for the first thrust, which he parried. He swiped his sword at the first man but missed. He yelled and swung again, and though his blow was blocked, it was all the Philistine facing him had courage for. The soldier turned and ran, stumbling into the two immediately behind him.

The other Philistine had chosen to rush into the bushes up the slope directly toward Keth. But Benaiah had time only to shout a warning up the hill before he aimed the tip of his sword at the base of the spine he saw in front of him and shoved in deep.

That man shook in a death tremor and vomited directly into the face of the soldier he had bumped into while fleeing. That Philistine, in turn, shrieked with fear but died immediately when Benaiah stabbed him in the throat.

Benaiah's sword caught up in a bush before he could kill the final soldier in the group. He could only smack him with the shield he held in his other hand.

There were more charging up the trail.

▲▲▲

Ittai emerged from the lake of blood and the fog and saw the forest, parched and dry, and thought of water. He fumbled for his pouch, trying to ignore the ache in his head, then shouted a curse for wasting so much time.

Groggy, he rolled over, head throbbing. He had to risk it—he lifted his head over the log again, but this time there was no arrow waiting for him, only the sight of the large Hebrew warrior in the path across the clearing killing his men.

"Attack him!" he bellowed. "Assault through it!"

His order shook the dozen or so around him into immediate movement. He directed them into the brush up the hill to attack their attackers, attack anything they saw—do *anything* so long as they did not remain on this trail.

And Ittai knew what he must do in order to lead his men. He charged up the slope, lowered his head, and smashed into the warrior. The Hebrew, looking down the path away from him, did not see him coming. Ittai threw his shoulder into the warrior's waist, knocking him off the path and into a bush. The Hebrew flipped from his belly, yelled, and immediately punched Ittai's face.

Ittai kept his head lowered and absorbed the blows, waiting for his opening. When the warrior's fists slowed, Ittai hooked his knee under the man's ribs and tried to pin him farther into the bush while the rest of Ittai's troops caught up, but the warrior felt the movement and Ittai wrenched away in pain as something struck his face.

The club came down again and again, striking him across the shoulder and against the plume of his helmet. It would have killed him had he not managed to pull away from the staggeringly powerful blows.

The warrior crawled back out of the bush. Ittai did not wait for him to get to his feet but ran at him again, muscles burning. He saw the black war club raised in defense and swung his scimitar wildly, trying to kill the man quickly.

It was a mistake. The Hebrew had only been feinting a defense, and now Ittai's jaw went numb as the club struck him under the ear. Warm blood sprayed into his mouth. The blow was shocking—he couldn't breathe, couldn't catch his breath at all.

He lifted his weapon to block another strike, but none came.

The Hebrew was escaping.

Keth was running down the trunk of a fallen tree, its branches long since rotted away and providing him a clear path to the ravine on the other side. He had heard Benaiah's warning about an escaping Philistine, but glancing left and right, he had not yet seen him.

A branch snapped close by, and he dove instinctively.

A Philistine had been lying in wait for him. The man swung his sword too eagerly, tangling it in the brush. Keth scrambled back on hands and knees, not wanting to give the Philistine another shot. The Philistine yelled, frustrated that his ambush had failed. Keth withdrew a flint dagger from his belt as he crawled and waited for the Philistine to swing again.

Keth jumped over the flashing blade and landed just behind the man as he turned. The flint dagger sank to the hilt in the man's neck. The Philistine slumped forward, and his head struck the boulder, leaving a smear of blood and vomit.

Keth did not pause. He checked over his weapons and gear quickly and then darted back onto the fallen tree. He halted in the center of the clearing of fallen trees, taking position at the exact place where he had killed the first two Philistines attempting to cross. He drew once more and sent another arrow into the narrow game trail opening where he saw figures emerging, but did not pause longer to see what happened, looking instead at where Benaiah had killed the troops on the other side. Archers were finally appearing on the trail. They were escaping just in time.

Keth ran as fast as he could, hoping that Benaiah had broken through and was going to meet him down the ridge at the designated rally point.

EIGHTEEN

Benaiah finished his climb up the shaft leading to the cave and crawled into the dark opening, the coolness of the refuge surprising him. Streams of sunlight speckled the ground and rocks around him. He panted for breath. His lungs were scorched. He realized he had forgotten to steal a water pouch in his haste.

He crawled to the rocks and stared through the small cracks out into the forest. Straining his eyes as he searched for Keth, he could hear the distant commands from the Philistine commander he had battled with his club. He and Keth would need to rush across the valley under cover of darkness. If they crossed during daylight, they would be pursued by the soldiers now encamped in the Elah or betrayed by a frightened Israelite trying to protect his wife and daughters from Philistine rape and destruction.

Benaiah could not fault such a man.

Ittai avoided the last arrow as he tried to regain control after the ambush, but one of his troops was not as lucky. The arrow sliced through the man's leg. He looked away from the shrieking young soldier and stared into the forest to see if there were more.

Ittai touched his jaw and felt along the bumpy and torn flesh where the Hebrew's club had struck him. It was a dull, numb ache. The jaw was not broken, though. Most of the force of the blow had been absorbed by the soft flesh under his ear. He would be able to chew again and not slowly starve to death like others who suffered broken jaws. Men preferred to die rather than be fed milk for the rest of their lives like a baby sucking on a breast.

He maintained his watch while his officers tried to regain order, but his mind was elsewhere now, years in the past. Ittai had seen the man assaulting his troops with arrows during the ambush, and it had shocked him. He had seen the garments and unmistakable profile of a Hittite darting down the mountainside. Bizarre—a Hittite fighting with a Hebrew.

And Ittai knew this particular Hittite.

Keth stumbled on through the undergrowth, stopping only when his tunic snagged on a thorn branch or when one of his braids became tangled in some brush. It was an endless source of Josheb's teasing, but he would never drop all of the customs of his people.

He saw the pile of stones on the canyon rim that Benaiah had described to him and looked around to ensure no one was following. He dropped out of sight from the hill over the ridge and crept along the base of the rock wall, in the hope that any pursuing Philistine that had seen him would assume he had continued his flight toward the Elah.

Keth was careful to step on the stones so as not to leave a trail. He found the opening in the small cliff and scurried up the crack, leaving his gear stashed under the same boulder that he saw Benaiah had used, concealed by a bush. The crack was wide enough for him to carry his weapons only.

He hoisted his legs over the cave lip and saw Benaiah waiting for him in the corner, but his friend's eyes were focused through an opening that faced up the hill they had just come from.

Keth lay still, feeling the heat of battle leave him quickly, replaced with crashing weariness and aching muscles. He worked his sandals off his feet to let the raw and bleeding skin under his heels cool. It had been too long since he had been on the march. Too much time wasted in the city, he thought.

"How is your wound?" he asked when he had caught his breath.

"I might have received others," Benaiah replied, still staring out at the hillside.

"No, you usually complain about new wounds, my friend."

Benaiah smiled. "And you?"

"Sore feet. I could use a rub from that new wife of mine."

"She would make you bathe first."

"I am her lord. She will do what she is told."

"I wonder when we will stop fooling ourselves into thinking that is true."

Grinning, Keth let his eyes shut and enjoyed the quiet darkness of the cave, full of cool stones that brought relief from the heat. Lying on his back felt wonderful. "I am slower than I should be. My body feels heavy, my movements sloppy."

"Mine as well. Did you get any water?" Benaiah asked.

"No. You?"

"No."

Keth ignored that dilemma and brought up another one.

"They will be wary after that. We need to be careful crossing the valley tonight."

"We'll wait until the third hour after dark when they usually change their shifts. They never pay attention during their shift changes."

"How far to the cave?"

"We can be there by morning so long as no one from Adullam sees us and no Philistines chase us. We can't lead them to it."

Keth nodded. "Do you ever find it strange that David has a bodyguard full of Philistines, and it is Philistines that we are now facing?"

"When I suggested foreigners, Philistines weren't my first choice. I told you when you joined us. He's a strange man."

"An hour watch each?"

"No, half an hour. You're too tired and would fall asleep," Benaiah said, his speech slurring from his own exhaustion.

The moist cool of the cave was calming, and soon Keth dozed off.

NINETEEN

Gareb walked through the nighttime streets of Hebron, having risen from his bed, unable to snatch the short hours of sleep he knew he needed. Quiet street shops and covered market benches smelling of spices and fruits stood silently as he passed them. Servants were sweeping the animal dung that collected in the market each day, the merchants trying to outdo one another to present the cleanest, most hospitable place to barter in.

He passed through dark streets, through the foreign quarter where the families of the mercenaries the king hired for his army lived. Gareb was routinely required to inspect this area. Many of the mercenaries brought their pagan gods with them into the city, and the king had issued the strictest orders to destroy any idols within the walls.

David himself would make surprise inspections, appearing on the doorstep of a suspected idolater at a late hour and demand to be allowed inside. Since he owned most of the housing in the city anyway, the families could not resist, and whenever idols were found, they were immediately destroyed in a kiln at the town square reserved for the purpose. Often the offending soldier was killed on the spot.

Gareb found Eliam sitting next to the city gate. Men of his tribe were frequently on duty there, and Eliam had taken to sitting with them on overnight watches.

When the guards saw Gareb approach, they stiffened their backs and held out their javelins. One of them did not notice him because he was sleeping. Gareb reached over and took the sleeping guard's javelin. The guard snapped awake, startled.

"What is this for?" Gareb said.

The man stared at him stupidly.

"What is this for?" Gareb repeated.

"Throwing," the man stuttered.

"At what?"

"The ... enemy?"

"I asked you the question, why are you answering with another one?"

"I ... throwing at the enemy."

The drowsiness in the man's face removed the last vestige of Gareb's anger, and he fought to keep from smiling. This was a new soldier in the army, Gareb could tell, a conscripted recruit who had drawn the short lot for the nightly watch duty. He decided to harass him a little longer. Eliam watched smiling from the shadows.

"I once shoved a javelin up a man's back when he was sleeping on the watch."

The young man swallowed hard.

"What tribe are you from?"

"Judah, sir."

"I thought you were going to say Simeon. I would have had to shove this javelin up your back and make you into my new battle ornament."

The soldier was shaking with fear. Softer, Gareb said, "Hold up that weapon and show me how you would throw it at me."

He backed away and gestured for the soldier to demonstrate. The young man looked at him fearfully, then picked up the javelin by the grip. Its oak handle was worn and chipped in numerous places, and the double-edged blade at the tip, thin from being sharpened so many times, would snap if it struck anything but flesh. This young man likely had been given the weapon as a gift from his father, who himself had had it for years. Sentiment had no place in the ranks, Gareb thought.

"Throw it at me," Gareb encouraged. The soldier glanced at Eliam, terrified. Eliam chuckled and nodded at him. The soldier positioned the blunt, weighted half of the javelin over his shoulder, holding the grip next to his ear, and steadied the double-bladed tip at eye level in front of him.

"Not bad form. Make certain you don't roll your wrist inward. Until you have trained with it for many hours, your grip will weaken, and it will fail you. You might cut your own ear off in the middle of a battle, and then I will be really angry and ram it—where did I tell you I would ram it?"

"My back, sir."

"That's right. I will ram it right up your back. Can you guess where the point of entry will be?"

"Yes, sir."

"Do you have enough rations?"

"Yes, sir."

"Stop calling ..." Gareb bit his lip. Actually, he was supposed to. One of the Thirty and all.

The young soldier waited nervously, trying to understand what the game was.

Gareb sighed and shook his head. Then he said, pointing to a watchman pacing the city wall, "Go relieve that man. The cold desert wind will keep you awake."

The soldier left, nodding his head gratefully. The other sentries at the gate feigned disinterest and resumed their watch. Gareb tilted his head at Eliam, who patted the sentries on their backs before walking with him.

The two of them climbed the narrow staircase to the top of the gate, stepped over a gear beam, and walked out onto the city wall. This section of the wall near the gate rose twenty-five cubits high, providing a marvelous vantage point for watching the sloping plains that angled away toward the distant hills. The grass that normally colored the countryside deep green was absent, and the landscape was pale and grim in the moonlight. In every direction the sky was clear, the sun had been red when it went below the horizon, and the citizens of Hebron had resigned themselves to another stretch of days without rain.

Eliam leaned against the gate shaft and ran his fingers through his beard as he looked across the plains. Gareb thought back to when he had first met the boy, now a man, as he worked as a servant in the tent of Saul. "Wonder if it will ever rain again," Gareb said.

"It's dry," Eliam answered.

Gareb nodded. "You ready for this?" he asked.

"I will be. Foot hurts some, but I think the new way of tying—"

"No, I meant, are *you* ready. For when we go out to drive away the Philistines."

"Who says they are coming?"

"You know they will come."

Eliam's smile faded, and he looked away again. "Of course."

"I made my peace. I think you should too," Gareb said.

Eliam nodded. "I have. It has been a long time. Everything fades in time."

Gareb scoffed. "You *have* made peace with him. That's the sort of thing that he would say."

"Didn't I tell you? I am the new court musician. I write beautiful songs."

They looked at the surrounding hills for a while. The breeze picked up and swirled on top of the wall. Gareb pulled his cloak tighter around his neck. He hated being cold. "I'm thinking about telling him," he said.

"What?"

"About what happened at Gilboa. He knows I was the prince's armor bearer."

Eliam glanced at him. "That was long ago."

"Yes, but he needs to know that I did not want to join him after Jonathan died."

"I thought about joining Abner. I never cared for Ishbosheth, but Abner was a man," Eliam said.

"I thought about it too," Gareb admitted.

"Why didn't you? You had more reason than anyone to hate David."

"I still don't like him."

"Then why are you here?"

"It's either him or a Philistine."

"There are others who could rule Israel. Do you believe Joab and Abishai acted on their own?"

Gareb shrugged. "They're capable of it."

"Maybe. Joab and Abishai are powerful. They might take the throne from David."

"They wouldn't try it. They're loyal family. Reckless, though."

"So is David."

"David is competent. And brilliant. Remember your rules of leadership. Competence above all. He is the only one who can lead us," Gareb said.

"But he is also reckless."

Gareb did not like where this was going. He turned his head and stared at Eliam. "You need to be careful. Others won't take that so lightly."

Eliam nodded and sighed. "Just thinking, that is all."

"Well, don't do that. You're too young and aren't paid for it. Focus on being the hero of Gilboa that you are supposed to be. Your feats on the mountain are legendary to the younger troops and are what will give you the chance to join the Giborrim eventually. You were the last one to speak to Jonathan before he died."

Eliam did not answer.

Unable to sleep, avoiding their dreams, they watched the mountains.

The youth was paid well for his ability to run long distances with dispatches from the borders. It was a fair wage, and in the chaotic years since King Saul had died, the youth was the envy of other young men desperate to be paid for their labor.

The messages were frequently a sealed parchment and nothing more. He picked them up from the Israelite garrisons and ran them to Hebron, delivering them into the hands of the member of the royal court who employed him. He knew that the king read them, and it was a tremendous honor. His father had told the men gathered at the city gates about his son's important royal responsibilities.

But this night, with this message, it was different.

As he sprinted down the moonlit road, perspiration streaming into his eyes, his panicked breath pounding in wild, terror-driven patterns, he saw the horrible monster coiling in his mind again. He saw the coming slaughter, the coming rape, and the flies in the heat, and he would refuse the treasure room of David himself to not have seen what he had seen that day.

He crested the last rise and saw the city walls and the watch fire of the guard at the top. He looked over his shoulder one final time and cried out in relief—he had made it.

He caught the scent of the city waste ditch as he crossed the bridge. The sheep gathered in the night pen snorted; their shepherds lying in the rocks nearby, wrapped in their cloaks, raised their heads sleepily and watched the figure dart past them.

"Philistines!" the boy screamed. "They are in the valley!"

Gareb swore and shook Eliam's shoulder. "That fool is going to send the whole city into a panic, get down there and shut him up."

Eliam sprang up and disappeared down the stairwell from the wall next to the gate.

Gareb called for a sentry and the soldier stumbled over to him, afraid of a reprimand.

"This might be a ruse. Watch that tree line. If you see so much as a suspicious shadow, I want you to try to avoid screaming like you were stuck by a child with a weaver's needle and come find me. Everyone stays alert. Spread the message."

The soldier nodded and Gareb descended the staircase. When he arrived at the gate, Eliam had pinned the messenger boy against the wall with an elbow to the throat. The boy was gagging and writhing and trying to shout. Fear had caused him to bite through his lower lip and blood was leaking down his neck and into his collar.

"Shut up," Gareb said. "When you stop screaming like a woman you can deliver your message."

"Philistines . . . in the pass!"

"There are always Philistines in the pass. They live among us."

"Thousands! An army!"

"Which pass?"

"From the plains leading into the Elah."

Gareb felt his heart flip in his chest. Philistines going into the Elah? So soon? "If you are lying ..." But when he looked into the boy's eyes, he saw terror.

Gareb spoke calmly so that he would not panic the shepherds running up to the gate and the sleepy-eyed traveling merchants camped inside the walls for protection. "Eliam, wake the king. And the Three."

TWENTY

Eleazar was in and out of sleep. He awoke for a while, listened to a bird chirping somewhere before flying away, and nodded off. It was quiet ...

... running again. Always running, always escaping, always outnumbered, always fleeing. Up the tall slopes of Mount Tabor, then higher up, on the run from Saul, need to hurry! Run away! They are too powerful ...

... the survivors in the towns after Gilboa. Women and children—the men are mostly dead. Defeat again, all is lost in the north, the king has been slain, Jonathan is gone, what will David do? Stay with the Philistines. Always the easy way. We will run again, Hebrews run, Hebrews flee, we always run, Yahweh must be ashamed of us ...

... killing Hebrews, we are killing Hebrews, young boys, that is all they are, our own kinsmen. We are killing Hebrews! I shove the body off my sword, it falls into the muddy water of the pool. Curse this place. Corpses are in the water, defiling it, unclean to touch the corpses, unclean

to touch the defiled water. Hebrew men, kinsmen, brothers, nothing but unclean corpses now. Yahweh, has it come to this? We slaughter our own tribesmen, and the other nations unite against us. Will it always be this way? I kneel, I cannot kill another Hebrew. Run, Abner, run from here. Protect those men from Joab, and from me. And Josheb. And Shammah. From all who live by the sword. Take the mothers' sons away from here, Abner. Hebrew killing Hebrew, son of Abraham killing son of Abraham. All because we do not listen, Yahweh. Mud in my hands, and tears. Many tears. And blood. The earth bleeds, our land bleeds. We run, we will never stand together ...

... lift the flap of the tent and duck inside. All is dark but the oil lamp, flickering in the middle. Rug spread out, cushions finely woven, soft as wine and shimmering like jewels. There she is, in the corner. Honey, grapes from distant vineyards, and other fruits I do not know. The idols surround her—here they worship their gods. Her face just out of the light ...

Eleazar woke with sweat drenching his blanket. His heart was beating fast. Every vein in his body throbbed, but his fingertips were cold, as always. Icy cold, unable to grip anything. He rubbed his hands together under the warmth of the blankets and listened to his wife's breathing. She slept soundly, never waking unless disaster was upon them. Sometimes not even then.

He slid out of the blankets and walked to the window of his house that overlooked the streets below. After staring at the brilliant stars over his town and instinctively checking every corner of the street unlit by the moon, he picked up a small clay pitcher that sat on a ledge next to the basin, then stepped through the doorway out onto his roof.

Eleazar sat on the brick ledge that lined the top of his house and took a drink of the water. A short one, though, because he did not want to drain their ration any more than necessary. As a member of the Giborrim, his family was allowed more than the common citizens, but he and the others refused. Another small way to protest David's new selfishness. The lower-ranking families had to drink too.

Eleazar's wife was skilled. She knew how to measure and ration to each member of the family according to their daily need, and they never seemed to run out. Much of the baking had to be reduced, and the bread was dry where it had once been moist, but they were managing.

The worst drought in anyone's memory, including the oldest of the elders, had put the farm and herding land into turmoil, and despite the lift in spirits following the recent coronation, many more of the tribesmen had been coming to the city to load their donkeys and camels with water pouches filled at the community wells.

Wells were drying up across the land. David ordered rationing at the Hebron wells, but it was only a matter of time before those wells ran dry also. Judah and Israel had both suffered bitterly from the drought while the surrounding nations, including Philistia, enjoyed abundant rain.

Eleazar feared the day he knew was coming—the day that they would have to load their ox carts with water vessels, load up their camels and donkeys with water pouches, and trudge to the plains of Philistia with their heads hung in humiliation to beg for water. Shame piled upon shame.

"We are their vassal," he spoke aloud to no one. "We live among them, our women whore themselves out to them, and now we will have to crawl into the royal courts of Gaza and Gath like harlots and beg for access to their wells."

Saying it made him angrier. The endless compromises would have to end. He would say something to David himself if he had to. Had the water in it not been so valuable, Eleazar would have thrown the vase into the street in disgust.

"We crawl. We beg. We lose heart and run. Never did *that* in the old days," he said aloud.

"You never had time with me in the old days, either. It's okay, though. You have handsome brothers."

Eleazar felt soft arms wrap around his waist. She was wrapped in a blanket, which soon covered him as well.

He pulled her onto his lap. She laid her head against his shoulder and nuzzled against him.

"I would offer you tea," she said.

"Save it for yourself. I might be leaving soon."

"Where?"

"I don't know. The borderlands perhaps. To convince your father that it was right to unify the kingdoms under David."

"He might have you killed."

"And who will be fighting for him?"

"My mother."

Eleazar kissed the top of her head. "I will concede that. She is meaner than—"

"Just because I said it does not give you the right to."

"Fair enough. I will express it this way. If our son fights even an ephah as fearsomely as his grandmother, we will be marching to conquer Egypt by the first time we celebrate the Feast of Tabernacles."

Rizpah moved her hand further up his chest and touched his chin. "How many more children do you want?"

"I am doing my part. About the *only* thing I have been doing worthwhile since we have been here."

"Don't worry. I am sure you will leave again soon."

"It's not you or the children. David is not the same. We need to be ... out there again. The kingdom will suffer."

"I know," she said. "He needs you to do what you do. All three of you."

He held her, savoring her touch and the softness of her neck. Then Eleazar saw the soldier running up the street.

I am running. Leaping over stones and trees, running as fast as I can, and I am terrified. Saul is hunting me, hunting my men. I see the top of the mountain next to me, wonder if I should climb, descend. Keep running! They are coming, they are coming! Eleazar pushes me from behind, yells at me to go faster, I see Josheb turn, fire an arrow at our pursuers, but they are coming, always coming, faster! What did I do? Why does he hunt me, Lord? Run faster!

... the rock is near, a fortress, the wilderness of Maon pours out beneath me. We must flee! Must go faster! Eleazar, help me, brother! Josheb, Shammah! My brothers are running. Michal loved me once, I loved her, but she betrayed me. Run, fool! Yahweh, strengthen my legs, carry me across the heights, teach me your ways, make me run faster. He is coming. The forest is ahead, if we can reach the forest we can evade them, but they are so close, on the other side of the mountain waiting for us, we are trapped, he has trapped me again. Yahweh, Abba, deliver me ...

... running, slower, growing weary, running slower, need to move my legs. Stop hunting me! Yahweh, make him stop hunting me. I see the forest ahead, the Lion is in the forest, his jaws are open, he is roaring, but I cannot see him anymore. Jonathan is dead, slain on the heights. Cannot do this without him. Cannot hear Yahweh anymore, cannot feel the covering, send me the covering, God of my fathers, forgive me, send the covering, show me where I have sinned, my people suffer ...

"Lord?"

David leaped out of bed and lashed out at the messenger with his foot. The kick sprawled him across the floor. David was on top of him immediately, a dagger pressed against his throat.

"My lord king, I . . . have news," the man gasped.

David, angry and panting, released the man and rolled to his side. The woman in the bed shrieked, and David glared at her, trying to bring his sleepy vision into clarity. The woman, a concubine from the harem. Nazreel? Nazira? What was her name? He was in his bedroom, the royal palace, in Hebron.

King of Judah.

King of Israel.

"Lord, my message," the soldier prodded gently.

Calming down, David nodded. He realized the man had drawn the short lot to be the one to wake him. David leaned against the bed and raked his fingers through his auburn hair. The woman shivered beneath the blanket. David vaguely tried remembering her name again.

"A runner says that Philistines are moving into the Elah. Thousands of them."

"Philistines live there. They have garrisons. Who told you to wake me for this?"

"Gareb of the Thirty, on the night watch."

David finally recognized the soldier.

"Eliam."

The young man nodded. "Yes, lord king."

Gareb did not indulge in frivolous warnings.

David struggled to his feet.

When David was gone, Eliam turned his attention to the woman in the bed. "Anything further?"

She rubbed her eyes sleepily. "Not yet. But I will let you know if there is."

Eliam nodded and left.

TWENTY-ONE

Within the hour, all of the members of the war council were in the meeting hall. This time, however, there were no vases of wine or bowls of dates. Some had been summoned despite being drunk. Everyone was somber, anxious to hear what was rumor and what was truth.

"You saw this army yourself," David said to the messenger, who was sitting in the middle of the room, calm at last. The presence of the fiercest warriors in the kingdom and their legendary leader had reassured him.

"Yes, my lord king. I saw thousands of them."

"Did you count standards? Regiments? Corps? The tents of their priests? Anything?"

"No, lord king, I did not know to do that. I only know that a sea of them gathered on the plains several days ago and are moving into the Elah."

"How fast were they moving?" asked Josheb, stepping forward and kneeling next to the map stretched across the sand pit.

"Slowly, sir. Some chariots, some scouts moving into the village of Adullam. They are not in a hurry yet, but they are moving."

David paced around the back of the group. Others asked question after question of the messenger, and he answered as best he could, but he was a courier, not a trained military scout, and his inability to provide detail was giving them a frustratingly vague idea of what they were up against.

David dismissed the messenger, and the boy bowed low before leaving. Eleazar watched him go through the door before he said, "This is why we have scouts on the borders. Whose men are supposed to watch that valley?"

"Those are Joab's men," answered Josheb, still crouched next to the map and staring at it hard.

"They might be dead. Philistines could have hit them before they could get a message out," David said, pausing long enough in his pacing to stretch out his sore shoulder.

"Philistines aren't that efficient. Someone would have gotten away. Or a civilian could have escaped and notified us. You know how it is. Every time we are invaded, a stream of refugees crowds our city," Eleazar said.

"But that boy was a runner," David said. "There might be people coming; he just outran them. He said he saw the army today, so that means he covered the entire distance from the Elah in just half a day. That's a pace we maintain. It might be another day or two before anyone comes for help."

"How can we trust his word?" asked Shammah.

"I've used him. You can trust his word," Eliam said. Heads turned. Normally, in war council, when the king and the Three were conversing, everyone else remained silent until they were called upon. Eleazar glanced at David, expecting him to reprimand Eliam, but the king had not even looked up from his pacing. David had been especially accommodating of Eliam since the day he had heard that Eliam was the last person to speak with Jonathan.

"Talk again without permission in this chamber and it will be the last time you enter it," Eleazar whispered to Eliam. Then he glared at Gareb, Eliam's training master, as if to ensure that a reprimand would come later. Gareb rolled his eyes and nodded.

Then, aloud, Eleazar said, "Lord king, I can go to the valley tonight to spy on it in the morning. I can confirm whether the Philistines are there, and how long till they are deep into our land. You can stay and rally troops."

David looked at Bether, one of the northern generals who had come in for the coronation.

"How many men do you have nearby?"

"I can have fifty thousand in three days. They are out in the villages on leave."

"But how many here in town, tonight?"

"Only one company. We thought we would have more time to muster—"

"We have no more time. None. Does everyone here understand that? I need to know immediately how many troops I can lead out of this city *this very night*."

Josheb drew a breath. "Lord, we don't know for certain whether—"

"Abiathar?" David stopped pacing in the corner and looked around for the priest.

"Lord, I will seek word from Yahweh about this." The priest shuffled out of the room and closed the door behind him.

"They are coming." David was now staring out of a small window in the corner that was opened each evening to let in the cool desert air overnight. He placed a hand on the sill and nodded to himself. "They are coming. I know they are. Yahweh has willed it."

David closed his eyes and ran his fingers through his hair. He scratched his beard. "I need to know the number of every man who can draw the sword. Every man who can march from this city tonight in an organized and intact manner, including the troops who watch the city walls."

Men spoke up in turn around the room, calling out from the shadows the numbers under their command, and as they did, Eleazar felt the discouragement become palpable. When the last commander gave his report, Eleazar added up the numbers in his head and winced.

"Five hundred," David said. "Five hundred men who can fight. How long until others can be ready?"

Again, answers came from around the room. Eleazar shook his head. It would be a week before a large force could muster in any semblance of order and discipline. Although there were a hundred thousand Israelites who could draw the sword, they were scattered over the countryside.

The standing force had been given a week to celebrate with their families before being recalled into the new units of a standing army. The people's army, over half of the total troops, those who could put down plowshares and come at a moment's notice to assist the new standing army, had not yet been organized and would likely cut each other down before they did any damage to a professional Philistine force.

David listened to each piece of bad news with only a nod, as though expecting it.

"We should wait until we can build up a proper army, as we spoke about today," Bether suggested, assuming he now had permission to speak freely.

"We don't have that kind of time."

"Why, if I may ask?"

David sighed. "This was going to wait until we had come to agreement on how the new nation is going to be governed, but I suppose I need to tell you now." He walked to the map and pointed at a mark at the end of the Rephaim Valley. "We are taking the city of Jebus from the Jebusites. That will be the new capital. It is in politically neutral territory. Benjamin surrounds it, so that will make you northerners happy, but none of our tribes have ever controlled it. It is high and defensible and has water year-round. We can strike anywhere in the kingdom within days if we are threatened."

And strike elsewhere as well, Eleazar thought, but said nothing.

"But if the Philistines reach it first, we will never take it from them. We have to stop them. At all costs. If they can fortify Jebus, they will be able to completely isolate us from the north. They already have a garrison at Bethlehem."

Another general spoke up apprehensively.

"The Jebusites have a fortress on the hill nearby that has never been conquered. How are we supposed to take it and turn away the Philistines?"

"We have to. Philistines first, then the city. By the end of the campaign season."

Now there were chuckles of disbelief around the room.

"But lord, you said yourself that we won't be able to stand up a full army for many months!" said the general.

"We won't attack the city until then, but we have to stop the Philistines from securing that area. And we have to do it with what we have."

The northern generals were exasperated. They shouted complaints as a group, declaring that they would not throw their warriors to slaughter at the hands of the pagans.

"The Giborrim will be there. I will lead the Thirty myself," Josheb said over the commotion.

"Lord Josheb, we all know of your exploits. My son sings the songs about you. But stopping thousands of Philistines and taking an impenetrable fortress in the same campaign season is beyond even what you and the Thirty can do," Bether said.

"We do not have a choice. Philistia cannot control that pass and that city. It would be the end of the kingdom."

"It can't be done!" Bether cried. "We have no supply chain! No water! The drought has destroyed everything. Our men will die of thirst!"

"Have you ever had a wife raped, Bether? A daughter? An infant child picked up by his feet and his head dashed against a rock? It will happen again if we don't march tonight," Eleazar snapped.

Bether stared at him, jaw clenched. "I have indeed, Eleazar. We did not have the services of the Lion of Judah to protect us over the past seven years in the north." As soon as he said it, the northern general Bether lowered his face.

The room was deathly quiet at the challenge. All eyes went to David, who stared at Bether.

"My lord king, I—"

"You are correct, of course," David said. He walked back to his window and looked out once more, his footsteps echoing on the smooth marble floor. Eleazar randomly thought about how much had been spent on building this house, using gold captured from years of raiding and plundering. In the old days.

The door opened, and everyone turned to watch the priest enter the room. He said nothing, but the look on his face confirmed their fears.

Softly, David's voice emerged from the dark corner. "Brothers, it has been a long time since I was worthy of leading men into Yahweh's battles. I beg your ..." He paused, shame on his face. "I beg your forgiveness. But I need you this night. And, I will not take a drink of water until we have stopped them. The lowest baggage carrier will drink before me."

"Don't be insane," Josheb said, but David raised his arm to cut him off.

The shadows of the men against the wall were still. The torch was dying. Eleazar waited for someone to speak in response.

Josheb stood. "Well, we are wasting time, lord king. Give us your orders. We are with you."

Gareb pulled Eliam aside as they left the council chamber. "You know better than to speak up without being addressed."

"Everyone else spoke up after I did!"

"But you're new."

"What difference does that make? I'll be a member of the Giborrim one day."

"You are in training to be a part of the Giborrim. You were in the presence of the king, the Three, and the Thirty only because you are assigned to me for your testing. Your opinions on military matters don't matter to anyone but your mother."

Then Gareb strode down the hallway with Eliam behind him, knowing he had much to do and only one hour to do it in.

Eleazar stood with Josheb and Shammah outside in the courtyard.

"You run the fastest, Eleazar," Josheb said. "You need to get down there and give us a proper scouting report before we bumble into the valley with five hundred new recruits who don't know their manhood from their sword. Shammah, you deliver the news to Joab that we are leaving tonight. He needs to organize the army when it starts arriving after the messengers have warned the people."

"David has banned Joab," said Shammah.

"No one else is capable of standing up an entire army within a week and marching it to Jebus to begin a siege."

David's plan was to rush the Thirty and the remaining available troops into the Elah and Rephaim valleys to cut off the Philistine advance and buy time for the full army to reinforce them. Once the threat had been delayed they would besiege Jebus and establish a stronghold from which to battle the Philistines.

That was the plan. But as Eleazar knew, most plans did not survive the first battle.

Josheb looked at Eleazar. "After the march has been assembled and departs, you can rush to the valley and give us your scouting report. We will meet you at the caves tomorrow afternoon."

Eleazar nodded, then reached over and hugged his neck. Shammah wrapped his enormous arms around them as well. They remained silent for a moment.

"Yahweh, you who spoke to our fathers Abraham, Isaac, and Jacob, and who gave Moses your divine Law, we do not trust our own skill, but your mighty hand," Josheb said.

Then they parted. Eleazar sprinted up the road that led to his house.

TWENTY-TWO

Joab walked down a fiery corridor. Flames were everywhere — torches on the walls, watch fires on the towers, heating coals in pits in the streets. But he moved into darkness, felt its cold grip, felt the rough leather of the dagger's handle. Abishai was next to him, his breath frantic.

At the end of the corridor ahead, he saw the figure of the man he hated. Closer now. Abner was smiling, smiling as though nothing had happened.

Joab slowed his steps, and everything slowed with him; Abner's arms raising for an embrace. Abishai rushing forward. The look of surprise on Abner's face as Abishai grabbed his arm, and Joab slowly, slowly raised the blade and aimed the tip directly at Abner's stomach, just under the ribcage where it would slash through to his treacherous heart.

And Joab, nearly delirious, felt the warm blood pouring between his fingers, down his wrists, soaking his elbows.

But Abner did not resist. Was almost expecting the blade.

"Blood for blood," Joab whispered to him, and Abner actually nodded.

Abner lifted his hand and placed it on Joab's neck. His grimace softened. Abner leaned and kissed Joab on the cheek. "Forgive me before I pass into Sheol," he said.

Abishai, suddenly remorseful, pulled Abner close, an embrace. Joab watched the old general fall, death claiming him ...

And then Joab was back in the room in Hebron with his brother, waiting. On the wall nearby a lamp burned low. The wick needed to be replaced.

Joab rolled over and looked at his brother sitting in the corner. "Are you hungry?"

"A little."

They reclined on the rug next to their food. Joab pulled off a chunk of bread and dipped it in olive oil.

"David will come for us. He needs us," he said.

Abishai sighed. "What makes you think we deserve anything from him?"

"He has punished us enough to make it look believable to the north. Secretly I'm sure he is grateful to us."

"He was truly angry."

Joab shrugged. "He'll forget about it. We're valuable to him."

"He's going to order us killed. And he'd be right."

As he walked from the council, his thoughts consumed with the Philistine invasion, David took no notice of the display of the desert night overhead as he dropped the hood of his cloak, entering the darkened doorway of the small house at the edge of town. He hated his task. He hated a lot of things right now, but this was chief among them.

The bodyguards who followed him took their positions at the corners of the building and crouched, out of sight, in the shadows. They would not follow him in, for this was a private matter.

The house was owned by one of David's officials who volunteered its use whenever the king wanted to conduct business of an unofficial nature. No one lived here, and no one even bothered to go near it—after all, it was known to be a former leper's home. Which was nonsense, but it served to keep curious eyes away.

The room was lit by a lamp stand with several low-wick lamps simmering in their dirty oil. The light was only just enough to provide a bronze glimpse at the room's other furnishings: a rug, some half-empty bowls of food, and the two men who reclined next to them. They sat up as he entered.

"Lord, we—"

"Don't speak. Listen first."

Joab sat back down. David pulled his cloak the rest of the way off his shoulders and tossed it onto the wall rack.

"Your lives are spared. The northern elders will not ask for your execution in exchange for their oath of allegiance to me."

Both men shook with relief. They grinned and hugged one another, exhaling a coarse laugh.

"I'm not done. You will not lead an army of mine. You will not be on my inner council. If I see either one of you consulting with any of the Giborrim without me present or speaking with any of the elders of Judah without my permission, I will have Benaiah execute you in front of the assembly, and your head will be buried inside the carcass of a pig. Your manhood will be cut off by women from the leper colony and fed to wild dogs."

David's face was murderous, and he'd spoken with cold finality.

"Lord, permission to speak?" Joab asked.

"Go ahead."

He managed to steady his voice, the images of his detailed fate still fresh. "We regret every day our vengeance on Abner, but we have served our penance for the crime."

"No, you do not, and no, you have not. You would do it again immediately if he was still alive."

"But we do! Yes, we had hate in our heart because of the murder of our brother Asahel—"

"It was the field of battle, it was not murder," David snapped. "What *you* did was murder, and you ought to be stoned for it."

"But we know it was wrong and have proven ourselves loyal to you since that day!"

David stared at him, incredulous. "Loyal to me? By murdering the greatest general in the Israelite army? What happened to Asahel was tragic, but we are outnumbered and surrounded by all of our enemies. Angering half the population of the kingdom does us what good?"

Joab looked at his brother Abishai for support. The more reasonable and popular of the two, Abishai was respected a great deal, and David had been dismayed to hear of his involvement in the crime.

"Lord, what we did was inexcusable," Abishai said. "On the blood of our lives and our vow to Yahweh, we will serve you as we will serve our God, in whatever capacity you would have us serve. Mercy, sire."

David felt his anger cool a bit. "Philistines are moving up the Rephaim and into the Elah. They are going to isolate us from the north and then come for us here in Hebron. They are likely planning on going to Jebus as well to keep us from reaching it first. I am taking men up to the stronghold at Adullam in a few hours. You need to stay here to call the tribal levy together and organize reinforcements."

Joab's face reddened. "Lord, please, you can't expect us to just stay here while the pagans invade our lands. We are your best—"

"You are fortunate that I am not ordering you to stay and learn the art of the weaving spindle from the women."

Joab had to stifle his outrage, but Abishai glared at him to shut him up.

"Who will command the army?" Abishai asked.

"I will until I find a replacement. Perhaps Benaiah."

This struck deep. Joab had to look away to hide the disgust on his face. David knew that Joab's hatred for Benaiah was consuming. But even worse was being tasked with guarding the city while the army marched. No glory and riches came to the man who settled fights among the women at the well while the others were killing Philistines.

David was satisfied. He knew it would sting Joab to hear Benaiah mentioned. "The only reason you two are alive is because half of Judah would rebel against me if something happened to you. They view your despicable, cowardly act as heroic. Since killing you would be unwise, you will stay behind with the women."

Joab lowered his face. David saw him clench his jaw several times. Abishai exhaled and nodded. And that was that. David stood. "We will stand up the people's army in a few months, after this is over. If you have shown me by that time that you are truly repentant, you will get a chance to redeem yourselves, nephews."

Then he walked back out into the night.

TWENTY-THREE

Ittai checked the woods for ghosts.

When he realized what he was doing, he sighed and rubbed his eyes. His jaw throbbed, giving him a constant headache. These forests were mysterious, and he'd heard the troops repeat the legends of the Hebrew god over and over all day long, until finally he'd declared that the next man to speak would be lashed.

He'd tried to send a team after the two warriors who had ambushed them in the woods, but none of the men showed the heart for it. He cursed them and sent them back down into the valley, and when they arrived back at the camp, he forced them to take over the duties of the slaves making food for the army.

Then Ittai made his way to the tent of the king of Gaza, the one ruler on this adventure who actually knew what he was doing. Ittai respected him, but he knew that it was the king of Gath who held the real power in the alliance. Both kings despised the Hebrews, but they had different ideas as to how to deal with the threat David posed.

After Ittai made his report on the attack in the forest, the king of Gaza had sighed and walked over to a servant holding a pitcher of wine. He drained a cup and dabbed his mouth with the cloth on the servant's arm.

"Only two of them?"

"Yes, lord king."

"We will need to move faster, then."

"Lord, he has mercenaries. The best. One of them attacked us today. I know him. A Hittite named Keth."

The king nodded thoughtfully. "David has acquired much gold in recent years. Much of it ours. Hebrews are backward and never organize into a proper standing army. He needs to buy an army."

"We need to move soon, lord king. In the morning. If he has more men like Keth of the Hittites fighting for him, it will go ill for your armies. Your spies should have known of such men."

"The foreigners have never been hidden from us. We knew he was recruiting them."

"But not men like Keth. Trust me, my lord, that is information you would have wanted to know before agreeing to come along."

"Our timing is perfect. David's army is scattered. The northern tribes don't fully trust him yet."

"Lord, men like Keth of the Hittites don't need armies. If David has a force of the best foreign fighters in his employment, and they have been training and learning this country for the past seven years, our numbers and timing will *have* to be perfect."

"How do you know this Keth?"

"He was in my unit during the civil wars ten years ago, when we were recruiting foreigners." Intent on not divulging more, Ittai changed the subject. "It ought to shock us into movement if David knows we are coming. No more lying around fondling ourselves, lord."

Ittai knew that this king permitted him to speak freely. This ruler respected him and his skill and knew that he could be won over through loyalty. Ittai wanted to keep all of his options available should everything go wrong in his own city.

He watched the king of Gaza walk to the center of the tent and sit down near a map that had been drawn by the most skilled artists in the land. The hide was beautifully tanned and the ink from the henna plant was thick and dark. The swells of the lowlands the Hebrews called Shephelah were drawn with exact detail of every ravine, every creek bed, every access point into the hills. The king poked at it with a staff. "You saw him here?"

"Yes, lord."

"And you did not know the other one?"

"No, lord, but I have an idea."

"Who? Was it he who wounded your face?"

Ittai hesitated. "One of David's Thirty named Benaiah. And yes, he wounded my face, lord. He was skilled. Much more so than other Hebrews."

"The lion killer."

Ittai had been expecting the king to chuckle and dismiss his words as the storytelling of women to children, but the king only stared at the map.

"They were traveling south?"

"Yes, lord king. They were trying to get through our lines. Normally when Hebrews ambush our troops, they strike and then withdraw in the direction they came. These two fought through to the other side and disappeared into a gorge near the valley."

"How long will it take them to get to Hebron to warn David?"

"David already knows. He has military scouts positioned along the frontier of his lands."

The king smiled. "Follow me."

They stepped out into the late afternoon light and eventually arrived at the corral where some of the royal horses were usually kept. Ittai saw twenty Hebrew men, lying naked and soaked in blood.

The king gestured to a servant, who pulled a rope fixed to a large animal hide. As the hide moved, it revealed a hole in the ground in the midst of the Hebrews. The ground started moving. Ittai squinted.

Scorpions.

Freed, the insects swarmed over the Hebrews, stinging them, and the men screamed in terror and pain. Scorpions crawled into their ears and mouths.

Ittai watched, but all he could see was the face of his armor bearer bursting in a bloody mess. If he could, he would catch more scorpions to stuff into Hebrew mouths.

"They will not be making any report to David," the king said.

"But what about civilians? Any shepherd or farmer could run back to Hebron and tell them we are coming."

"True, but they won't know what they have seen. Philistines in the land? There are always Philistines in the land. David won't mobilize an army unless a trained eye delivers a complete report. It will be too late by then. But these two warriors you fought with worry me. They have likely spied us out."

The scorpion-covered Hebrews were begging, pleading for death. The servant looked up at the king, who nodded. One by one, the servant brushed aside scorpions from each man and eviscerated him, pulling out the heart and liver for use in sacrifices.

The priests would fire up the ceremonial kiln later that night, offering the hearts of their enemies to Dagon to ask for domination over the Israelites they hated.

Now, Ittai sat back among the men in the shadows at the entrance of the Elah. Wary commanders quietly voiced their concern about ambush by more demons. Ittai rolled his eyes but remained quiet. If demons attacked, their weapons would be useless anyway.

Everywhere he looked, he saw his armor bearer's bloody face.

Reclining on blankets next to a small cooking fire, he stabbed at a slab of beef from a butchered cow soldiers had found wandering by itself in a nearby Hebrew village. It fed the entire company heartily, and now men relaxed near their fires, satiated. But there was uneasiness in their ranks. The rumors about the forest ambush were starting to spread out of control.

"I don't suppose the kings have told you their plan, lord," his new armor bearer said, sitting across from him. Ittai had picked him earlier. He seemed capable.

"They have."

"What is it?"

"The king of Gaza has ordered me to lead a battalion farther into the valley tomorrow in order to meet up with the Sword, coming in from that Hebrew pit called Bethlehem."

The armor bearer sat forward. "Should we tell the men? That will lift their spirits."

"Not yet, because the king of Gath cannot know about it. He will want the glory of the march. We are to slip out before sunrise, day after tomorrow."

"Any further word from the spies?"

"None. Whoever in David's court has been informing our kings has been silent for weeks."

"What if the Hebrew king has an entire army on the other side of those hills? David may have sniffed out the spy and could be using him to spread false information to lure us into a trap."

Ittai shook his head. "I am told that David spends more time in his harem than scheming with his generals. We have them completely off guard."

"What if they have an entire army full of warriors like those two?"

Ittai decided not to tell him about Keth of the Hittites. "They won't. Perhaps he has a bodyguard of those warriors, but not an army."

"What else do you know of him? The Hebrew Lion."

"Rumors, mostly."

"I heard he is their god in human form."

"That would make a nice prisoner."

"What if it is true?"

Ittai glanced at his face and saw apprehension. "Afraid of him?"

"Afraid of their god. I've heard the stories. They said that the Hebrew Lion has a cave near this valley protected by enchantments. That every time our men are led to it by a traitor or search for it in the woods, they become disoriented and confused. And then they are slaughtered. Probably by those two demons you saw today."

"You sound like a new recruit," Ittai said, smiling. "Haven't you fought Hebrews before?"

"That's why I am afraid."

"What do you mean?"

The armor bearer shook his head and licked his fingers. "We fought them when Abner led them, but nothing strange ever happened. It was when their prince Jonathan led them that it would become odd."

Ittai looked back at the fire, thinking. A log snapped over the coals and sent a wave of sparks drifting up into the night. "I was in the valley away from the fighting during Gilboa, but I heard about Jonathan. They say he was a man, more than his father. They say the same about David. Maybe their god favors certain warriors."

"Why do you suppose Saul marched against us in the first place?"

"There are four Hebrew tribes in that region. He couldn't abandon them."

"Which tribes?" the armor bearer asked.

"Naftali, Zebulun, Issachar, and Asher. Issachar men usually serve as their scouts."

"I heard that his people hated him. Seems strange he would come to their rescue."

"He had his reasons, like all kings do."

"Their god is terrifying. They say he even makes the mountains shake."

Ittai pulled his necklace out and fingered Dagon's amulet. The green stone glowed dully in the firelight. "We are protected," Ittai said.

The aide looked at him, looked at the amulet. "Will Dagon be able to defeat their god when it comes time?"

Ittai did not reply.

TWENTY-FOUR

Eleazar crept into the dark room where his children were sleeping. He made his way to the girls first. The two oldest were nestled together under the same blanket as they always were, having stayed up far too late talking and then falling asleep face-to-face.

He reached out his hand to touch their faces, then caught himself. He held his hand steady, feeling their breath on his skin. They would marry not many years from now. He wondered if he would be there to see it.

He made his way slowly to the other side of the room, where the two younger girls had also fallen asleep side by side. He slowly pulled the blanket at their feet over their waists. They stirred but did not wake. He looked at their faces, their necks, the way their hair was tangled.

The memories he had of all of their births were fading. He could only recall a few details, like how the midwives had made the announcement, or what joke Josheb had said when he heard it was another girl. *Yahweh, forgive me for not being a better father, and for every time I pushed them aside.*

Then he found his son where he always somehow was in the middle of the night, curled up under the bench in the corner. No matter where Eleazar or Rizpah would lay their son down, he would always wake up the next morning under the bench. For a while it had been out in the alley. "My brothers were that way too," Rizpah had said once. "Maybe boys are born restless."

Eleazar rested his hand on the boy's ankle. As he sat still in the darkness, listening to all of them breathe, he saw his father walking toward him across a field. He had weapons in his hands, and his face was proud. Eleazar saw his own son practicing with the bow, and chasing his sisters with the spear.

And then he imagined that he was sitting in a still forest, listening for Yahweh's voice in the trees as the wind passed, whispering. The days of his life were growing short and cold. He knew it in his soul.

Eleazar sat a while longer, wondering what it would be like to live in peace, only fighting off scorpions in the common room and marauding crows from his crops. Then he stood and crept back out, his heart aching with love and grief.

Eleazar, carrying his weapons and a few days' worth of hard bread and water, found Josheb and Shammah at the back entrance of David's house, along with three members of the Kelethite and Perethite foreign bodyguard that Benaiah had formed. Josheb was in a heated debate with them as Eleazar walked up.

"You can go wait with the rest of the troops at the gate."

"Lord, Benaiah has ordered—"

"Benaiah does not intend for you to hang around the king like a yipping dog. You will have the chance to do your job, Philistine, but for now, as we march out to fight against your kin, I simply do not trust you."

The man looked at his partners, who could only shrug their shoulders. The leader sighed, exasperated, then walked down the dark street toward the city gate with the others behind him.

"You have to feel for those fellows," Eleazar said. "They never get to do anything. David sends them away all the time, Benaiah gets angry at them for leaving David even though they have been ordered away, and you prattle at them like a mother-in-law."

"If they were men, they would be marching against us in the Rephaim right now."

"David pays well."

Josheb rubbed his forehead. "The king told Joab and Abishai that they would not be coming along."

"We should not leave them here alone when the army starts to muster. Orders or not, Joab won't sit still with all of those men waiting to be led into battle," Eleazar said.

"That's why Shammah is staying behind to watch him."

Eleazar was stunned. He looked at Shammah, who lowered his head. "Leaving Shammah? On the eve of battle? Why not leave a messenger for Benaiah when he returns? Benaiah should muster them. What kind of foolish—"

"Joab would kill any such messenger and inform Benaiah that David had left him in charge."

"Unlikely, even for Joab."

"We don't know who in the court is sending the Philistines information. It might be Joab. After Abner, I'm putting nothing past him."

"Joab is a fool, but he is not a traitor. And Abishai regrets Abner's murder. He would hold Joab accountable."

"Shammah stays here to wait for the army. He will let Joab muster the troops while he tries to find out who is feeding information to the Philistines. When the time comes to lead them out, Shammah will bring them down the Bethlehem road to hit the Philistines from behind and pinch them against us."

"Is the garrison marching?" Eleazar asked.

"We have to assume that every Philistine in the land is converging on us."

Eleazar stamped his feet against the chilly night air. "Did you say good-bye to your family?"

Josheb looked irritated. "Yes, of course."

"Not long enough," Shammah said.

"Forgive me, I didn't know you had emerged from the goat shed where you sleep to give me family counsel."

David stepped out of the doorway at that moment and approached them, looking up and down the street. "Where is the bodyguard?"

Josheb said, "I told them to meet us at the gate."

"Are we ready?"

"I just finished telling Eleazar about Joab."

"We could really use Shammah and his spear," Eleazar said.

"I know. But I need him here. Joab cannot be left alone."

"You're the king," Eleazar sighed.

"Have the preparations been made for the sacrifice?"

"Yes," answered Josheb, "Abiathar is ready. As you requested, the people have gathered at the city gate."

"Each man has a water ration and three days of food?"

"Yes, and each is carrying all of his weapons. Gareb is organizing runners to bring us resupply at the cave as often as possible, but supply is tight right now."

They walked down the street past the silent homes of the Giborrim in the direction of the city gate. A few moments passed, then David said, "Just a few valleys. That's all that stands between that army and our homes."

"Three," said Eleazar.

"What?"

"Three valleys."

David sidestepped a bit in order to kick a rock in the path. It tumbled and bounced until it struck a wall.

"Leave Eliam behind with Shammah."

"Why?" asked Eleazar.

"Just keep your eyes on him, Shammah," David said quietly.

Shammah nodded but said nothing.

Eleazar let his mind wander while he walked. To his children as he had kissed them in their beds, and to his wife.

"You love this, don't you?"

"It's better than kicking down the doors of harlots trapping our men."

Eliam watched as Gareb stood with his foot on the back of a soldier who had left his sword lying in a mud puddle next to the well. The soldier tried to lift his head out of the mud but Gareb pushed it back down.

"That tastes better than your guts at the end of a Philistine spear. I heard that they eat the liver of their enemy."

Eliam looked away to hide the smirk on his face. Gareb finally relented and let the soldier stand up, wheezing through mud-covered lips.

"Will you leave your sword in mud again?"

"No, sir."

Gareb nodded and clapped him across the face.

"If it rusts, let it be because it has been drenched with the blood of Philistines, not because it was left in the mud. Fifty leaps and then you can get back to your section."

The man began to jump into the air and land on his chest repeatedly as Gareb and Eliam walked away, continuing their inspection of the troops being assembled in the early morning darkness.

"Do they actually eat the liver?"

"Shut up."

Eliam chuckled, then changed the subject.

"Where are Joab and Abishai? David would not leave without them, not with a Philistine invasion coming."

"Over my head and yours. I am trying to figure out how to move these girls to Adullam by the end of the day, attack a force that outnumbers us by thousands, and do it without water or resupply for days."

They reached the gate and looked back over the column of troops preparing to march. It was a mixture of veteran soldiers and new recruits, every man who could muster within the hour as instructed. Messengers had been dispatched across the hills to rally the armies, but it would be days before they could all come. Gareb hoped that the discouragement he felt was not showing on his face.

In the column, wives were clinging to husbands; husbands were speaking deep oaths of love back to them. Gareb rolled his eyes. "I have, for a fact, pulled most of them out of the arms of whores myself. Funny how a man suddenly remembers that his wife is the only woman who cares about him, in the end."

Louder, to the group, he said, "You'd better drink your fill now. Each man carries two pouches of water, to be distributed by your section leaders. It won't be enough to live on for more than a few days, so either kill a Philistine and take his water, pray that there is water at the well of the cave, or plan on drinking wine in Sheol by the end of the week."

While they scurried to do so, Eliam said, "Where do you want me on the march?"

"Nowhere. You need to stay here."

"What? Why?"

Gareb shrugged. "Shammah told me that you need to remain behind with him to keep an eye on Joab. They suspect he is up to something."

"Up to what? And Shammah is staying behind from a battle? Have they gone mad?"

"Up to what we have been talking about—spying in the court. Somehow the Philistines know our movements and that we don't have an army assembled right now."

"But Joab's been barred from the court. He doesn't know all that David is doing. And he's David's relative!"

Gareb sighed. "It really doesn't matter for us, does it? Those decisions are made over our heads."

"But you're one of the Thirty!"

"But not one of the Three."

Eliam scowled. "I will go put my equipment back," he said.

"Sometimes our duty requires us to be away from the front. It's no less important."

Gareb watched him walk away. He was maturing and had potential, but Gareb did not like the thought of him spending time around Joab. He reached down to pull a pebble out of his sandal. When he stood back up, he noticed that everyone had gone silent.

On top of the city gate stood David, visible in the light of the watch fire. Next to him were Shammah, Eleazar, and Josheb. The soldiers in the street were paying close attention. Many had not seen the king in months, others never. Gareb thought that David looked comfortable in his armor and that his eyes were finally tight and focused.

"Brothers, it all depends on us. If Philistia can isolate us from the north, we will never recover from it. I know that many of you do not trust me, but I promise you, my blood will be spilled in this fight just the same as yours. It is the blood of Abraham, Isaac, and

Jacob. My tribe is Judah. Your tribe might be something else, but we are Yahweh's people, and it is in Yahweh's name that we will go.

"One day, we will again have the Ark of the Lord in our midst, and we will know Yahweh's presence among us. That is my vow! But first we must destroy what threatens us, and we ask the Lord our God, keeper of our safety and salvation, to march before us into battle!"

Josheb raised his arm, and people began to part from the rear of the column as a group of warriors passed through, making their way to the front. They were large and fierce, Gadites and Gittites both, foreigners and Hebrews marching together.

The crowd sensed who they were and a cheer began to rise, because no matter how dire their circumstances, *these* men were marching out to battle.

The Thirty.

Gareb could not help but smile.

David gestured toward the street, where an altar had been hastily constructed from the stones of his own house. A robust, thickly muscled bull was led out by two Levites. Abiathar the priest laid his hands on the animal's head and spoke a prayer to Yahweh. Then he took the sword that Gareb handed him and pierced the animal's throat, skillfully severing the arteries. At first the bull did not know what happened, then as it felt its body grow weaker, it began to thrash. The Levites pulled it over the altar and held it in place while gouts of blood splashed out of it onto the altar.

When it died at last, Abiathar directed another group of priests to begin cutting off the animal's head and legs and removing the entrails. His arms bloody past his elbows, Abiathar arranged the pieces of bull carcass across the altar. It occurred to Gareb that the smell of butchered cattle resembled the smell of butchered men. He had never seen a sacrifice this close before and felt slightly nauseated.

After long moments of work, for it was his task alone, Abiathar pulled several handfuls of the animal's fat over the rocks and reached for the pitcher of oil. He poured it out over the remnants of the carcass that covered the altar and then cried out with his bloody hands outstretched to the heavens.

A Levite handed Abiathar the torch, and as Gareb watched the flames erupt on the altar, he glanced at David.

Eyes open, the king was muttering something and staring hard into the fire.

Holding a shawl over her head and wrapped in a cloak, standing in a blackened corner of an alley where no one would bother her, Sherizah watched the sacrifice of the bull. She saw the crowd begin to sing the song that David had written for use in times of war, listened to the sound of the many voices echoing firmly along the stone corridors. She cried out to Yahweh in her spirit to watch over her husband, Benaiah, still gone.

The knock on her door had come several hours previously, and once she was certain that her children were sleeping soundly, she slipped out into the night to find out what was happening. The news about the Philistine invasion had gripped her heart with worry. Was Benaiah now dead, and would her sons be fatherless at last?

She shivered as a breeze swirled through the streets. Her ankles were sore from carrying water to the poverty-stricken widows on the edge of town all day, those too weak to carry it for themselves. She and the other wives of the Giborrim busied themselves with such tasks, and she loved the solace of it.

There was a noise, and she searched for its source. Something falling? A step? The orange glow of the altar fire flickered down the dusty street, and she suddenly felt afraid to be alone.

Sherizah worked up the courage to walk forward toward the

crowd. The breeze died, she heard the noise again, and fear emerged once more. It was a footstep. Something was following her.

Monstrous images filled her mind. Brutal men with rough hands grabbing at her, pulling her down, the smell of her daughter's blood drowning her.

Screaming and running down the street now, sobs shaking her, then the Amalekite raiders pinning her down, tearing at her clothes, the pain of violation. Benaiah was not there, and she screamed as she ran from whatever was chasing her.

She was back in the dark room. The girls were screaming. A man held a knife to her oldest child's throat. Sherizah turned her head and screamed. The knife made its cut, and Sherizah passed out from the terror and grief of it. She awoke and found the same man on top of her, hurting her, her daughters no longer screaming. Her vision swirled in waves of black and red, the icy cold of the table beneath her cutting deep into her flesh. There was hideous laughter, the smell of wine, cries of anguish in the distance. The smell of smoke.

Sherizah stopped running at the edge of the crowd and collapsed, sobbing. She raked her fingers through her hair, trying to scrape out the horror that kept returning to her mind. But it would never leave. *Yahweh, it will not leave!*

She opened her eyes and saw the men marching out of the city and the families gathered and the children who would be fatherless before the end of the week.

Whatever had been following her was gone, but the despair remained.

Eleazar was to run to the valley to scout the Philistine force. He should have left immediately after the sacrifice. But he did not care at this moment.

He waited until the last of the column of men cleared the city gate and marched away toward the north, then retreated to the alcove outside the wall where he had instructed his wife to meet him. She was there, still wrapped in the blanket, unconcerned with what others might think.

He picked her up and carried her to a dark corner of the woods. He pressed his face against her neck and felt her shiver from the cold night air. "Do not let Josheb choose your husband if I fall."

"Don't speak like that."

"He will have a face like a pig if Josheb chooses him. Ask Benaiah to do it. Remind his wife."

"Enough."

They watched the orange flicker of the watchtower fires in the distance. Eleazar pulled her closer, stroking her back lightly with his fingers.

"I have loved you every day. Even when I have failed you."

Rizpah was quiet. Then he felt a small tremor in her chest. The tears dripped down her face until they touched his.

TWENTY-FIVE

At midmorning the next day, the army took another break in the march. Josheb found the nearest rock his body would fit on and laid his pack down beside it before stretching out. He covered his face from the midday sun with a water pouch. It was still cool inside, and he resisted the desire to take another small sip. Only one per third hour, he reminded himself. Needs to last until ... just needs to last.

David walked past him to the front of the ranks where the Thirty waited for the march to continue. Josheb knew that these breaks tried their patience; being forced to wait for the new recruits to keep up on a forced march was a different experience for them. The Thirty traveled alone and fast and usually left the tedious nature of organized marching to the regulars.

They were crossing the hills and forests on a route parallel to the King's Highway trade road in order to remain unseen by any Philistine scouts who might be traveling on it. The highway was used by merchants and soldiers alike, as well as pilgrims seeking the Ark of the Lord.

Josheb peeked out from under the water pouch at the sky. Despite the delays, they were making good time. Regulars were always inspired by marching with elite troops and were able to march and fight above their abilities. Wisely led, men could do remarkable things, he remembered David saying once.

But the men were drinking water too fast. He heard section leaders growling reprimands at their troops for guzzling too much of the precious liquid in the heat of the day. He sighed and prayed that they would find the well at the caves filled with water, or a pond that had not grown bitter.

They would be at Adullam by evening.

Benaiah awoke to the sound of men talking outside the rock hollow he and Keth were hiding in. It was daylight. He had no idea what time it was or how much time had passed. He heard Keth's steady breathing, but very gently his friend's hand raised, and Benaiah knew he was awake as well.

He held still and tried to listen to the quiet voices. Philistines. Two of them. He translated their tongue in his head as he emerged from the groggy realm of sleep.

"... leading along the back side of the cliff."

"He saw it there?"

"Yes, going up to the cliff. Their tracks. Somewhere here."

Benaiah realized in an instant what was happening. These men, stragglers possibly, knew the approximate location of their hiding place and were trying to trap them. He and Keth would make great prizes for the Philistine kings down in the valley if David's army was now their enemy.

He rolled onto his belly and eased himself across the dirt to the entrance of the tunnel. Below, against the sunlight now streaming onto the bottom from the outside access, he saw a soldier's head appear. Keth was next to him.

"He won't crawl up here, will he?" Keth whispered.

Benaiah tried to think. The weariness of his journey and their battles left both of them so exhausted that they must have slept through the entire night.

"We have to break through, or they'll just wait for us with arrows," he whispered back. Keth nodded. Benaiah was grateful that their pouches had not been discovered yet. The hideaway cave was a good spot, but the shaft to crawl up into it was too narrow to carry any gear besides weapons. If they had been able to spot a track, it meant they were skilled woodsmen, possibly an elite team sent from the army below. He had to get down the shaft before they were able to come up.

He held his breath and strained his ears to hear them. More whispered voices, grass bending as it was pressed down by feet.

Below, down the shaft, he thought he could hear a man moving. Crawling.

He had to make a decision. Go now? Wait? He looked at Keth, who raised his fist and moved it up and down slightly with a hand signal.

Go now.

Benaiah rolled over the entrance of the shaft, feeling himself dropping. The soldier beneath him heard the movement and tried to pull his head out, but Benaiah landed on the man's neck. He felt the spine snap beneath his foot, killing the man instantly, but not before the soldier was able to yelp.

Benaiah heard scuffling on the cliff top above him as he crawled out of the space. He looked up and saw the archer on the cliff. The soldier pulled the arrow back and released it very fast. Benaiah slammed his back against the cliff to avoid it. A lance dropped down from above.

Keth appeared behind him holding their weapons. Benaiah took the club and the sword and slid the shield onto his forearm. No more arrows or lances flew at them because they were hidden from the warriors above by the lip of the cliff.

They waited a moment, then Benaiah darted along the base of the cliff and climbed up the steep ravine disguised from above, grateful that they were fighting on their home soil and knew the terrain. They emerged in some bramble scattered along the top of the ravine. Benaiah could see the two remaining soldiers, one with a bow and one with a lance, staring down the cliff at the spot they had just left.

Benaiah clapped Keth on the shoulder and charged. The man with the bow turned and sent his arrow flying. Benaiah rushed forward to close the gap between the two. The Philistine calmly and methodically pulled another arrow out of his quiver and fixed it to the string. Benaiah heard Keth next to him panting. He saw the second soldier throw his lance. Keth caught the weapon in mid-flight and tossed it aside as he ran, and then they were on top of the Philistines.

The archer managed to loose the second arrow, but Benaiah saw it coming and ducked out of the way, swinging his club. The archer rolled. The club struck the ground and clattered away. He tossed the sword from his left hand into his right and cut at the archer rolling away from him. Knocked off his feet by a powerful swing of the archer's heavy bow, Benaiah collapsed on the edge of the cliff. The archer, instead of charging him like Benaiah had assumed he would, pulled another arrow out of his quiver and fixed it to the string, brought it up to aim, and tilted it sideways from only an arm's length away.

Benaiah kicked out in desperation and his foot caught a rock.

The rock flew into the air, not hitting the archer but forcing him to pause in his aiming, allowing Benaiah to lurch forward and grab him by the ankles, yanking him to the ground. The warrior's arrow flew up into the canopy of trees.

Benaiah reached for his fallen sword and stabbed it toward the man's chest, but the man twisted and it slid into his thigh instead. Benaiah pushed the blade in deep, deep enough that his fingers dug into the wound. He tore away at the exposed skin, trying to withdraw the sword and strike again, only to be blocked by the Philistine's shield.

Keth was having similar trouble with his man, who had produced a sword and was slashing skillfully. Keth blocked a blow so that the man's weapon was pinned away from him, preventing him from blocking. Keth brought down his sword. It clanged off the man's helmet. The man rolled away and swung a rock that smashed Keth's face, causing blood to pour out of his nose.

Keth rubbed blood out of his eyes and avoided the next blow. He jerked a dagger out of his waist belt and plunged it forward as his opponent tried to swing the rock again. The dagger ripped off the man's ear. The man screamed. Keth grabbed the soldier's hair to brace himself and turned the dagger's tip inward, shoving it through the Philistine's jaw into his skull.

Keth dropped the dying man and turned to where Benaiah was struggling a few paces away. He rushed across the clearing and drove his knee into the arm of the mercenary as he was about to swing his sword at Benaiah's head. The man yelped.

"Kill me and I—"

Keth shoved his fingers into the man's mouth before he could finish and thrust his dagger as hard as he could, cutting all the way to the spine. The mercenary jerked several times, air hissing out of his lungs. Keth felt the death tremors ease and then fall still.

He rolled away from the unclean corpse and pulled Benaiah with him. The two lay gasping for breath in the bright morning light of the clearing next to the cliff.

"Those ... weren't ordinary ..."

Benaiah coughed. "No ..."

"They must have heard about the fight yesterday and tracked us down for the bounty."

"Get their water."

They tore into the Philistines' water pouches and took long, deep drinks. Both fought the urge to fill their bellies too quickly. When their breath had calmed somewhat, and Keth had checked to make sure his nose was not shattered, they examined the dead soldiers. Each had an armor breastplate with a black engraving of a serpent, a sword, and the snarling figure of a half-man, half-fish demon.

Keth knew the symbol. He cursed.

Josheb found David at the head of the march.

"The men are already fighting and bickering. Some want to rebel. Just like that day after Ziklag."

"What's the matter with them?"

"They're undisciplined, afraid, and drinking too much of their water. They're going to run out soon."

"Tell their leaders to force them to abstain. Designate carriers."

"We have done that. They still don't listen and are refusing to relinquish their rations."

David ran his fingers through his hair. He wiped his face on his sleeve and exhaled. Josheb heard him whisper something.

"What?"

David shook his head. "Nothing. I will speak to them."

He walked to the front of the ranks and stood on a small rise so that all could see him. The Thirty and a few of his Gittite bodyguards took up their positions nearby and waited to hear what he would say.

David stood with his arms crossed a moment, staring out at them. The murmuring died as they waited. Then he pulled his untouched water pouch off of his shoulder and tossed it to the nearest rank of soldiers.

"You are thirsty. I know this. As I told your commanders last night, before Yahweh, the God of my father Jesse and my forefathers Abraham, Isaac, and Jacob, I will not take another drink of water until we have defeated our enemies and you have enough."

There was murmuring again. A few soldiers gasped. "Lord, you must drink!"

David shook his head. "Yahweh is sufficient. He will provide in his good time."

Josheb beamed with pride. *The old David.* He stepped forward and was about to offer to do the same, but David caught his arm and whispered, "No, my friend. This is my burden alone."

Gareb was standing in the ranks of the Thirty when he heard David's vow. Afterward, he went back to inspecting the ranks, but his mind was elsewhere—on a hilltop at Micmash when Jonathan had looked him in the eyes and told him *we can do this.*

"Does he mean that?" one of the troops asked.

Gareb looked at the soldier, back at David, then at the soldier again. "I've watched him many years. Yes, he means it."

The troops began talking about it among themselves. Gareb moved on.

David had been a coward for abandoning Jonathan. He'd even fought for the Philistines!

But the water vow was something Jonathan would have done, and the thought made Gareb's eyes burn.

Do not let these men down, king, he thought. *Because your blood brother never did.*

TWENTY-SIX

Eliam wandered aimlessly through the streets of Hebron, angry that he had been forced to remain behind and frustrated that Gareb had not fought harder to keep him in the ranks. As the hours passed and his frustration mounted, he found that he had made his way up to the city wall. His limp was improving, but the pain of the old arrow wound in his foot still bothered him when he climbed.

There were only a few sentries left, and most of the city guard were old men, but soldiers had begun to arrive late that morning, conscripts from the countryside and regulars returning from their interrupted liberty.

Eliam watched as groups of threes and fours appeared on the roads. It was a stunning day, with blue skies and no clouds anywhere but the far west near the Great Sea and the far east over the Jordan Valley, where the rains would reach and then stop, as though Yahweh had built a mighty wall keeping them away from the central lands.

Just as he was considering returning to the royal residence and finding the girl again, he sensed someone standing near him.

"You should be marching with them."

Eliam recognized Joab's smooth voice and turned. He inclined his head slightly to acknowledge his superior. "I would, lord, but I was told to remain here."

"Frustrating, isn't it?"

"Very."

"What reason did they give you?"

"Shammah needed assistance organizing the army."

"I believed that to be my task."

"The king thought you might need assistance."

Joab nodded and smiled. "I am still not trusted."

Eliam remained quiet.

"What did Jonathan say to you on that mountainside? Have you ever told anyone?" Joab asked gently.

Eliam closed his eyes, saw the prince's noble face, the courage and fire in his eyes, the scene of valor where he had attacked the Philistines by himself, right before Eliam had . . .

I will look for you when this is over.

Eliam shook his head. "No."

Shammah watched Joab and Eliam from inside the house of a friend with a view of the city wall. The darkened interior shielded him from their view. Shammah watched the younger man depart and make his way, limping slightly, toward the stairs that led to the street below. It had not been a planned meeting, he guessed, or else they would have chosen a less conspicuous place. Perhaps Eliam was simply bitter about not going with the army.

Perhaps, he thought, Joab knew this as well.

TWENTY-SEVEN

Eleazar crawled to the top of a boulder hidden among the branches of a sycamore and held still. His breathing went shallow. Beads of sweat formed around his eyes, but he did not wipe them because he knew he was being watched.

The sentry was young but alert. He had refrained from snapping his head forward too eagerly when Eleazar had first crept into his field of vision, instead slowly rotating his head so that he could watch out of the corner of his eyes. Any further movements would confirm the threat, and the commander would be alerted with a shrill blast from the small trumpet curled between his fingers.

Eleazar clung to the boulder. He watched the sentry ease his gaze toward the edge of the forest casually, his eyes flickering to the very spot Eleazar clung to, his fingers slipping. Eleazar glared at the sentry, calling on all of his discipline to keep his fingers tight on the stone. Heartbeats passed.

Something clanged nearby and the sentry jerked his gaze away for a moment. Eleazar used the distraction to leap the rest of the way onto the boulder and flatten his torso against it. He let out several quiet gasps of relief and finally wiped the sweat from his eyes.

He counted to ten, then slid his face along the coarse surface of the boulder until the edge of it slipped away and he could see the head of the sentry. The Philistine was still looking at the boulder, but his eyes were trained on the side Eleazar had just leapt from. After a few moments, the sentry shook his head as if to clear his vision and turned his face toward his section leader, who was giving out commands.

Satisfied, Eleazar began the task he had been sent here for: scouting the enemy armies now swarming at the mouth of the Elah Valley.

The ranks nearest his position consisted of heavy infantry, carrying long pikes and heavy cudgels forged with iron. Eleazar shook his head, marveling at their arrogance. Clumsy, heavy weapons that could not be wielded in the rugged hill-country terrain. They did not feel the need to be cautious, which meant that they were underestimating their ragged enemy. Not that we have given them any reason to be cautious, always running, he thought.

There were units of archers and slingers and men with skirmishing weapons in a line stretching back down the valley. Sunlight glinted and sparkled like the waves of the sea on shields and lances, spearheads and swords. Slaves scurried about with water skins. Orders were shouted. Laughter.

Eleazar was finally able to pick out the supporting companies. These were the most important numbers for his particular task. Inexperienced scouts merely counted the number of men at arms, but Eleazar took careful note of the supply carts and wagons, armorers, and craftsmen who accompanied the army. No force of fighting men could last long away from its supply, and if commanders had brought along a multitude of support and supply companies, it could be assumed that a full campaign was underway.

Looking up and down the valley, Eleazar saw a large force of fighting men, but a minimal amount of supply. This had been a hasty mobilization. Few of the usual groups accompanying an army on campaign were here. No merchant caravans following the army hoping to capitalize on the new plunder that the soldiers would be acquiring, no treasure carts to pay the soldiers while on campaign, no prostitutes and wives and squalling children bringing up the rear.

Their sluggish movement and lack of motivation was obvious to his trained eye. Smart commanders never let troops lie around waiting for action; they kept them busy to keep their minds off home and meals and women.

Even so, there was a multitude of soldiers in this Philistine army, and more would come every day. If the right king or general were to lead them, their devastating weaponry and sheer size would be overpowering. Eleazar counted ten divisions on the approach to the mountains, plus the scouts and archers that he either could not see or was not able to count because of their fragmented traveling formations. Three divisions were moving through the entrance of the valley. It appeared that at least thirty thousand soldiers would soon be moving through that valley in the direction of the objective Eleazar had feared—the Jebusite city.

There was good news. They were bringing chariots. The trade road carved through the valley was passable for chariots, but they would be useless in an open fight. Surely their commanders knew that. The Hebrews were at their best when they could turn the massive, clumsy nature of the enemy against itself.

Eleazar watched the sentry glance back toward the boulder one more time, his face uneasy. With a clenched jaw, the young man pulled his helmet straps down near his ears to secure his helmet tighter and settled back in with the rest of the army. A few of the officers snapped instructions in their tongue that Eleazar assumed were warnings to be alert at every moment.

The breakaway formation of charioteers and infantry snaked forward along the bed of the creek. Farther up the valley, it would eventually pass under the ridge of a hill that, years before, had been the site of Philistia's greatest defeat. A barley field had been planted since that day, Eleazar had noticed earlier when he was sneaking up on the army, and he now imagined it basking in the sun as though it were trying to hide the history of the spot.

Eleazar could not help but smile when he had passed the legendary field where the two champions had met and the young shepherd had made his magnificent stand with a sling. It was a day Eleazar would never forget, the day that kept him believing that David would always come around no matter how far he strayed. Just a young regular soldier in Saul's ranks that day, only there to please his father, Eleazar had seen the covering for the first time.

The barley grew near a place between the ridges where water runoff would be most advantageous. Not the best place for a crop normally, as floods could wash it away, but an attempt by the farmers to gather as much water as possible in the drought. It also formed a natural pincer that forced the regiments to condense into tight ranks to move through. A highly defensible position if one was in need of it.

When the last of the Philistine advance party had moved out of sight around the bend in the valley, Eleazar let go of the boulder and dropped to the ground, careful to keep the boulder between himself and the sentry now lazily swatting at flies. Eleazar's knees crackled, and he winced. He had been on the rock longer than he realized. The sea breeze picked up, arriving at the same time it always did, the middle of the afternoon, and the sun baked the portion of the valley exposed to it. The air of the forest was cool and dark on his water-starved flesh, and Eleazar enjoyed it for a moment, wondering if he could ever relive the memory of this valley enough times. Then he shook his head, knowing he needed to hurry, because that same shepherd boy was now his commander, and he would be waiting for his report.

Even so, he waited an hour longer to ensure that rogue scouts were not waiting to catch him spying, then trotted back into the forest.

TWENTY-EIGHT

The caves above Adullam were impossible to spot from the valley. The slope rose sharply through dense undergrowth on a mountain buried deep in the forests of Judah's northern tribal lands. The land had never been cleared. Many thought the woods were haunted. Native Canaanites did not want to disturb the forest spirits and rarely ventured into them. The Philistines suspected there might be Hebrew hiding spots in the region, but every attempt to penetrate the thick growth had met with discouragement and occasionally disaster. An entire platoon had once been lost without a trace during the reign of Saul, courtesy of a feisty band of bandits who eventually moved south to Ziklag with their leader. David had used this area to his advantage many times, discovering the paths that led to the caves and using them to hide troops whenever moving through this part of the country.

The entrance to the main cave itself was a tall crack in the cliff face. It was used by their army when there were operations in the north, its proximity to the major valleys and trade roads making it an ideal hideout. David had found it when running from Saul, and here Eleazar, Josheb, and Shammah had found David years before.

In the clearing near the entrance of the caves, Josheb spotted Eleazar emerging from the trees.

"How many?"

"Ten divisions on the plains. I couldn't count the archers. There is already a smaller force moving up the Rephaim. Champions and giants. Everything we love about fighting Philistines."

"Chariots?"

"Yes."

"Praise Yahweh for that. Good to know that some things never change."

Eleazar slid down the wall of the first cave on the path. The Israelites always approached it from the south, which meant they were rarely seen by enemies approaching from the west, as the Philistines always did.

"They're going to set up their base in the Rephaim and then isolate the Jebusite city before attacking Hebron. The invasion of Judah will be easy picking. I would sell a daughter on it," Eleazar said.

"You wouldn't get much. Better go tell him." Josheb nodded his head toward the forest.

"He's not in the main cave?"

"No. He said he would be praying in the forest. He might be passed out from thirst. When I told him that the men were going through their water too quickly, he repeated his vow to abstain from drinking until there was enough for them. It's foolish, but it worked. They haven't exceeded their rations since."

"Why would he—"

"Does anything he does ever make sense? At least he didn't make us sing it."

Eleazar nodded. He rocked to his feet, his body tired from running since before daylight.

"Should I wait for him to finish?"

"No, we need to plan."

Eleazar rubbed his forehead. "I assume the well is dry."

"Our men are thinking about drinking their own urine. So, yes."

"How much longer do you think we can go without water resupply?"

Josheb shook his head. "Day or two. They can live past that, but no way they could fight."

"Any news from Shammah about more troops?"

"No, but it's only been one day. And more troops won't do any good anyway without water. He's probably praying as well. This whole army should have been priests."

Eleazar walked toward the trees, crossing the clearing where the five hundred men who could be mustered from Hebron were inspecting weapons. The Benjamites among them were now examining bowstrings, testing the tension and rubbing oil on the strings to prevent them from becoming brittle and snapping in the dry weather.

The approach of evening made the area peaceful, and Eleazar stopped to collect his thoughts before proceeding into the forest. He had hard news to give his king, the man he had known as his commander for many years, long before there were thrones and kingdoms, and he wanted to be sure that he drew on the memory of those days for strength.

He thought of the morning he, Josheb, and Shammah had arrived at the caves, long ago now. Eleazar and the other two had been removed from Saul's army because of their loyalty to David. David had been the commander of their unit in Saul's forces, and under his leadership they had done things that men were not supposed to be capable of doing, great feats of valor and courage so magnificent ...

He shook his head and kept walking.

Men looked up from their work as he passed, but before they

could rise in respect he waved them down. He was one of the Three, and it was difficult to escape notice. Eleazar left the steady clamor of the field, nodding to the sentries perched high above on the top of the cliff. From where they were, they could see in every direction, all the way to the Rephaim, the region Eleazar had just come from. They nodded back respectfully.

The first of the foreigners that comprised David's bodyguard greeted him inside the wood line. They called the challenge, and Eleazar gave the response word. The guard knew who he was, but Benaiah's discipline was ruthless, and any infraction in procedure in regard to approaching the king meant harsh consequences. The man who stepped from behind a tree was a Gittite, Eleazar noticed. A Philistine. Eleazar thought again about how strange it was that the king's hated enemy also made up his bodyguard.

The man nodded a greeting. Eleazar returned it.

"He did not want to be disturbed, sir." The man's eyes were glazed and his throat croaked from dryness.

"He needs to know this."

If it were any other soldier in the army, the Gittite would have held firm, but this was one of the Three, and after hesitating, he stepped aside. Eleazar thanked him and continued on through the forest. He knew where the king was, because it was the spot he always came to when they were here and he wanted to be alone.

The trees and brush began to clear as Eleazar walked farther in, until he found himself on the edge of another cliff, one that rose from the valley below to a narrow point surrounded by jagged stone walls. The cliff faced north, and Eleazar could make out hazy ridges in the distance lining the Elah and Rephaim Valleys, and somewhere in those valleys was the monstrous Philistine force. Eleazar knew the advance corps he had seen was only one of many. Issachar scouts would come with new reports every day.

Philistia had dominated the lands of the Hebrews since the Gilboa disaster seven years before, but before his death, Abner had managed to drive them back to the plains with little more than a scrap of the old army. Now they were coming again. It would be nice to have the old war horse now, Eleazar thought.

He paused to let his eyes adjust to the late afternoon sunlight after emerging from the forest.

He was not the only one still lamenting the recent loss of Abner. Eleazar pushed aside the anger creeping over him, grateful again that Joab had been left behind at Hebron.

Somewhere a bird cawed. Insects were beginning their evening swarming. Golden light sprinkled the landscape below him, the trees glimmering with the soft sea breeze rustling their leaves. It was an idyllic spot, and Eleazar understood why the king enjoyed this place. He walked along the cliff face until he had come around a small bend, and then he saw him.

David was kneeling, holding the carcass of a bird in his left hand and a dagger in his right. He was facing a small altar he had built, clearly preparing to make a sin offering to Yahweh. Eleazar wanted to speak up to prevent such a heresy, as only priests were supposed to offer sacrifices, but he was mesmerized by how passionately David was calling out to the heavens. He shouted and cried out all of his sorrows, including many things Eleazar had not known about, and it was anguishing to hear.

David dropped the dead bird, apparently deciding not to perform the sacrifice himself, however fervently he wanted to, and the quiet sounds of evening replaced the sound of his shouting. David stood and gazed for a long moment at the distant ridges angling toward the center of the hill country. He held his hands over his head. The voice began to sing, an aching melody of praise and grief. Eleazar had not heard this song, so he remained hidden and listened to the words.

It was an offering to Yahweh, to go instead of the bird, and it pierced the land around them with its beauty. Eleazar closed his eyes and let it soothe him, remembering long-ago ages when he walked with his father and listened to the old stories, the stories of his people and the God who delivered them.

Eleazar's heart was full, and for a few moments, he was no longer on a ridge in drought-ravaged country in an army surrounded on all sides by their hated enemy, but with his father, in the good days . . .

. . . the great man is standing in front of the assembly. He holds out his arms wide to me. The people sing, are grateful for his generosity, the most revered man in the area. Men cry out to him, give thanks to Yahweh for him. The town adores him. He is a mighty general and warrior. If I am like him in every way, perhaps he will be pleased with me.

He embraces me, I smell the warm, sweet smell of the forest on his cloak, the heat from his neck against my eyes. His embrace is true. Burning tears in my eyes. Father is pleased. I did nothing special, and yet he is pleased. My heart will burst—father is pleased.

Father raises his voice and proclaims to the assembly that I am a man. But I did so little, and he is so great, and he tells them how proud he is of me. The crowd cheers. It was nothing, but father is smiling at me.

He leans in close and says something. Say again? The noise.

"I am proud of you. You are a man."

"It was nothing, father, just a leopard that threatened a child. This feast was not necessary."

"A man proves himself in the small battles, my son. If your courage holds in the small battles, it will hold in the great ones."

He covers my face with his hands, speaks a prayer of gratitude to our God, he of the mountains . . .

David's song ended, and there was perfect stillness. Even the birds and the insects had stopped moving to listen. Eleazar opened his eyes, wiped them with his sleeve, and waited. He wished his father were with them now.

David remained with his hands up in worship. He stared hard at the distant ridges, his mouth moving and muttering words that Eleazar could not hear.

Then it was over.

David dropped his hands and turned back to the forest. As he approached the tree Eleazar leaned against, he stopped. "Your report?"

Eleazar cleared his throat, wary. "Ten divisions on the plains."

David closed his eyes and shook his head. "Yahweh, deliver us. What else?"

"A battalion in the very front, approaching the Elah, moving toward the Rephaim. Champions and giants, infantry and archers. They aren't carrying enough supplies to occupy our lands, but enough to tell me that they are making camp. Enough to take the city if they are well led."

"Chariots?"

"Whole platoons of them. Still haven't learned."

"Other movement?"

"None that I saw, but our scouts keep reporting other regiments like it. They're amassing from all over Philistia. Seems they don't trust you."

David stared at him, thinking, and Eleazar had to fight to look in the amber eyes. Then the king softened his stance and sighed.

"I think it will be wise to leave part of the army in Hebron," Eleazar said. "It might be tough to hold them out here with only a few companies. Men might stand a better chance behind the walls. We can only suffer one Ziklag."

David nodded. "Send a messenger to notify Joab and Shammah that they need to leave a force behind."

Eleazar watched him nudge a rock with the tip of his sandal and stare at the ground. Then he knelt and cleared the surface of the ground with his hands until there was a span of dirt a square cubit in size. He picked up a nearby stick and tossed it to Eleazar, who knelt beside him and began to sketch.

"This is the Rephaim, and here is the saddle that leads to the Jebusite city. They are two days of mass-marching away from Jebus with that main force, assuming others are going to be joining them along the way and force them to go slower. When the rest of the army gets here, we can use the Sansan-Gilo hills to screen our movements and meet them where the valleys approaching Jebus converge. They will move cautiously. For all they know, all of your regiments are either inside that fortress or are lining these ridges leading up to it. They're proud, but they know about us. When I was scouting I overheard them talking about how one Hebrew attacked a pride of lions with his teeth."

"I wonder if that is the only thing Benaiah will be remembered for," David chuckled. "So, they don't know there is only a handful of us, Philistine divisions are moving up the Elah from the plains, a battalion in front, but a larger force is gathering. Anything else?"

Eleazar hesitated, not looking up from the ground.

"Water is dire. I took one of my last rations when I returned from the scout this afternoon. It might be days before we can drink again."

"Yes. There wasn't time to bring much. The spring has not flowed in months here. I sent out squads to get water from other brooks, but they haven't returned. Philistines might have captured them," David said, then exhaled.

Eleazar studied him and noticed that his lips were cracked and dry. He looked worse than any of the others in the camp. *Because he gave his men all of his rations.*

"It was a necessary risk," David continued. "When the report came that the Philistines were pushing, I did not have time to confirm that the spring had water in it."

Eleazar waited for further questions, but David only studied the map sketched in the dirt in the fading light. Moments passed. Eleazar pinched the bridge of his nose and squinted away sweat.

"Yahweh will deliver them to us," David said with finality.

"Your orders, then."

David stood up. He kicked one of the rocks. "Until Shammah can get more troops here, we can't stop them from invading. But we can cut them off from the Jebusites."

Eleazar glanced at the map. "At the boundary?"

David nodded. "They won't push south or start a siege of Jebus unless they have free access to the valleys and plains for reinforcements. If we strike that advance force hard right away, the main force will hesitate and give us time to gather. They won't penetrate farther into the hills of Judah without a supply route. Abner taught them that much." He glanced at the map on the ground. "If we cut them off here—" he pointed to a spot on the map near the entrance of the Elah Valley—"we can stop more of them from coming into the pass. The troops already in the valleys will turn to hit us, but at least it will give Josheb and the Thirty time to get to the Bethlehem road. A scout reported movement from the Bethlehem garrison. It makes sense. Any Philistine reinforcements will have to come from that direction. If the Thirty can hold, we can eventually fortify those routes with slingers and archers."

"There are rumors that the Sword of Dagon is in Bethlehem. They won't miss any of the action of an invasion."

"The Thirty will be able to handle them."

"We have never led any of these northern troops. They might run."

"Yahweh will go before us."

"They all have iron in their armor. We only have a handful of skilled archers who can shoot between it."

"Then they will need to aim well. Yahweh will guide them."

Eleazar tried to suppress his frustration, but David knew him too well. "How many more battles do we need to win for all of you to believe?" David asked wearily.

"I know Yahweh is with us, but we have five hundred troops, mostly green. The Thirty have not fought in ages and will be rusty, Shammah will be trying to get the Simeonites, the Naphtali commanders, the Benjamites, and the Gadites to stop squabbling, and while they are terrific for slitting throats, the Gadites aren't diplomatic negotiators. Benaiah and Keth—"

"Uriah."

"—Benaiah and Uriah are missing. There is no more water. Joab and Abishai might well march with the Philistines instead of rallying the army ..." He let his voice trail off. "Your nephews ..."

"I know that. Joab was punished," David snapped.

"But not enough. He is a murdering—"

"I know that! Let it be!"

Eleazar said nothing further. He was confused as to where his despair had come from. What good did it do to bring these things up? Why did they matter? They would still fight, wouldn't they? He held still and waited for his orders.

David's eyes were glassy from stress and lack of water. He looked across at the ridges lining the valley again. The sun was shimmering red and low on the horizon. Purple streaks in the dry heavens above them were bringing twilight to the hill country. Once more Eleazar searched the west vainly for any sign of the rain breaching its barriers.

"You and I will hit them at sunrise," David said finally. "Near Pas Dammim. Josheb and the Thirty will go to the Bethlehem road to hold off whatever is coming from that direction."

Eleazar smiled in spite of himself.

"There is a barley field at Pas Dammim now. Seems no monument to your victory was constructed by the Philistines."

David laughed hoarsely. "Perhaps we should remind them of the last time we met in that spot."

"How will we get word to Benaiah and Keth?"

"I have a feeling Benaiah and Uriah are coming back this direction after seeing all of the Philistine movement. They'd know to go to the cave first whenever plans are disrupted. Shammah can keep Joab under watch back at Hebron while he works out a solution to all of the complaints among the tribal levies. The men just need to fight again. Lying around the city has made us soft and unfocused. They don't understand the danger we are in. Get some sand under their feet and the petty bickering will stop. We need to hold the pass until our army can get here. All of this happened very quickly, so no plan we make will be perfect."

Eleazar hesitated. "There has to be a traitor in the Thirty. No one in Philistia could have known about your plans to mobilize the new army after acclamation by the elders so soon, especially not fast enough to dispatch messages to the outposts and mobilize thousands of soldiers."

At this news, David raised his hands and covered his face, rubbing his eyes as though he wanted to rub away images.

David's voice dropped to nearly a whisper. "My friend, this is my doing. I have become lazy and greedy. I let Joab become too powerful, my men grow soft, my kingdom—"

"Clear your head. You made a covenant with the elders. It is Yahweh's kingdom, not yours, now protect it as he told you to."

Eleazar's rebuke pierced the cool forest air but did little to awaken David from his dreamy state. *He needs water! Yahweh, bring us water. Why have you taken it from our land in our time of trial?*

"Our people have lost their heart for war. Sometimes I feel as though we are alone, throne or not," David said, rocking back and forth on his knees.

"That's why they need you."

"They need Yahweh."

"They need you to lead them to Yahweh."

David stopped swaying; his hands dropped to his waist and he appeared to be looking at the map sketched in the dirt in the fading light.

Eleazar wiped away more sweat.

David collapsed forward onto the map.

Startled, Eleazar took David's shoulder and pulled to turn him onto his back. "Wake up!"

He cupped his hands around the king's face and shook him.

David's eyes fluttered open and he coughed. "Sorry," he rasped from a parched throat. He rolled over with his hand on Eleazar's shoulder. "Don't tell the men," he said.

"You need to drink water."

"My troops are thirsty."

Eleazar jerked him upright in frustration. "You need it more than the rest of us. We all die if you die. You are in no condition to fight anyone right now."

David's eyes rolled back into his head. Eleazar realized that David must have begun his water fast long before that afternoon. He shouted into the woods for the bodyguard, and he heard branches slapping as they ran toward them.

"Oh, for a drink of cool water from the Bethlehem well ...," David muttered in delirium.

Three troops from the foreign bodyguard charged into the clearing on the edge of the cliff, blades drawn.

"Take him back to the cave once it is dark and try to give him something to drink. Give him my final ration," Eleazar said, tossing them the pouch. The Gittite leader nodded his head and leapt forward with the others to pick David up. Eleazar watched them help him to his feet, and they walked with David, coughing and rasping, suspended between them back toward the camp.

Eleazar stood and glanced in the direction of the altar, thinking. David had probably vowed to Yahweh that he would abstain from water out of repentance. He prayed that Yahweh was seeing this, and that he would be with them tomorrow.

In several hours they would be moving again, slipping through the forest under the shield of darkness to take positions at Pas Dammim. He said it aloud, and the name had meaning.

Pas Dammim.

Boundary of blood.

TWENTY-NINE

The sentry stepped aside as Benaiah approached.

"I could have been anyone," Benaiah said, irritated.

"Yes, sir," the sentry replied with an awestruck expression on his face. He was young and new.

"Whether you recognize us or not, you always challenge people coming to the perimeter."

"Yes, sir."

Benaiah nodded and continued walking, Keth falling in step behind him, tilting his own head at the nervous sentry.

"He was probably raised on your song," Keth said after they had passed out of earshot.

Benaiah grunted. "They need to learn new songs."

"Be kind, friend. Young men need their heroes."

The gaping void of the caves appeared in the darkness at the edge of the field. They returned the quiet greetings of the soldiers gathered around the entrance, eating hard bread and dried meat.

Eleazar approached them and embraced Benaiah.

"Was he with you on the frontier?" Eleazar asked when he had released him.

"Who?"

"The king. I assumed he was with his bodyguard."

It took Benaiah a moment to realize that Eleazar was teasing. "You tell him that. I have tried and failed for years."

"He might listen now. He's not doing well," Eleazar said more soberly.

"What is the matter?" asked Keth.

"Lack of water. We had to rush here so quickly that we could not bring a proper supply. Usually the spring is flowing, but now it's dry, along with every other creek and well in this area. The troops think Yahweh has cursed the land."

"Who is spreading such lies this time? Hekia?" Benaiah had had many dealings with the rumor-mongering soldier. Hekia had once been a part of the king's bodyguard, but his tendency to stretch the truth and spread hearsay had led Benaiah to dismiss him. Now, due to his formerly privileged position in the king's inner circle, he fancied himself the consummate royal court insider. He claimed to still have sources inside the guard, but Benaiah had investigated and found that claim to be false.

"Hekia is back with Joab," Josheb added, walking up behind them. He embraced Keth, then pulled on Benaiah's beard. "Your boy is going to have one of those before long."

"That's how I know he is mine. Growing a beard in his seventh year. Only men of Kabzeel can do that."

"There are other men in Kabzeel. Didn't your wife go visit family after we moved from Ziklag? Any enemies you left behind there? Old rivals? The boy could be one of theirs."

Benaiah shoved him, but then Josheb's smirk faded. "What is it?" Benaiah asked.

Josheb swallowed hard and struggled to speak. "Abner was killed by Joab just after you left."

Benaiah felt as if he had been kicked. He sat on a nearby rock. Keth knelt next to him. They both stared at the ground. Benaiah was full of questions, and yet it was as though his throat had closed.

"He and Abishai lured Abner into the city gate and stabbed him," Josheb added.

"Abishai too?"

"He regrets it," said Josheb. "David made Joab ride in the chariot at the head of the funeral procession to shame him in front of the people."

"So where is he now?"

"Back in Hebron. He's been banned from leading an army, but David needs him to muster the remnant. Shammah stayed behind to help—and to watch him."

Benaiah wanted to know more but fought to push it out of his head. The politics, the ramifications of Abner's death—all of it had to wait. "So what are we doing?"

"We have five hundred green northern troops here. Philistines are packing into the Elah by the thousands. They sent two regiments in advance, according to our sometimes reliable Eleazar. We attack the scout battalion tomorrow. The king said we need to prevent them from reaching the Jebusite city at all costs."

"Keth and I saw their army coming south," Benaiah said. "The report is accurate. Had to fight through them. Green troops? Where are the Thirty? The other mercenaries?"

"The Thirty are here. Right after you two left, the army was granted a few days' leave to celebrate the coronation. Many men went back to their homes. We think the Issachar scouts were captured—it was only a messenger who reached us with the report. Someone leaked the information that we were too scattered to muster. The king rushed us here with everyone he had. Joab and Abishai are scraping the army together at Hebron as fast as they can."

Benaiah sighed. "Does he ever get tired of wet-nursing Joab? Especially now?"

"Joab has become powerful," Keth said.

"Not more powerful than David. If Joab hadn't killed Abner, we would be invading Philistia instead of the other way around," replied Benaiah.

"Do you really believe David can afford to anger half his tribe? Joab also owns half of the army of conscripts. We don't have a standing force yet, so we can't just replace him. David's own brothers stayed behind in Hebron and wouldn't come with him. He has enough to worry about right now," Eleazar answered.

Benaiah nodded in resigned agreement.

"Don't worry," Josheb said, "David thinks he has a way to deal with Joab."

"How?" asked Benaiah.

"He would not say, but he made it plain that it would happen soon."

"We're wasting time here," Eleazar said impatiently.

"Looks like our Philistine alliance is finally officially over. I can't imagine why they don't trust us. Not many Philistines besides Achish ever really liked David, he of the two hundred foreskins," Josheb said.

"We have worse news," Benaiah said, and Josheb and Eleazar looked up, alerted by the dark tone of his voice.

"Worse than what we have already been discussing?" Josheb said. "What is it?"

"Keth and I killed three men who bore the emblem of the Sword of Dagon on their armor."

Josheb sighed. The group said nothing for a time.

"That might be who is coming from Bethlehem," said Eleazar.

"An Issachar scout finally earned his pay and arrived earlier today to tell us there is a company mobilizing out of the Philistine garrison in Bethlehem."

"Is David holding up?"

Eleazar shook his head. "He looks bad. I think he stopped drinking water before this afternoon. I was in the forest with him earlier when he passed out. Seemed out of his head—said that he wanted some of the water from Bethlehem."

"The men need something," Keth said.

"Yes. Water," Josheb replied.

"No, I mean they need *something.* Something that will inspire them. These troops may have heard about us through songs, but that won't inspire them to hold the line in the coming days. Especially when we have to besiege that fortress in Jebus."

"We will be there with them. They can watch us," said Josheb.

"No, he's right," Eleazar said.

"Well, Keth and I will go with the Thirty tomorrow. Wish we had Shammah with us," Benaiah said.

"I will come up with something to inspire the men," Eleazar said. "We'll meet up again tomorrow."

They parted. Benaiah looked around at the men coming and going in the darkness, speaking nervously to each other and laughing at strange moments. They checked their weapons repeatedly. Archers swung up bows over and over, practicing the drilled motion. Slight tilt, hold the arrow in the notch, pull and release, look at the target and not the arrow. Others sat and held their knees to their chests, rocking back and forth—thinking of home, Benaiah knew.

THIRTY

Late that night, Josheb, Eleazar, Benaiah, and Keth gathered with David one final time before battle. The king had briefed the commanders of the five hundred earlier and they were back with their troops.

Now with his closest circle, David sketched in the dirt of the cave. As he did, Eleazar studied him. The king looked better, more alert, but his voice cracked through his dry throat.

"Here is the Rephaim Valley. That's the knob that juts into it where it meets the Bethlehem road. That is Jebus." He pointed at the junction where a road intersected with the Rephaim. "Josheb, I want you, Benaiah, and Keth to take the Thirty with you to that point and stop any attempt by the Philistines to send troops to reinforce from Bethlehem. That might be the Sword of Dagon. If Benaiah and Uriah spotted a few of them across the valley, they might not all be moving together. Let's hope not. Eleazar and I will attack the regiments that have reached the end of the Rephaim. We will crush them at their front and then drive them back down the valley."

He pointed at the spot where the valley narrowed before becoming the Elah. "That is where Eleazar and I will destroy their lead element and seal off the pass from any reinforcements coming from their encampment. The commanders of the green troops will need to attack down the sides of the valley precisely when I signal them. This has to be perfectly timed and perfectly executed. Yahweh has given them into our hands, and I do not want to squander this opportunity."

The group stared at the map, each of them memorizing the steps.

"Eleazar, where will you and I be?" David asked.

"At the place where the Elah and Rephaim meet, where it is narrowest. We are to destroy the advance battalion and cut off the Philistine army massed on the plains from meeting up with the Sword of Dagon or reaching Jebus."

"Correct. Benaiah, where will you be?"

"Should be with you commanding your bodyguard and protecting you."

"Just answer."

Benaiah's eyes darted across the map once more before he replied. "We will attack the Sword or any other approaching Philistines out of that point on the Bethlehem road where the Rephaim bends just before it reaches Jebus. We need to destroy them so that they can't meet up with the army coming from the plains. If we don't see any, or after we defeat them, then we will move down the valley to meet up with you."

"Splitting our army into two parts," David said, "is an act of faith on its own, so my best warriors have to be divided between the two parts. Eleazar and I will be with those blocking off the valley at the rear because they are the greenest. They will need to see me. The archers will attack first, we will charge and hit their line, and the two unit commanders will strike farther up the valley to cut off their head." David looked up again.

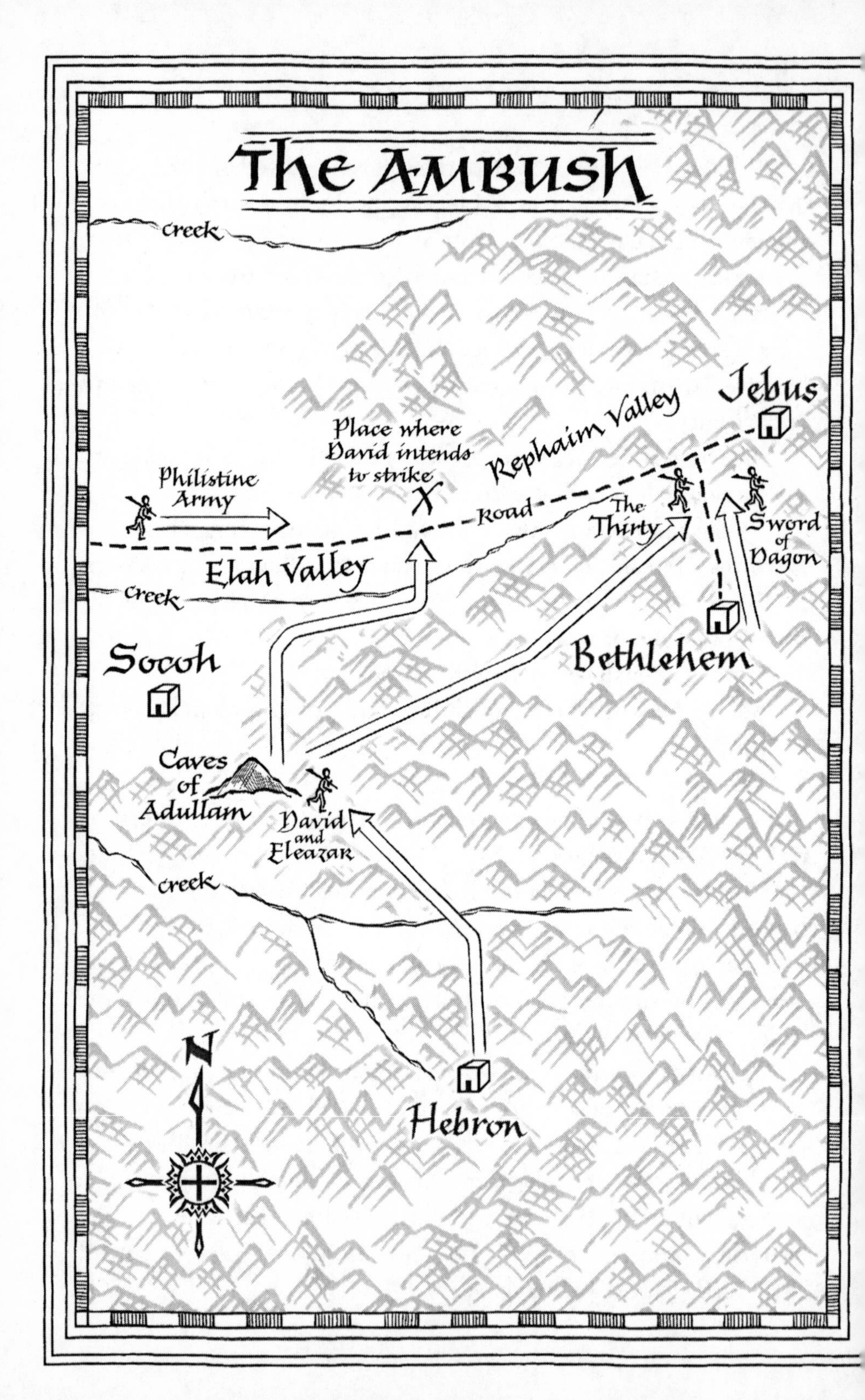
The Ambush
creek
Jebus
Place where
David intends
to strike
Rephaim Valley
Philistine
Army
X
The
Thirty
Road
Sword
of
Dagon
Elah Valley
creek
Socoh
Bethlehem
Caves
of
Adullam
David
and
Eleazar
creek
N
Hebron

Eleazar inhaled and held his breath a moment to calm his nerves. It was an exceedingly risky maneuver. Normally an ambush was a concentrated attack on a single line, not divided into parts as spread out as this one was.

David sighed, as if hearing his thoughts. "It's the best we can do. We could not get here in time to hit them before they got to the valleys, and I have to send troops to the Bethlehem road. We cannot let them take Jebus."

"As you said, lord, Yahweh has promised victory. Praise to our God," said Josheb.

"Arrows to our enemies," they all echoed.

David nodded, satisfied. In the torchlight, Eleazar saw vigor in his depleted face and thought that there was nothing like a desperate fight to revive a tired mind and body.

Plans finished, they sat together in the quiet for a while, listening to the men in the woods. Eleazar wished, briefly, that he was one of the regular troops again, uncaring about strategy and tactics, only knowing that they would have the man next to them when it came time. The world of the foot soldier did not involve command and politics. Just wine, women, and the man next to you.

Then he shook his head. His wife always made fun of his wandering mind. He would stare vacantly into the distance, and she would ask him what he was thinking about. He never had an answer, only that he was thinking.

"Well, come on, then. They're already moving," Josheb finally said.

But no one moved. Every man hated this moment. It might be the last time they ever sat together in this life. Perhaps they would meet up in Sheol. No one knew.

Finally, they got to their feet and embraced each other. Eleazar kissed Benaiah on the cheek, then clapped Keth on the side of the face.

"Watch out for him, Hittite."

"I always do."

Gareb gently kicked the dozing soldier squarely in the back of the head.

"Come on, wake up. It's the last day of our lives, might as well end it like men."

The soldier scrambled away. Gareb had spent the better part of the night wandering among the troops, too anxious to sleep, walking from soldier to soldier, trying to encourage the green ones. He would not be marching with them but instead going with the Thirty to the Bethlehem road. He knew that many of these troops would not survive the day. It was never easy to say good-bye to them, no matter how many times he had done it in his life.

The rest of the troops following David and Eleazar disappeared into the forest, making their way to the valley. Many mothers' sons. Many fathers, he thought.

Spotting Benaiah and the others at the edge of the forest, he trotted over, preparing to race northeast to battle a foe that would probably destroy them.

Across the forest at the entrance of the valley, Ittai could not sleep. He rose from his mat to inspect his chariots again. He passed through the bedrolls of men, stepping around cookware and weapons scattered sloppily. He almost woke everyone up to yell at them about it but decided that they needed their sleep. There was no way of knowing what surprises the Hebrew god had for them in the woods.

He made his way to the chariots, lined up at the edge of camp for fast hitching, and examined them in the torchlight. He wasn't sure what he was looking for. All seemed in order.

He handed the torch to a sentry. "Go rest. I will take the next two hours," he said. The soldier left.

Ittai crawled up on a boulder and settled in to watch. The Elah gap opened in the distance. It was a dark night. Clouds had moved in from the west over the Great Sea. He sat still watching the valley.

Something emerged. Movement. Ittai blinked to clear his eyes a few times.

Dagon was crawling out of his lair.

Ittai watched the sea god slide over stones and through the trees, slithering his way toward their army. The horses in the corral whinnied and stamped their hoofs.

Darkness covered the figure; Ittai couldn't see him clearly. A breeze picked up, and Ittai was back in the ocean in his youth, his test of manhood, swimming as hard as he could, fighting the water as it pulled him down into the black. Ittai pulled at the waves with every stroke, but it was no use, he couldn't fight it any longer. And the monster circled closer from beneath the waves, its eye always watching him, and Ittai cried out to his god and clutched the amulet, but his god would not come to him, would not let him stand on his scaly hide.

Then Ittai was back on the hillside, staring at the darkness of the valley entrance. He felt something pass over him—a shadow, a figure, he couldn't tell.

He turned and looked at the sky over the coast. A bank of clouds. Watch fires on the perimeter. All seemed well.

He shook his head, blamed it on his weariness. No, he was certain he had not seen Dagon fleeing the Israelite hill country.

Part Three

THIRTY-ONE

Eleazar sat in the darkness, waiting. The early morning air was cold. He wrapped his arms around his legs and pressed his face between his knees.

For a moment, he was a boy with his father again, standing in the field outside their home.

His arrow fell to the side—he had missed the target again. His head dropped. He would never learn it. Never learn ... he felt a hand on his chin, lifting his head up.

"That one was closer," his father said.

"But farther than the first one. I am making no progress."

"Keep your arm steady and look at the target."

"Men of our tribe do not learn the bow, father. Why must I?"

"Yahweh has other plans for you. You must learn every weapon. Courage. Shoot more arrows. I want fifty more before dark."

"Mother will be furious."

"I will suffer her wrath, do not worry."

He lifted the bow and notched the arrow. Tilted it to the right, letting the shaft settle, then pulled it back as far as he could—not as far as his mouth; he wasn't strong enough yet. His eyes blurred.

He released the arrow too early. It struck the tree above the sackcloth target. He threw the bow down in anger. It was quiet. He looked at his father.

"Control it, Eleazar. Do not be afraid to let the stillness come."

"Yes, father."

"Again."

He tried again and again, and again after that ...

... and then Eleazar was in a dark room, the purification ritual over. He didn't remember what is was even for, what sin he had committed. But he remembered the priest leaving when it was over. Eleazar was clean again, but his heart was heavy. His father stared at the ground, silent.

"Forgive me, father. I will memorize every letter of the Law; I will never miss a dot."

He sighed, looked at Eleazar. "Son, it is not memorizing the Law that pleases Yahweh. What grieves him is your heart. You behaved in an unclean manner because your heart is unclean."

"No one else follows the Law as strictly as we do!" He regretted the words immediately, but they were out, and they stung his father worse than anything he had ever said.

"I am sorry."

His father nodded, eyes closed. After a moment he rose and left the room. Eleazar was alone. He had broken the great man's heart. But none of the other boys, not one, had fathers who made them visit the priests, made them memorize the Law ...

Eleazar lifted his head. He glanced down the line of men. Nearby, David stared down the valley, his eyes vacant, his breath labored.

Eleazar closed his eyes again. The battle would come soon. First, just a moment with her.

She was gazing at him. It seemed like she glowed with the sun. Two children in two years. Father was proud, said the men of their family were robust and virile. She rolled her eyes at this when no one was watching but him. She wanted many of them, many children, many sons.

"I am afraid to meet the others," she says.

"Women talk and chatter a lot. You will make friends at the well quickly."

"Do you know any of the other warriors?"

"Yes. Josheb and Shammah have decided to come as well."

She lay her head against his chest and pulled his arms around her waist. She always wanted him to hold her this way. The others laughed at him for it. He lowered his face into her hair. It smelled like saffron.

"Was this the right thing to do?" she asks.

"Father says he is our future. Yahweh has anointed him. He will join David one day as well."

"Your father is a good man. Mine wasn't."

She was still, melted further into his arms. The children slept quietly . . .

Eleazar shivered. It all disappeared again.

He was on the ridge, with David, about to die.

Don't think that.

Eleazar sat up. His muscles felt tight and stiff from crouching against the cold stones for an hour while they waited. He opened and closed his fingers to keep them warm.

"As soon as their morning watch is over we move," David said.

Eleazar looked down the slope of the ridge they were on where a Philistine watchman was doing his best to remain hidden among the rocks of an outcropping that overlooked his camp. Moonlight glinted off his helmet. With the approaching dawn, he had become careless, likely thinking about the breakfast his growling stomach was demanding. "At least our enemy is green as well," he said, nodding toward the careless watchman.

David followed Eleazar's nod, then shook his head. "That is the sort of thing I have never understood. Disciplined in so many areas, stupid in so many others. Only the most foolish of commanders fails to inform his troops that helmets are useful only in battle, and not on lookouts where they are a beacon for all to see."

The Hebrew deputy commanders were nervous as well, Eleazar noticed as he turned to check them. They met his eyes and looked away quickly, probably wondering how he was able to speak so casually with the king. Eleazar rubbed his forehead with his wrist. He checked his sword again out of habit.

To his right, visible in the moonlight, he could see the beginning of the Rephaim in the distance as the pass from the Elah narrowed. That valley led straight to Jebus and was intersected by the Bethlehem road, toward which Josheb, Benaiah, and Keth were currently rushing to stop the Sword of Dagon.

Eleazar had not yet seen the Sword of Dagon here himself. Perhaps it was simply an attempt by the Philistines to spread fear among the Hebrews. They did such things. But Benaiah and Keth had said that two Philistines they had fought gave them a real battle, and for men who easily killed dozens at a time to have trouble with only two was cause for worry.

Below him, the Elah stretched left, with the barley field he had seen earlier nestled near the ridges where the man lying next to him had begun his life as a warrior. "Do you ever think about that day still?"

"What day?"

"Goliath."

David pointed toward a shallow ravine in the middle of the valley where the creek, now almost dry, trickled through sandy banks. "That was where I waited for him," he said.

"I saw you from the ranks as you approached the stream, but you disappeared behind the bank for a bit. I never asked what you were doing."

"Finding stones. And waiting for the covering."

"Were you certain Yahweh had delivered him to you?"

"Yes."

"How?"

"I heard him through the covering. His spirit. The voice is ancient. Gentle. Powerful. I just knew, like I know he is going to deliver them to us today."

Eleazar saw it play out again before him in an instant. The giant on the opposite bank, his army behind him on the slope, the Hebrews lined up on the hill to Eleazar's right. He remembered the very smell of that day, the taste of the dust on the wind, the thrill of watching their enemies finally running from them instead of pursuing them.

Eleazar shook his head. *Send it to us once more, Yahweh.* "Why do you continue to trust pagans and foreigners?"

"They might always be foreigners, but they won't always be pagans. Yahweh loves them as well."

"But as your bodyguard?"

"How else to convince them that Yahweh loves them?"

That made no sense to Eleazar, but he let it go for now. He prayed silently for the man next to him, still so young, with the weight of kingdoms on his head. He carried burdens none would ever grasp.

They waited. As daylight arrived, they could see hundreds of Philistine soldiers marching up the pass into the hill country, led by squadrons of chariots assigned to each platoon. In each chariot was a driver and a soldier who wielded both the war bow and the lance. The charioteers rode next to one another, forming a column of twos in a tight formation. The horse teams snorted and stamped at the billowing dust of the dry valley floor.

The Philistine camp these advance companies were now departing was still pitched, left in place for the regiments that would follow after the passage to Jebus was secure. Eleazar could see it far to the left. When he descended the slope during the attack, it would not be visible. But destroying it would be their objective as soon as they defeated the advance troops.

Ranks of infantry and archers followed the chariots closely, using them as a screen against any ambush. Once more he noticed the lack of support regiments and traveling riffraff that followed an army on an extended campaign. Eleazar started to count them but lost track, then decided it did not matter. There were a lot of them, and that was all that mattered. He wished Josheb and Shammah were with him.

"I am sorry for my behavior," David said.

Eleazar, surprised, shook his head. "I have not been at my best in recent years, either," was all Eleazar could come up with for a reply.

"Without you and the others, I would be in the pit."

"Without you, our wives would already be slaves."

"How is yours?"

"I keep things from her."

"What?"

Eleazar looked around to make sure he was not being overheard. "After the battle at the pool of Gibeon, I went to the tents of the Ammonites outside of town."

David nodded. He took a deep breath and nodded again. An anguished expression briefly crossed his face. "I have not set the best example with women."

"Should not matter with me."

"It begins with me, and I have failed."

"When I was there that night, I went into a woman's tent. I didn't—"

"Bring it into the light."

Eleazar frowned. "What do you mean?"

"Yahweh heals when it is in the light and not in darkness and shadows."

Eleazar wondered if David was talking more to himself.

David reached over and clasped his arm. "But it is a new day. Yahweh's mercies are new every day. The light comes, and the day is new, and there are wars to fight."

Eleazar decided to let it be. He patted his water skin. Almost nothing left from the captured Philistine skins. The day would be hot.

Then, quietly, hidden from the Philistines behind the rim of the hills lining the valley, they began to follow the Philistine army on a parallel course.

Ittai's morning had been rough. He didn't have his armor carrier to help him organize a scout. He missed the man. He'd lost many companions on battlefields, but this one hurt. He would feel his absence today.

Now, riding his chariot into the valley, cursing the kings and their foolish insistence on bringing chariots into the mountains, he searched the ridges above them carefully. He was frustrated at having been sent into the valley without a proper scout and was anxious to be reunited with his Sword of Dagon unit. There could be ambushes and traps laid for them around the next bend.

He tried to focus on what he knew: that the Hebrews were disorganized and scattered, their tribes divided, and there was no way that they could have sent a sizeable force this quickly to stop them.

But the horses were uneasy. They neighed and pawed and jostled his chariot. Horses always knew when something was about to happen.

Ittai called out to his team soothingly as he rode through the gorge. If there was to be an ambush, it would happen soon.

THIRTY-TWO

"After this last group moves through, we take the field," David said. "Yahweh has promised victory. Make sure we have destroyed all of them in the valley before going back to attack their camp."

Eleazar nodded. They would charge down the slope covered by their archers, stationed in a clump of trees down the hill to their right. Their archers would protect them from the Philistine archers, who would take cover behind the chariots. He guessed it would be five Philistines against one Hebrew. Not the worst odds they had ever faced, but considering they had no water or resupply or reserve forces to aid them, it would be close.

He hoped there would be enough time to cut off the east and west ends of this part of the valley. The rest of the Philistine army was already plodding through the Rephaim. If David's troops could destroy this force, they would be able to stop any more encroachments from the plains, then hold the narrow gap between the Elah and the Rephaim until Joab and Shammah could bring a larger force.

David gave final instructions to his subordinate commanders. Eleazar waited until the other commanders had crawled back to their men to lead them to their ambush points.

"You want the two of us charging to that ravine near the barley field?"

"My voice will echo off the hills better in that spot. I want them to hear me."

"You're going to sing to them?"

"Remind them of something," David said.

"Are you ever going to use your bodyguard? You're the king of the whole nation now. Many people hate you. You ought to give Benaiah a chance to actually do his job."

"Benaiah stays busy in garrison. But I don't want them bothering me in the field."

"Say something inspirational. I could use one of your speeches right now," Eleazar said.

David started to speak, but his voice caught and he coughed harshly. It was a dry, wheezing cough. Eleazar thought about holding him down and forcing water into his mouth.

David licked his cracked lips. "Something inspirational? Don't be afraid. Fear comes when we see only the enemies before us and not the beheaded champions behind us."

"You write these down, don't you? All of these riddles."

"Every one of them."

Eleazar waited a moment. "Why did you want Michal returned to you?"

David fiddled with a stone for a bit as he considered it. "She was my prize. I had won her," he said simply.

Eleazar let it go. The moments passed. The last of the chariots in the squadron crossed through the gap to their left.

David knelt down and pressed his face into the dirt. He muttered something that Eleazar couldn't hear. Then he slowly sat up and took several deep breaths. He looked at Eleazar. "Are you ready?"

"I'm with you."

David nodded, then stood up. He raised his fist to the sky and shouted, "Lord, the God of our salvation, you have always shielded our heads in the day of battle. We call upon you again!"

Then he sprinted down the slope. Eleazar followed.

They leapt over the small boulders in their path, trying to get to the middle of the field before the next regiment appeared in the pass. The Philistine commanders had let their units drift apart during the morning march. They would pay for it dearly.

It was not the cowering, soft man in the council room at Hebron but the fiery champion of his people who charged into the valley ahead of Eleazar. It seemed like David ran faster than a deer, and Eleazar had to concentrate to keep up. He watched the large sword of Goliath slap against his king's back, the prize taken so long ago not far from this very field, returning to bring more death to its former masters. Eleazar sucked in the cool morning air and pushed himself faster, glancing down and to the right at the rear ranks of infantry as they marched farther up the valley.

After running out onto level ground, the two men reached the ravine in the middle of the field and stopped, panting. David, his auburn hair and beard streaming with sweat, pulled the sword from over his shoulder out of the leather scabbard securing it to his back. He held it over his head.

His powerful voice, trained and strengthened from years of singing war songs and shouting commands over the noise of battle, stopped the entire column of Philistines, was no longer weak and raspy sounding. It surprised Eleazar.

"Sea filth! Come back to me and let Yahweh finish what he started in this valley!"

▲▲▲

Ittai heard the voice and ordered his rider to halt the chariot. He had instinctively pulled the war bow out of its carrier when they entered the narrow area of the valley the Hebrews called Pas Dammim, knowing that if there was going to be an ambush, this would be the place.

His was the first chariot in the squadron, so he had to look back over the top of all ten chariots in his lead platoon. The king who marched for glory this day was in the rear of the battalion, and Ittai hoped that if there was an attack, he would fall immediately.

Ittai saw two Hebrew warriors standing near the small ravine they had passed moments before. He cursed the man who was supposed to be watching their rear, though he was actually angry at the commanders who would let the units stray so far apart in the dark.

The Hebrew shouted in the Philistine tongue, and since Ittai had heard every word, this could be only one man. Ittai clasped the amulet of Dagon he wore around his neck and spat to ward off evil. But he was glad; no more waiting, no more wasting time.

"Form the perimeter! Ambush is coming! Grab your loins, men; that is David himself, and he carries the sword of Goliath. Let's get it back!" he shouted, bringing the war bow up. The Hebrew was foolishly within range of his ten chariot archers. He pulled the string to the corner of his lip, tilted the bow slightly sideways, stared hard at the Hebrew's torso, and released the arrow.

The shot was perfect, but the Hebrew king leaped away from the bank before it struck him. Ittai saw him roll when he hit the ground and crouch behind a bank of sand. His partner did the same.

Ittai's platoon stood frozen, unwilling to believe that the dreaded warlord was actually attacking them.

"Get moving! Ambush is coming! Ambush is coming!"

"But there are only two of them, Lord!" his chariot driver shouted over the noise of men suddenly jumping to action.

Ittai pointed up the ridge to his left. "They're up there, watch for them! Our scouts have succeeded in warning us again, I see."

He directed the chariots to circle, but that was difficult in the hilly and boulder-strewn terrain. He cursed the Philistine kings once more for foolishly ordering chariots to accompany them. The Hebrews were not, contrary to the rulers' assertions, afraid of them on sight.

David replaced the sword on his back and tugged out his sling, two cords of goat hair with a leather notch tied between them. Eleazar peered over the sand bank watching the rear Philistine platoon form their perimeter. He desperately wished that water would suddenly flow down the creek bed to quench his thirst.

"They aren't attacking. Their commander is smart."

"Yahweh has given them to us," replied David, reaching over and plucking another stone out of the creek bed. He had a full pouch of them already but apparently had a ritual. Eleazar saw him whispering something as he handled the stones, as though blessing them. An arrow hit a rock next to his arm.

"What are you doing?" Eleazar asked.

"Reminding them how this went last time."

David fitted the stone into the notch and held it to his heart, muttering things Eleazar could not hear. Eleazar waited for two more arrows to whistle over his head before stealing a glance over the top of the sandbank.

Then the Hebrew archers on the hillside began shooting their own arrows into the Philistine ranks. There were precious few of them, but enough to divert attention momentarily from the bank where David and Eleazar crouched.

David used the distraction.

He shouted and jumped up at the same time, leaping across the creek in a bound, the muscles in his legs twitching furiously. Eleazar watched him scramble up the side of the opposite bank, swing the stone three times, and then release it as he ran across the field.

Eleazar did not see the stone fly, but he saw one of the Philistine troops pitch backward, a spray of blood from his crushed face showering the chariot he was climbing out of.

David flung another stone, then another so quickly that Eleazar did not see them actually release, but he heard the sound of terrified men as the hail of stones from the running warrior killed Philistines.

Ittai ducked as a stone hit his aide in the eye. The man fell over without a noise, blood pumping in spurts onto the rocks. Ittai slipped on the blood, and on the blood of other troops of his that had fallen from the arrow assault, and he shouted orders to form the perimeter with the chariots, heard the terrified horses neighing in fright and kicking at their handlers. *Hardened war horses behaving like colts!*

He joined in the effort to calm them, but the horses were frothing at the mouth and slinging sweat, shrieking in agony.

"Their god has attacked us!" one of his men screamed.

Ittai crawled to the nearest perimeter chariot and peered through the wheel spokes to see what the rest of their army was doing. Each platoon had circled as they were supposed to, but they were too far apart to link up to coordinate a counterattack. He cursed in frustration. The amulet of Dagon thumped against his neck. He stuffed it down the front of his armor.

Need to move. Who? Where? Their king—kill their king!

Ittai spotted the Hebrew king, still charging and slinging stones from the pouch at his waist. Ittai knew that Hebrew slingers could be formidable adversaries, but this man *did* move like a god, running and leaping over tremendous distances and firing stones with deadly precision, hitting every target he chose. Ittai had never seen such a display.

"Hit him with everything! Every archer! Take him out and the rest of them will run!" Ittai shouted to his lead platoon.

Eleazar roused himself from his awed stupor at David's attack. He raced out from behind the sandbank and shouted and waved his sword over his head, staring at the hillside he and David had just come from.

At the signal, two columns of Hebrew troops poured over the ridge into the valley, shouting with battle rage. The Philistine platoon closest to him, the one suffering most from David's murderous assault and the swarms of arrows from the grove where the Hebrew archers were positioned, turned to face them.

Philistine arrows flew sporadically, the troops unsure where to direct their fire and afraid to raise their heads over their chariots for fear of David's stones. None of them noticed Eleazar.

He raised his sword again and then pointed it at the huddle of Philistines. He saw that their commander had directed his men to concentrate all of their arrows at David. *Good strategy—won't work.* Eleazar dropped his sword sharply. The Hebrew archers sent arrows in the direction Eleazar was gesturing.

The two Hebrew foot-soldier companies reached the bottom of the valley, one on the east end and one on the west, trapping the Philistine battalion and cutting it off from the rest of the force out of sight down the valley.

▲▲▲

Ittai, between directing the fire of his remaining archers and trying to settle the horses, saw the trap close. He saw the company of Hebrews disappear over the bend in the valley to the east, where he knew they were setting up defensive positions against a counterattack from soldiers that might be arriving farther up the Rephaim. He was able to see the western approach from where he crouched, and he watched as the Hebrews formed ranks on that end as well. There were only a few companies of them, but if they were stout men, they could defend that gap against assaults long enough to allow a third charge to come directly over the hill and rush across the middle, overwhelming his battalion and completing the ambush.

Ittai glanced furtively between the Hebrew king, still slinging rocks like some awful shepherd war god, and the top of the ridge, where he expected the next wave to come from. A soldier next to him, a youth who had just joined his lead platoon before the march, took an arrow in the leg. It cut deep, and blood spurted. The boy cried out and grabbed Ittai's waist in pain.

The boy screamed for help and pleaded with Ittai to stop the blood. Hopelessly, Ittai simply pulled him back against his chest, holding him while his sobs became weaker and weaker. The horses shrieked. Stones and arrows struck necks and faces. The boy whispered something.

Ittai did not hear it. He released the boy and started moving.

Eleazar, still standing in the open, was waiting for the chariot ranks to break.

He watched as the horses in the Philistine chariot platoons broke loose all at once, driving open the perimeter ranks of the battalion and scattering men and equipment everywhere.

A chariot team whirled and raced into the valley, out of control, then veered straight toward him. He darted to the side to avoid it. A wheel struck a rock and burst into splinters, sending the chariot cartwheeling. Horses and men screamed in pain. A horse from the chariot team caught its leg in a hole in the ground. Its leg bone snapped so loudly that it pierced the din.

The charioteer was tossed from the back and landed in front of another runaway team, which tried to avoid the fallen man but veered just enough to sever his head with a wheel.

More chariot teams charged away into the field where the rocky ground caused them to stumble and fall. Wheel spokes burst, men were trampled, and still the arrows flew.

Eleazar sensed no command or control in the Philistine ranks. Officers shouted orders sporadically. Troops cowered behind their section leaders. He overheard men screaming that the avenging Hebrew god was going to cast them into the sea to be judged by Dagon.

When the horses of the platoon closest to him had all scattered, Eleazar raced forward to join the fight. A Philistine archer swung his bow toward Eleazar, who rushed at the man. The archer released the arrow a moment too soon—high and to the left. Eleazar tackled the archer, sending him crashing into another soldier before he killed them both with his sword. They were his first kills in a long time. He leapt back to his feet, regretting the deaths for a moment, loving it the next. Then he tossed his head back and shouted with battle rage.

David took cover behind a boulder. The pause in the fighting came at just the right time. His arm was weary from the sling, and he was gasping for breath. *Lying around in the palace harem makes a man soft. Forgive me, Yahweh.*

He checked the valley's east and west ends and saw his troops in their positions. The other two commanders should be rushing down the hillside at any moment to sweep across the ambush line and destroy the demoralized Philistine remnants. Eleazar had charged the platoon nearest the barley field and was finishing them off. All was going as planned.

Bless you for your covering and your strength in the day of war.

David closed his eyes, felt the sea breeze stirring up. He caught the smell of sweat and gore swirling on the wind. It was getting hot. Dust scratched in his eyelids. He coughed. Thirsty. So thirsty. All he could think about was water. He opened his eyes and stared hard at the ridge across the valley.

The Philistines were scattered and disorderly across the valley floor, their perimeters had been broken by their foolish attempt to bring chariot horses into the hill country, troops were losing their discipline. This was the best possible time to hit them.

Where was the second assault?

THIRTY-THREE

Ittai saw another Hebrew running between the overturned chariots, almost upon him.

He swung his bow at the warrior, but too late—the warrior blocked it easily with his short sword. Before Ittai could move again, the Hebrew had cut down two more of Ittai's troops. Ittai shouted warnings, but now his entire lead platoon was gone, along with the horses. He cursed and spat on the ground. The Hebrew darted away from the last corpse and charged Ittai again. Ittai was ready this time and held up his own sword to meet him.

The Hebrew feinted high. Ittai anticipated it and met him with a low block when the sword cut low. He twisted his shoulders away to absorb the force of the blow, trying to trip the Hebrew as he rushed past, but his opponent knew it was coming and pivoted at the last second.

Ittai caught the edge of the Hebrew's armor with his sword and tripped him. As the man hit the ground Ittai was on him, trying to choke him, screaming in his face, feeling the man's hot breath. Sweat flowed into his eyes. They rolled and wrestled, then the Hebrew squirmed out of his grip and jumped up.

Ittai blocked a strike, tried kneeing him in the ribs. The man was too fast—he avoided it, and Ittai tried to toss him again, but the Hebrew stepped out of reach.

Ittai thought the next move would come low again, but the Hebrew's fist smashed into his face and knocked him flat. He felt his nose break. Warm blood streamed down his lips into his mouth. The blow had aggravated the injury to his jaw, still painful from his fight with the other two Hebrews days before. His vision went blurry, his head numb.

The Hebrew was on top of him, the sword point at his neck. Ittai closed his eyes and prayed to Dagon that it would be quick.

He waited. Horses shrieked throughout the valley. Men yelled. Nothing came.

He opened his eyes and saw the Hebrew squinting at him through a sweaty brow. He was holding the tip against Ittai's throat, muttering something in the Hebrew tongue. The two men glared at each other, breathing hard.

Then, to Ittai's surprise, the Hebrew jumped up and ran in the direction of the next platoon.

Ittai sat forward, reached up to touch his broken nose, and coughed out some of the blood in his mouth. His anger raged. *Dagon, where are you? Give me vengeance!*

A bug crawled on a gore-splattered rock between his legs. He watched in a daze as it struggled to make its way through the mess, getting stuck every few steps. He thought of helping it along. An arrow struck the chariot he was sitting near, rousing him. *Move!*

He moved to a crouch and watched the next platoon being decimated by the Hebrew warrior, then flicked his eyes to the top of the ridge where the final wave of the ambush would soon cross.

Still nothing. He coughed again, wiped his face on his tunic. Sweat burned in the cut.

Ittai left the bow and quiver, slid the sword into his waistband, and decided to charge the archers shooting relentlessly at them. Assaulting through the ambush would be the only way he and any of his men would survive, and he had to do it before the final wave of Hebrew troops attacked.

He was unsure why he was still alive. The Hebrew god was pouring out his wrath on the invaders from the coast.

Ittai willed the amulet against his chest to do something as he charged toward the grove from which the Hebrew archers were raining violent terror on his men.

David was outraged that the third assault still had not come.

His throat burned with dust and he ached for water. Eleazar had destroyed the rear platoon and was attacking the next, but David knew that he could not keep up such an attack unless the next wave of troops came down.

Angry, David ran back across the field to show his officers on the ridge to attack *right now.* He whirled the sling once, measured again, measured a third time, released it. It glanced a fleeing Philistine harmlessly on the side of his helmet.

David arrived back at the sandy bank and darted across the streambed. Dead Philistines lay in the sand where Eleazar had killed them. The valley went quiet before David reached the top of the bank. He crawled to the lip and checked the ridge. *Still no assault!*

The valley had grown quiet because his archers had run out of arrows.

The Philistines, seeing this, had mustered several squads to charge the trees, knowing their only chance to escape the ambush was to assault through it. Philistine officers had regained control of their troops and were directing a counterattack.

David shouted in frustration as he stared at the ridge above him. *Decide! No hesitation!*

He turned and sprinted down the creek toward the gap where one of the two first assaults had taken its position. He kicked sand up his legs as he ran. His feet slid around in the sandals. He kicked them off. Always preferred barefoot. Need the armorers to—*focus!*

He reached the gap where his men were supposed to be lined up. Instead, they were fleeing back up the slope they had come from.

"Stop! Get back down here!" he yelled, more furious than he had ever been.

One of the section leaders looked over his shoulder at him and stopped. He pointed west toward the gap. David followed his gesture.

The next Philistine battalion was already coming, and another behind it.

Eleazar killed one more man before he knew the time had come to escape. There were too many. The planned third assault had never come, and the Benjamite archers were trapped in the woods with the Philistines about to run through them.

Eleazar ran back the way he had come, stabbing wounded men who still lived as he went to ensure they would not fight again. He headed for the sandy bank and heard the rustling noise of Philistine arrows as they flew toward him. He knelt behind an overturned chariot, waited for the thumping of the arrows striking the carrier to cease, then continued running.

He searched for David but did not see him. *Must have gone to rally the fleeing troops.* They would need to escape the valley before it became a slaughter field. He stamped his feet in frustration as he ran. *We had them!* Where was the third assault? Why had Yahweh stopped him from killing that Philistine commander?

He smelled smoke. Turning, he saw a Philistine with a lit torch running across the valley toward the barley field. Eleazar looked away and kept running, but he could not prevent himself from looking again, and then finally stopping. The enemy troops behind him were finally in an assault formation and coming his direction. He glanced at them, then back at the soldier.

The drought had killed most of the crop anyway. It wasn't worth his life to stop it, was it?

Eleazar looked at the barley field, then the soldier, then the platoon chasing him, then back to the field. He could not see David anywhere.

Ittai burst into the cover of trees expecting to be struck by an arrow at any time. None came. Instead, he saw most of the Hebrew archers scrambling to flee the woods. The few who still wished to fight were out of arrows, for now they came toward him with sickle swords.

Now Ittai made these archers a target for his rage. He slit the belly of the first archer, spun and killed the next. He knelt as another swung his bow. Ittai caught the beam of the bow, jerked it out of the man's hand, and rammed it against his nose.

But as he bled profusely from the blow, the third Hebrew did a strange thing. He grasped frantically at Ittai's waist, as though searching for something. Ittai kicked him away, but the wild-animal look on the man's face made him pause.

What was he looking for? The man's lips were frothing with spittle, his eyes crazed with lust for something.

Water.

The Hebrews were not charging them just to kill them. They were trying to get their water.

Ittai shouted to whoever could hear him, "If you get hit, slash your water pouches! They are dying of thirst! Don't let them take your water!" He stabbed the Hebrew archer in the belly before moving on.

Inspired by his actions and words, his men charged faster behind him. Ittai yelled them forward to kill more Hebrews. The remaining archers fled up the hill away from them.

It was obvious to Ittai now that the third ambush he had expected was not coming. Either the Hebrew commanders had lost their nerve or they had already thrown everything they had at the Philistines in desperation.

Yet David himself would not have led a suicide mission. They might not have had time to organize, but surely he had thousands of soldiers in his command. Was the drought so bad? Were more Hebrews out of commission than the Philistine rulers had thought? Where was Keth of the Hittites?

Ittai leaned against a tree to catch his breath and steady his nerves. Daylight filtered down above him. He watched the dust kicked up by the fleeing Hebrews and his pursuing men. Dust covered every leaf, every blade of grass.

There was a renewed sound of commotion behind him back in the valley. Squinting and searching through the gaps in the trees, he saw two things. The first was the Hebrew warrior who had spared him emerging on the slope to his left in a full sprint, and the second was one of his troops from another company carrying a torch in the direction of the barley field on the other side of the valley.

Ittai realized what was happening and laughed. If the man with the torch reached the field and set it ablaze, there would be serious harm done to the farmers of the region. What little remained of the crop during this drought would be destroyed. A last spite to the Hebrews.

The Hebrew charged toward the barley field, holding his sword out in front of him, his tunic and armor drenched with sweat and covered in blood. Ittai wanted to race after the Hebrew and slaughter him, but he needed to rally his men.

His nose ached, his jaw throbbed. Blood was all over his face and neck.

How far away were his Sword troops?

And where was the Hebrew king?

THIRTY-FOUR

Farther up the valley from where David and Eleazar had begun the attack, at the point where the road from Bethlehem met with the Rephaim, Benaiah elbowed his way through a bush before pausing against a tree trunk. He waited briefly, then pulled his head just high enough to see through the forest.

It was now midmorning and the sun already raged overhead. Patches of sunlight were visible down the mountainside from his position. The valley opened into grasslands, crisp and brown from the drought, with a road cut by parallel ox-cart ruts long since dried out.

The trees blocked most of his view, but he could make out glinting Philistine armor as the column of troops marched along the road. It looked extremely hot on the road. The troops would be suffering under their metal armor. A possible advantage.

Benaiah let himself slide backward until he was even with Keth.

"They're on the road. Just like David said."

"Any chariots?"

"No, looks like the garrison commander in Bethlehem has more brains than the kings from Gath. Light weapons. Mobile. Javelin throwers. Looks like more Sword of Dagon troops. It will be tough."

"We have the best warriors in the army with us."

"We're also outnumbered. Vastly."

"David said Yahweh promised victory."

Benaiah nodded absently. Sweat dripped from his brow. He raised the edge of his tunic and wiped his forehead. He saw the scattered figures of the Thirty behind him. It was their task to be the first into a fight and the last to leave, and they met this responsibility with pride. But he had to wonder if this was going to be too much for even them.

Josheb crawled up beside him.

"Two hundred," Benaiah said.

"Less than we thought, at least. But we still can't let them meet up with the others."

"Agreed."

"Do you think they are as good as we have heard?"

"If they fight like the two that found us in the hideaway, yes."

"I thought you said there were three."

"There were. I killed one quickly."

"Then they aren't that great."

"I jumped from above and landed on his neck. He wasn't expecting me."

Josheb nodded, then took a short drink from his nearly empty water pouch. He swished the liquid around in his mouth, savoring it, before swallowing with a pained expression.

"Terrible last drink for a man to have. Warm and smelly."

"They're carrying water," Benaiah said.

"Bethlehem has wells that are still full," said Keth.

"And that's the only place in the land. They know about the drought just a half day's walk from the town. Anyone who doesn't want to die of thirst has to walk a day to reach Bethlehem. It's why they fortified the town. They know how valuable it is to us."

"How well do you think they are coordinated with the force coming up from the plains?" asked Josheb.

"They can't be. None of the movements we have seen the past few days tell me that they are taking our threat seriously. They're acting like they just want to snatch as much land for themselves as possible. It's a risk to draw troops from an important garrison like Bethlehem."

"Unless they have reason to believe we are not prepared to do anything about it."

Benaiah cursed, then looked back at the other members of the Thirty scattered in the trees. He saw Gareb a short distance away watching him. He lowered his voice. "When we are done here, I will find the jackal who is spying on us."

"How can we be surprised when so many members of David's inner circle are foreigners?" Keth asked.

"You're a foreigner," said Josheb.

"No, I have a Hebrew name now. That clears me of all suspicion."

"I'm still keeping an eye on you."

Benaiah picked up a twig and chewed on the end of it, ignoring the jokes. "Might be a woman from the harem. He is susceptible to them."

"We're wasting time," Josheb said. The other two nodded.

Josheb sketched on the dirt. "Standard ambush. I will go first. They will expect a trap, then you two go next to make them think you are it. They are used to a handful of men at a time coming just close enough to kill an officer or two and then retreating into the woods. They also know that our army is concentrated on the Rephaim right now. When they believe you are all there is and have their backs turned, the rest of the Thirty can hit them. 'The Lord is a warrior, the Lord is his name,' as Moses once sang."

"We are with you," Keth said.

"If you fall, Benaiah, I am picking your wife's new husband. I'll give her to Shammah."

"Yours is nothing but trouble. I'll give her to Shammah as well."

"Shammah wouldn't know what to do with all of those women. Probably turn himself into a eunuch."

They hugged once more. Then Josheb crawled up and over the stump and disappeared. Benaiah made eye contact with three of the subordinate leaders and motioned them forward. He whispered the plan of attack to them and made them repeat it. Then they eased their way back to their squads.

Now they waited.

Josheb picked out the first officer standing at the edge of the road. He was pausing to squeeze a few drops of water out of a pouch and growling orders at his armor bearer. The column of Philistines was marching five abreast, more disciplined and orderly than the mass of troops they had seen staggering through the Rephaim over the ridges behind them.

Every man was outfitted with light armor of leather and iron pieces and carried short swords for tight skirmishing in the thick brush crowding the mountain slopes. They also carried javelins should they be forced to fight through an ambush. They were stopping for a rest after pressing hard throughout the day, but none of the soldiers ever fully relaxed his guard.

They have skilled commanders. Yahweh, go before us. We need your armies.

He raised his war bow and aimed at the officer's head.

▲▲▲

Benaiah reached out his hand to Keth, who took it. They clasped wrists and spoke blessings on each other's families. Keth prayed to Yahweh for the sake of Benaiah's family in his native Hittite. Benaiah returned the blessing by asking Yahweh to bless the womb of Keth's new wife, who still had not conceived. It was their private ritual, shared before every battle.

When they were finished, they waited for the sound of the first man to die.

From a short distance away, Gareb watched Benaiah and Keth go through their battle ritual and wished he had his own comrade to share such a moment with. Eliam was more of a son to him than a comrade. They had suffered much together, but he always felt as though he were teaching the young man. What he wanted was someone to bleed with as an equal, like he had with Jonathan.

He wiped his face. He looked around at the other men to see if any were drinking too much of their water out of nerves, then reminded himself that they were the elite warriors and he did not have to watch over them like a father.

There were insects flitting around his face. Gareb ignored them, even as they hummed into his ear and landed in his eyes. No sudden movements, nothing to break discipline. A fly crept into the corner of his mouth and worked its way up his face. Hazy sunlight trickled into his senses from the canopy above. It was hot. Very, very hot. He hated bugs.

He was suddenly afraid. He hated being afraid.

THIRTY-FIVE

The gut string snapped as it released the arrow. Josheb watched it fly and then at the last second dip too low, its flight path warped by the valley breeze. The arrow hit the commander directly on his breastplate, which pinched inward before the arrow shattered on the iron. But the force was enough to knock the man over, and he collapsed against his shield bearer with a loud grunt.

Josheb had pulled out another arrow as soon as he fired the first, and this time he accounted for the breeze. As the officer started to pull himself up, the iron-forged tip burst through the gap in his helmet next to his ear. The Philistine's head jerked and shook with spasms several times. The shield bearer tried to help him up as the ranks of the troops began shouting and forming into battle formations. The shield bearer screamed and pulled away when he saw the shaft protruding from his commander's ear.

Josheb stormed out of the woods, dropping the bow and wielding a cudgel in one hand and a sickle sword in the other. The first blow caught the stunned shield bearer in the side of his head, the second was a sword stroke into the throat of a nearby squad leader who had begun to take command.

The Philistines recovered from their shock quickly and formed into defensive positions, ignoring Josheb as he had said they would. He sprinted away, moving in and out of the range of javelins and ran up and down the ranks taunting them and calling out their best champion to face him. But they were disciplined troops, watching him restlessly and keeping their eyes trained on the wood line.

Keth jumped at the same time as Benaiah. They rushed out of the trees and into the open. A flurry of javelins met them. They dropped to their bellies in the small dip that ran parallel to the road and heard the clatter of the weapons as they fell.

Then they were back on their feet, each man snatching two javelins and hurling them at the ranks of Philistines. They darted back into the woods, arrows thumping against tree trunks and shredding the leaves overhead, running through the brush, ignoring the scratches it left on their legs.

Benaiah and Keth emerged farther down the road and crossed it, drawing more shouts and javelins from the Philistine ranks. The full detachment of archers was in the rear of the formation, hastily attempting to assemble in the narrow gap of the valley roadway.

They pulled up next to Josheb, who was still shouting taunts. Benaiah saw that still no arrows came, and then he realized that something was about to happen. Something unexpected, but he could not tell what.

The Philistines had not faced them as they had hoped, had not placed their archers in a neat formation and exposed their backs to the forest where the Thirty were ready to tear them apart.

As they watched, the Philistines turned away from them, surged together, and charged away from the three Israelite warriors into the trees.

Gareb cursed but did not delay further. "They didn't fall for it! Get into your teams!"

There was mass confusion as hundreds of Philistine troops rushed into the forest, hacking and slashing at anything they saw, urged forward by their officers who bellowed threats and curses at them. There was shouting. Gareb saw the other two men in his fighting team and pulled them together.

"Don't let them retreat, we have to hold," he said as resolutely as possible, and they nodded and understood. To the death.

As bad as it was, Gareb knew that they now had a slight advantage. A battle in the open could have been disastrous, but in the trees, where his men were at home, they had a chance. Commands shouted in the woods were confusing. The enemy was too large and their commanders would have severe trouble keeping them fighting in unison. But they had correctly anticipated the ambush, and the mass counterattack was the right strategy. The Sword of Dagon had been trained well.

He hid behind a rock until two Philistine soldiers stumbled past, then he cut them across the backs of their legs. They screamed as they thrashed about in the dry brush, their blood spraying the brown leaves. Gareb could hear the other members of the Thirty doing the same, trying to wound the Philistines where they could in order to terrify the others with their painful cries.

Josheb, Benaiah, and Keth reacted quickly to the Philistine counterattack. Since they were the only targets in the open, they had to draw the fire of the archers, the only Sword platoon left in the roadway.

Josheb gave the order, and the three Israelites rushed forward in a wedge. Benaiah thought desperately that they had no protection, no shields to block the impending fury of the arrows that would rain down on them. He heard Josheb saying something, and realized he was asking for the covering. *Covering in the battle, covering in the day of war.*

The arrows came. They were so close that the archers did not even need to raise their aim to gain elevation. The deadly shafts flew directly at the running Hebrews. Benaiah winced and begged Yahweh to shield them in the last instant before the arrows struck.

Gareb picked up a rock and smashed it against a Philistine's face. He struck another face with his fist before sliding the sickle sword between the scales of armor in a third man. The soldier collapsed against him. Gareb strained to push him off, but he was trapped, and a flurry of weapons came at him at once. His arm was trapped, the sword too slow to block any thrusts, and he winced at the hot metal waiting to penetrate his neck.

A body fell across him and stopped the blows. It was a Hebrew warrior, and Gareb thought he had tripped in front of the blades before he saw that the man was already dying, and in his last conscious act he had thrown himself over Gareb's head. Gareb madly wanted to thank him for his sacrifice but could not recognize him. Igal? Zelek? Who was his father?

Move!

There was a Philistine on top of him. He shoved the body

aside, then a dagger was coming toward his face. Gareb grunted and turned his face right before it struck, and he felt the blade cut through his cheek and pin his head into the dirt from the side. Searing, blinding pain. Crumpled flesh hung loose in his mouth, and he gagged and vomited.

Without thinking, he released his grip on the sword and jammed his fingers into the eye sockets of the Philistine. He felt warm liquid as the eyes ruptured beneath his fingers, but he could not see what was going on, his face was still pinned by the dagger. The Philistine gagged.

Gareb pulled his fingers out of the man's eyes and found the hilt of the dagger next to his cheek. He jerked it out of the dirt and slid it through the flesh of his cheek, tears filling his eyes. He screamed. He stabbed the dagger into the foot of another Philistine soldier nearby, then realized that man was already dead. He had stabbed a corpse. He searched for another leg, another piece of human flesh to kill, but the shouting had passed him by; the battle was moving farther into the grove.

Blood pouring from the wound in his face, Gareb shoved with as much strength as he could muster and crawled out from beneath the pile of bodies. The Philistine who had stabbed his face was still alive, shrieking. Unsteadily, Gareb knelt and pulled a sword from under the leg of the dead Hebrew who had saved him. He didn't have time to see who it was.

He stumbled forward into the woods, the sunlight shining in patches on the ground in front of him, the deep forest echoing with the sound of souls wailing and entering darkness.

On the road, the arrows had missed them.

Josheb hit the Philistines first, lowering his head and ramming them before they could prepare another volley. He spun several times quickly, dropping two with his own sword while tripping another. He stabbed the downed man, then repeated the movement again, faster. Keth did the same, and Benaiah. They were fresh and angry, and before long the archers were all dead.

Benaiah did not let himself dwell on the failed arrows, on the impossible miss, because now Keth was running into the woods, and he followed him. Ahead of them, Josheb bellowed his fearsome war cry, the cudgel and sword prepared. Benaiah's club was out. They pursued the Philistine troops.

THIRTY-SIX

The battle spread up the mountainside through the forest. The Thirty were taking advantage of the concealment to lash out from hidden burrows and behind tree trunks. It was a storm of shouting and metal striking metal, sudden pauses and shouts, then more clashing of metal.

The gash in Gareb's face hurt badly. The bleeding had not stopped, only slowed, and he hoped it would go away soon; it was making him lightheaded. And thirsty. He slouched against a boulder and fumbled for his water pouch.

He could hear Sword commanders shouting orders in their heathen language. He treasured the tiny sip of water, felt it prickle his bloody throat, reigniting the terrible pain in his face. Water drained out of the hole in his cheek. His arms shook. He stared into the opening of the water pouch, willing more of the liquid to appear. He tied it shut and let it sling on his side again.

And then, suddenly, he heard a series of shouts, clashes of metal, and the thumping sound of men running echoing across the mountainside. Then silence, then confusion, then more voices. The wind picked up, the trees overhead began to sway, and just when Gareb was about to climb a trunk to see what was going on, a hoard of Philistines erupted into his little clearing.

He leapt to his feet, sword ready to plunge into the first torso that got near him, when he saw that the Philistines were battling each other.

Battling *each other*?

Their eyes showed madness, their screams primal and animal-like. They clawed at each other in horror and stabbed wildly. A sudden gust shoved the trees overhead viciously. Gareb could smell something in the air; he could not identify it. He darted to the edge of the clearing as the Philistines, dozens of them, continued to kill each other.

Then something appeared out of the trees. Gareb froze.

It was a figure, a man-like thing, but it had a massive sword covered with fire. The warrior with the flaming sword raised his huge arms above his head and yelled a war cry that resounded and shook the earth, as if a lion as vast as the mountain itself was on the hunt, and Gareb covered his ears in fear.

The fearsome warrior slashed his sword in blazing arcs, cutting down Philistines. There was smoke and fire.

Then the warrior vanished.

The horrified Philistines who remained ran into the forest, where there was another outburst of clashing, and then all was still except for the noise of coughing, gagging, and men calling for help.

The sounds roused Gareb out of his shock. He stumbled forward on numb legs again. He looked at his hands. His fingernails were caked with gore.

All the things he should have been thinking about, and he was thinking about his fingernails. There were remnants of the Philistine's eyes under them. He shook his head. The wind was dying, his ears ringing. He was so very, very thirsty.

Who had the warrior been? A demon?

Branches gave way as he staggered forward, and he found himself standing in another clearing. Josheb was there; he tensed up as Gareb appeared. Benaiah and Keth were there also, on either side of nearby trees, waiting to ambush him.

He stared at them. They stared back.

"What happened?" Josheb asked. His eyes shot back to the thicket surrounding them.

"Don't know," Gareb mumbled, his mouth swollen nearly shut from the dagger wound. "Heard something, saw something, and the Philistines all started running."

"Saw what? And what was that roar?"

Gareb shook his head, unable to speak.

"We killed the rest of that pack as they ran by," Benaiah said, gesturing at the bodies on the ground, "but they were already doing the job themselves."

"Thirty! If you are disengaged, rally on my voice!" Josheb called out. The four of them took up defensive positions on the edge of the clearing to be ready should any remaining Philistines arrive as well.

In a few moments, teams of three began to appear in the clearing, some warriors leaning on each other. Gareb counted them.

Twenty.

With the four of them, and Shammah and Abishai elsewhere, they were still missing four. After waiting a moment longer, Josheb called out again. No response came from the woods.

"What happened? Why did the Philistines go mad and start killing each other?" Josheb asked the group. They all answered with shaking heads.

"Someone attacked them. It wasn't any of us."

All eyes snapped to Gareb. He was having trouble finding words.

"A warrior. Not like a man."

Josheb lifted his face to the sky, his eyes closed and his arms outstretched. "Our God has delivered us, men. He has kept his promise." There was murmured agreement. Josheb lowered his arms and looked around. "I can't see all of you, so I am calling out names. Answer if you hear. Elhanan!"

"Here, sir."

"Igal!"

"Here, sir."

Josheb counted them all. They were still missing four men.

The silence hung, suspended in the heat of midday. Each man stared at the ground, gasping for breath from his exertions, trying to hold back his grief. Gareb clenched his jaw several times to ease the stiffness in his face.

Josheb finally nodded.

"We will mourn them later. We need to get back to the king now."

THIRTY-SEVEN

"Reposition the men! We can hold them!" David shouted up the slope.

He called out order after order, but none of the men would turn around. Behaving like the green troops they are, he thought, desperate now. He had no way of knowing whether the Thirty had been able to stop the Sword troops, no way of knowing what happened to his third assault. He knew nothing.

He stared at the Philistine platoons charging toward the gap, then felt a glimmer of hope when he saw that it was not a full regiment after all, merely a few platoons moving side by side.

"Get back!" he screamed. "Hit them!" But his men were gone. *Yahweh, what now? Pull back with the men? Stay in the fight? What about Eleazar?*

No answer.

Shouts. Philistines coming up the valley toward him. They had taken heart at the sight of the fleeing Hebrews and were in proper formation to attack him.

David closed his eyes, took a weary breath, opened them again. He raced toward Eleazar.

The Philistine with the torch did not see Eleazar approaching behind him. He lowered the flame to the tops of the stalks, setting the edge of the field on fire. The sea breeze was stirring and would whip it into an inferno quickly.

Eleazar did not slow. He seized him by the back of the tunic, swung his sword, and severed the man's torch-bearing arm. Then he yanked the soldier backward on top of the small flame that had been ignited. The Philistine screamed, the bloody stump of his arm spraying Eleazar in the face.

Eleazar rolled the man several times over the fire. After a few frantic seconds of rolling and stamping, the flames died away, but there were several spots where embers still glowed.

He felt the empty Philistine water skin on his side, sliced open by an arrow.

How to put it out?

Eleazar grabbed the Philistine's arm and held it over the site of the flames, letting the blood seeping out of the wound drench the embers, then picked up the fallen torch and dipped it into the blood pool gathering under the Philistine.

He fought despair. They were coming. Vast hoards of them would be filling the valley soon, and they would overwhelm every town and village and settlement in the land, and they would slaughter and rape without mercy or end.

And the people would run, he thought. The people would have to run away again, always fleeing and cowering and hiding and begging and pleading with other nations. They were weak, just like he was weak, as he had been when he had gone to the tents of the Ammonites, running away like a coward from his wife and home ...

But Yahweh delivered me then. He can do it again.

Eleazar saw David at the western end of the valley running toward him. Also approaching were the Philistine remnants, who had been organized and were now charging forward.

David was fast, much faster than any of the Philistines chasing him, so he outran them and slammed into Eleazar, hugging him and giving him a kiss on the cheek.

"Thought you went to rally the men," Eleazar said.

David was panting heavily. "I did. The men are ... too green. Never should have brought them ... so many foolish decisions."

"We didn't have a choice." Eleazar pointed south. "Our homes are only three valleys that direction. You said yourself—if we pull back, the Philistines take this valley and we'll never get it back. By the time you rally the men, they will have filled this gap with too many troops. I have to hold them here."

"We can regroup later. Let's get moving."

"I am holding this field."

David, leaning forward, hands on his knees, to catch his breath, looked up at him. "Is it worth your life?"

"This farmer would think so," Eleazar said, gesturing at the field. "His wife and kids are probably nearby."

David nodded. "Then we will do it together."

"Don't be a fool. It's not worth *your* life."

"If you think I am going to abandon—"

"You die and the whole kingdom falls," Eleazar snapped. "Get back and rally the others. I have to hold here."

The pursuing Philistine troops were close now. David looked at them, then at Eleazar, who raised his arms impatiently.

David shook his head. "Your woman and children—"

"—will be enslaved with the rest of our people if you die. Now get back and rally the others!"

Eleazar's shout seemed to stun David. No one had given him orders in many years.

"You're certain?" David asked.

Eleazar seized David by the tunic. Pulling him close, he pointed south again. "Didn't you hear me? I said our homes are only *three valleys over* from here! If I don't hold this ground right now, and you don't rally the men for a counterattack, my family dies anyway!"

"But if we run back now, the Philistines will—"

"All they *ever* see is us running!"

David stared at him, and Eleazar saw that he finally understood.

The Philistines were almost to the edge of the field. Eleazar saw David's eyes narrow, fighting emotion. David placed his hand on Eleazar's forehead. He whispered something. A prayer. "The Lord wills it. Make your stand, brother. I'll be back quickly."

"Care for my family ... if I fall."

David looked down, then back into his eyes. "I will. Your family will never be without." Then he nodded firmly. "But you will make it. I will not see you in Sheol yet."

David left. Eleazar watched him run across the field back to the slope, where he would eventually find his men and demand to know why they had lost heart and abandoned them. His anger would be terrible. A Philistine officer dispatched a squad to chase David and they veered away, already losing ground to the fleet-footed Hebrew king.

Eleazar planned fast. The Philistines had lost their archers, so they would need to get close to kill him. As it was, all they had to do was run him down in a concentrated assault. They were heavy infantry with war axes and spears, able to lock shields and deploy their weapons through the gaps.

But the Philistine foot soldiers were too consumed with battle rage to listen to the efforts of their officers to organize them, and they charged side by side at Eleazar, standing in the middle of the field.

Eleazar lifted his face to the sky one final time, his eyes closed.

He was back in the woods outside the city gates, and the woman was there in the tents, offering herself to him, and he reached out to touch her roughly. But her skin was cold as death. The skin of a slave. He saw her as someone's daughter. A child. And in that moment he remembered the words of his father.

If your courage holds in the small battles, it will hold in the great ones.

And Eleazar had turned away from the woman and stumbled out the tent, and Yahweh had sent a cold wind to refresh and revive him. The tents of the Ammonite camp were blown down by the wind, and Eleazar screamed with relief as he escaped darkness, delivered by the hand of Yahweh.

The Philistines were almost upon him now. His eyes opened; he blinked in the hot sunlight.

His wife, his children. He wanted to see them married, wanted to toss grandchildren into the air and tell them of the old days. He did not want to die in this lonely place. He saw his father again, saw him holding his face between his hands and kissing his head. He remembered when Yahweh saved him in the tents of the Ammonites, and a thousand other times. He understood now what David had told him, and he saw not just the enemies before him, but the beheaded champions behind.

If your courage holds in the small battles, my son, it will hold in the great ones.

"God of my father!" he screamed through blistered lips. "You have delivered me on countless battlefields, both in my heart and on earth! I have not forgotten! Now show the power of your covering!"

Then they came, and he lifted the sword to eye level to deflect the first attack and guided the point into the throat of another soldier.

Then he leaped, kicking a weapon out of a hand and slicing a deep cut across a fourth man's arm. The last two men in the squad rushed him, and he killed them.

The deaths of an entire squad of soldiers within the first minute of the fight caused the rest of the onrushing troops to balk. Eleazar called out to them to attack, feeling something crackling in his muscles begging for release. He was now surrounded, the company having formed a perimeter around the barley field. They held their weapons up, over a hundred troops, angry and frightened at the same time.

Ittai, panting from running across the field, came up behind the crowd of soldiers on the edge of the barley field surrounding the Hebrew warrior. He'd almost joined the chase for David, but the man was too fast.

The Hebrew, crouched like an animal in the center, was keeping the troops at bay even though he called for them to attack. Ittai saw the pile of dead Philistines at his feet and knew that many more would fall before this man died.

Spears flew toward the Hebrew, who spun in a tight circle and knocked all of them out of the air with his sword. He then snatched one of them and flung it with such force that it impaled a man through his armor. When another soldier charged, the Hebrew flung another spear, then kicked another up with his foot and threw it at a third, who crumpled backward with the spear shaft jutting out of his skull.

The man shouted something, his eyes wild with battle rage, his muscles and arms twitching as though possessed. Ittai looked away from him at the surrounding ranks and searched for an officer's helmet before realizing his was the only one. The Hebrew had killed all of the remaining officers but himself.

"Attack him! Everyone! Rush him!" he bellowed. His voice was loud and authoritative and troops began to move, but not fast enough. "If you attack one at a time he will kill all of you! Everyone go, now!"

Spears flew and were deflected, pikes were thrust, but the Hebrew held his ground, swinging the blade with blinding speed, cutting down ranks of soldiers. The barley was trampled and covered with blood and bodies, dozens of bodies, and still the Hebrew fought, moving forward without fear or mercy. Ittai saw demons in his eyes.

He gripped the amulet again.

THIRTY-EIGHT

Eleazar was no longer afraid, did not care how much his arm was beginning to hurt. He knew only that there were more enemies, and he would slaughter them until there were no more, until this field and sacred valley was free of the pagan filth that trespassed here. He saw fire everywhere. Fire consumed his eyes and arms. Fire burned in his nostrils, blood sprayed his face, his arm blocked and thrust, parried and sliced, blocked again, sliced again.

Bodies piled up around him. There were many left to kill, so he stabbed his blade into a man's guts and pulled the soldier close to his left side to use as a shield. A Philistine pointed a pike at him and Eleazar cut his fingers off when the pike got close.

His sword arm burned with fatigue, but the fire burned brighter and hotter, and men died.

At the top of the slope, despite his fury at the deserting troops, David paused and turned, afraid that he would see victorious Philistines carrying the headless body of his friend over their heads as a war trophy. Instead, he saw the scuffling of massed bodies kicking up dust.

The fight went on, and somehow, Eleazar was holding the ground.

Eleazar's own sword snapped in half when it struck someone's armor, so he caught the hilt of an incoming sword, guided it with its own force back toward the Philistine's eye. It missed and hit the helmet. He smashed it again, this time crushing the ear and forcing the man to his knees. He ripped the helmet off the Philistine with his left arm and swung it into the face of another charging soldier. Still they came, and he fought them.

He had mad thoughts, thoughts of songs in the camp, of his son's rapid growth, his wife's oddly shaped feet. He slapped the broken blade's side across an arm that reached in too far, then kicked out and tripped two charging warriors. Against all common sense, the Philistines were still charging him in ones and twos and dying by the dozen.

His right hand was tightening. He'd squeezed the sword hilt so hard that his fingernails had snapped off, exposing raw and painful flesh.

Eleazar winced as an enemy sword slipped through his block and nicked him on the forehead. The Philistine withdrew his weapon quickly to strike again. Eleazar brought his broken sword up to deflect the blow, but not in time—the hot metal burned into his chest.

The Philistine shouted hoarsely in triumph, believing he had made a killing blow. Eleazar lurched backward, landing on his back on a trampled patch of barley, wrenching the Philistine's sword away from his grip with his foot.

He shook his hand to free his broken sword from his grip. It did not release. He pounded his fist on the ground, and still it did not release.

There were shouts, shadows blocked the sun in the dusty air. He bit at his rigidly frozen fingers, still not releasing their grip on the sword hilt.

More men coming!

David rushed into the forest following the tracks of the fleeing men, anger powering his steps. Branches slapped across his face. Hundreds of men stampeding like cattle through the forest left a distinct trail.

As he crossed another dry creek bed, he saw motion ahead of him in the forest. *A cloak, a tunic?* It came from the direction of an old rally point, a gnarled tree with a dead top that jutted out from the edge of a cliff. They were not far from the caves. He heard shouting through the trees.

David pulled his sling out again and withdrew three stones from his pouch. He entered the clearing to see his troops bent over with their hands on their knees, crowding next to the old tree like it was a mighty sentinel that would shield them from their enemies.

"Korah, Ribai, and Hurai!" David shouted the names of the three northern commanders so loudly that everyone snapped their heads up.

Ribai, standing on a rock near the tree, raised his arm. "My lord, you are safe! There were so many of them, we were going to come back—"

David dropped one of the stones into the sling notch, never breaking his stride. He whirled it three times, and before the man had finished speaking his skull had been splattered, showering the men around him with bright crimson blood and bone fragments.

Men gasped in horror and fell away from the carcass.

"Majesty! We were—"

David sent the next stone at a man who had emerged from the front ranks of panting troops, and it struck him in the lower jaw, tearing it away and exposing his upper teeth grotesquely. It was Hurai. He clawed at the wound in shock, unable to find the lower half of his face. A burbling sound erupted from his throat, and he raised his hands toward the heavens.

"Mercy, sire!" one of the other soldiers howled.

David reached the group and grabbed a javelin from a cowering man nearby, his eyes cold and murderous. He showed the weapon to the dying man struck by the stone.

"Your orders were to throw volleys of these into the Philistine ranks to finish the attack," he said, his teeth clenching together and his voice quaking with fury.

The commander, Hurai, tried to speak but could not with his ruined mouth.

An aide stepped forward. "Lord, we—"

"Cowardice on the battlefield cannot be tolerated."

"Forgive us—"

David rammed the javelin into Hurai's open throat. The man twitched and convulsed.

Men wailed at the sight. They threw themselves on the ground and tossed handfuls of dirt into the air.

"Mercy on us, Majesty, mercy on us!"

David walked past the second corpse and searched the crowd. "Where is Korah?"

Fingers pointed to the tree, where the third commander stood shaking. David walked toward him.

Korah fled.

Watching him scramble up the slope, David dropped a stone into the sling and held it silently, letting the man run for a moment. He was especially angry at Korah's cowardice; all of his bluster in the council at Hebron had meant nothing.

As the terrified officer reached the crest of the slope, David whirled his sling once through the air in a slow arc, sped it up, and whirled again.

A hand caught his elbow, and the stone and sling jerked to a halt. "In the name of Yahweh, have mercy!"

David turned angrily. It was an old man. His eyes held David's gaze, firm. It gave David pause. David did not recognize him, yet he seemed familiar.

Then the old man crumpled to the earth. He grabbed the king's feet. "Kill your servant, lord, but let that man live."

David's face twisted in hatred. The old man kissed his feet and begged him again.

"Mercy, great king, mercy."

The soldiers around David also threw themselves onto their faces in the dirt, reaching their hands toward him in complete subservience. Voices howled, songs of death were hummed through fear-tightened lips, dried and cracked from lack of water.

David turned back toward the ridgetop just as Korah disappeared over it. He yelled. He kicked the old man in the ribs in frustration. "Never, ever abandon the attack! You should all die for this cowardice!"

"We should, great king, we should! Mercy on us!" the old man rasped, holding his side.

David wondered briefly why such an aged man was in his army. But he pushed it out of his head. "I want an immediate rally back to the valley. Eleazar is caught there, alone, defending you and your families. If you fall back against my orders again, Sheol will be a relief after what I do to you!"

The men shouted their approval, still calling for mercy as they gathered themselves off the ground. David pointed at three different men and promoted them on the spot. Still terrified, the three urged their men back through the forest, trying to regain a semblance of order.

David, panting and furious, wiped the sweat from his forehead on the edge of his tunic. He squeezed his eyes shut to calm his rage. After a few quiet seconds, the stillness of the woods and the sound of birds told him that all was well, and he opened his eyes once more.

Mercy, God of my salvation. I hear you.

"Where did you come from?" he asked the old man he expected to see still cowering at his feet.

But he was gone.

THIRTY-NINE

Benaiah, Keth, and Gareb staggered after Josheb through the forest. Benaiah thought of water. He saw it everywhere in his imagination. It poured from treetops, out of rocks, washed over his feet. He found himself swimming in the Nile again, taking gulps of water with each stroke.

But there was only dust and stone in front of him.

The rest of the Thirty were fanned out around them on the hillside, attempting to sweep out the remaining Sword of Dagon troops as they made their way back to the place where David and Eleazar were likely battling for their lives.

"How is your face?" Josheb asked Gareb.

"Ugly before the dagger wound, so I can't imagine what it looks like now."

Benaiah grinned. He loved Gareb's wit.

"Does anyone have any water left?" Josheb asked.

They looked at one another. Benaiah swallowed painfully, his throat filled with dust. Heads shook.

"Stay alert," said Josheb. "They'll hit us again."

"They lost many when our helper came," said Keth.

The hillside rippled with small gullies. They rushed through them one at a time, up and down each hump in the earth, and it was just when Benaiah was realizing that they should probably slow down that the Sword of Dagon counterattack began.

Benaiah ducked away from a javelin, but before he did, he saw that each gully on the hillside had a squad of Philistines defending it, and with steep rock on their left and open valley on their right, the Thirty would have to battle through the ambush.

Josheb ordered all of them down. The men split into their battle teams and then took turns charging forward. A team of three would assault through the brush and into the next gully under a hail of javelins and blades, and when they engaged the enemy, another team rushed forward.

Benaiah, Keth, and Gareb immediately formed their own battle team and made ready to rush when it was their turn. They heard the shouts, and then they were running. Benaiah charged forward with his shield and sword out. Keth covered his left side, Gareb his right, and the Sword troops reacted perfectly, deflecting the attack.

Shammah was in the busy streets of Hebron when he felt the call in his spirit. He put down the fruit he was examining in the market while waiting for Joab to reappear and looked heavenward. All sounds of the busy market ceased in his mind.

His eyes closed, and he mouthed the words of prayer that were so frequently on his lips. His frustration at being left behind while his brothers marched to war was gone.

They needed him now.

In the open, in front of all who were watching, he raised his arms and cried out loudly to Yahweh. Many stared at him as though he was mad, but he did not care.

Josheb glimpsed Benaiah struggling through the gully and saw that his men were losing ground. The Sword troops, entrenched, were not budging from their positions. It was going to be costly trying to force them out through the usual strategy.

Josheb pulled out his spear. He had no equal with it. It was his burden and his blessing.

Then he ran to the lines and attacked.

Benaiah was able to kill one soldier, but lack of water was slowing him, and his arm was tiring, and he failed to raise his shield in time to prevent another Philistine's blade from striking his shoulder. His sideways roll saved his life, and as he was about to move back into a braced attack posture, a spear impaled the Philistine and was withdrawn faster than he could blink.

After spearing him, Josheb spun the man around and used him to block the next few blows, and then he ran toward the next gully. Benaiah, Keth, and Gareb followed him.

Josheb plowed through the next rank, moving too quickly to be hit by the weapons aimed at him, and then he penetrated the next, and the next, and Benaiah, Keth, and Gareb had to summon all of their remaining effort just to keep up with him.

The rest of the Thirty saw that Josheb had penetrated all of the Philistine lines by himself and surged after him to divide the enemy.

Benaiah was hit from behind—he whirled, caught a sword with

his club before it could slice through his neck. He smashed the club into the Philistine's face.

Another man dove at his knees and wrestled him to the ground. Benaiah elbowed the man's neck, then tried punching him in the ear but only caught the helmet. The Philistine shoved a dagger near his face. Benaiah blocked it, but the Philistine was strong and thrust it again.

Benaiah released his grip on the Philistine's wrist and jerked his head back, letting the dagger swipe near his face, then caught his thumb on the hilt. He shoved the tip back into the Philistine's eye.

Someone else bumped into him. Keth, fighting off two Philistines.

Benaiah picked up his club and struck the Philistines down from behind.

"They're breaking off into wedges, just like how we fight," Benaiah panted.

A wedge of Sword troops appeared just as he said it and made him leap over a ledge into a bush down the hill to avoid them. Gareb and Keth leapt after him, and as they landed they scrambled together to make their own wedge.

Up the hill they could see the rest of the Thirty trying to fight their way out of the counterattack. Then the Sword wedge that had chased them down the hill hit them.

Benaiah ducked out of the way when the huge man leading the Sword wedge swung a cudgel like it was a piece of straw.

"Why don't any of our tribes have giants?" Gareb grunted.

It was the first time that Benaiah, Keth, and Gareb had fought together in a wedge, but they knew it instinctively. Keeping their space from one another, they protected each other's flanks and took turns attacking to keep the wedge tight.

A wedge of Sword troops charged them. Benaiah waited for

them to break apart at the last moment, but their discipline held, and Keth had to yield a few cubits of ground to set his attack.

That was when Josheb, appearing out of nowhere, assaulted the rear of the Philistine wedge. He killed all three Sword troops with three perfectly timed strikes.

Benaiah whirled around, looking for more. He saw Philistines pulling back into the bushes and scrambling through the nearby wadi.

"They're withdrawing," he said.

"They need to retreat, not withdraw," Josheb said.

"We need to get back to David before they organize again," Gareb said.

The four of them slipped through the trees to find the rest of the Thirty.

FORTY

In the Elah Valley, a huge warrior stepped out of the ranks, and the others backed away. It was one of the champions that Eleazar had seen gathering in the valley. He had broad shoulders and arms the size of trees, taller than any other soldier by a head. Eleazar had no time to catch his breath before the giant was rushing at him.

He pulled at his fingers to break their grip on the hilt so he could get another weapon for his right hand. They remained frozen, and the shattered sword stayed in his hand. Tired and confused, he could not understand why the sword was not falling out of his hand. The warrior threw Eleazar to the ground and raised a spear.

Eleazar rolled to his left, yelling, swinging his blade across the giant's knee guards harmlessly as the spear hit the dirt next to him. The Philistine giant stabbed with the spear again, hitting Eleazar's broken sword as he held it up to block.

Need the covering!

Why weren't the others charging him while he was down? Even the giant balked momentarily, staring over Eleazar's head at something.

Eleazar saw his opportunity and shoved his broken sword forward. The jagged tip cut into the giant's thigh. Eleazar twisted the blade, feeling the muscles shred. The warrior knelt, grabbing at the wound.

Energy came again. Eleazar rolled to his feet, yelled furiously, and sliced the blade across the only exposed part of the giant's neck, buried under layers of armor. The giant fell.

Eleazar heard the sound of more swords clanking and breaking as the battle continued. But with who? Who else were they fighting? The giant had paused to stare at something just before Eleazar had stabbed him. What had he seen?

Eleazar's eyes were blurry. He wished he could look behind him, but the threat was in front. He crawled to his knees to be ready for the next attack.

But the others were running in terror.

David crested the bank. He felt the end of his strength coming and coughed out a song of praise to his God for renewal. He kept running forward, ignoring the awful pain in his throat and weakness in his bones.

Finally, Eleazar came back into view. David was overjoyed. He was still alive, and the enemy was fleeing!

But who was that with him?

There were but two Philistines left, the rest having fled when they realized that swords, spears, and javelins would never bring down the foe they faced this day. The dozen remaining Philistines had stepped back from the Hebrew demon with the fiery strike, shouted to their god Dagon, and spat in the dust before running toward the entrance to the pass to escape the counterattack that might come from the Hebrew Lion.

Eleazar, his fingers still rigidly wrapped around the hilt of the broken sword, took short, quivering breaths. His throat was so dry it choked him. The missing fingernails and the spots where blades had found flesh were numb, but he knew they would hurt later. Hurt badly.

Eleazar was kneeling, his legs too tired to stand, but he was ready, and spoke to the Philistines standing in front of him in their tongue.

"When you are ready."

Hearing the challenge in his own language, the foot soldier lost heart and sprinted after his comrades, but the other, a commander by the design of his helmet, held his sword at eye level and continued watching something behind Eleazar, an amulet dangling from his free hand. Eleazar recognized him as the Philistine officer he had spared at the chariot.

"Tell me why you spared me," the Philistine said, as though thinking the same thing, his eyes darting over Eleazar's shoulder every few seconds. His face was covered in blood, his nose broken, and his jaw was swollen and distorted.

Eleazar chuckled, wiped his dirty lips on the back of his hand, and spat. "I won't do it again, if that is what you are asking."

"What sorcery do you use?"

"No sorcery. Our God is powerful."

The Philistine's mouth twitched as though he was about to reply, but he just stood holding the sword up. They glared at each other.

The Philistine finally lowered the tip of his sword into the churned-up dirt and rested his weight on it. Eleazar saw him take several deep breaths and glance around the field. Whatever the man had been nervously watching was gone.

Careful to not draw attention from the Philistine, Eleazar

resumed trying to move his fingers. They were as solid as limestone. His knuckles were pure white and there was no blood left in the muscles of his hand to move them with.

They heard rumbling, and Eleazar and the Philistine turned toward the other side of the valley. The companies of Hebrews who had abandoned Eleazar and David in the fight were rushing up the slope from the creek bed. They crossed the lines of destroyed chariots and some broke off to find water pouches and weapons from the soldiers. David was in front of them.

The Philistine looked at Eleazar one more time, nodded his head slightly, and knelt while leaning on his weapon to wait.

"I will stay with you," he said.

"Why?"

"My own people will kill me after today's loss. I would rather go to the afterlife killing Hebrews than being executed by my own army."

"Then try to kill me now."

"You spared me. I am honor bound to do the same with you. I will wait for your men." He looked up over Eleazar's head again. "And you have sorcery that I don't know."

Eleazar watched him curiously, but then let his head fall against the earth, beyond exhausted.

The broken, blood-covered sword was still firm in his hand. He wondered if it would always be there, wondered if he would have to take it to bed with his wife when he returned, wondered whether it would frighten his daughters.

He laughed, wiping away sweat. Dust gathered in the corners of his eyes was burning. Or was it blood? And who was this Philistine that Yahweh wanted to be spared? He did not know.

All he knew was that his courage had held.

▲▲▲

Ittai couldn't stop himself from searching the sky overhead, where the demon warrior had disappeared after defending the Hebrew.

Then he stood back up and readied himself for the first few Hebrews. They were charging madly, unskilled. Ittai avoided all of their strikes and managed to stab one of them while tripping the other. He buried the blade between the shoulders of the man who fell. Another Hebrew came at him and died by another strike.

He yelled and jerked his weapon free. He challenged them, hating their sorcery, confused and despairing that he had been abandoned by his patron god. He killed another Hebrew, then another, a young one. He smashed the boy's face and felt teeth breaking beneath his fist. It felt so good that he tackled the boy to the ground and kept pounding his teeth and jaw into mush. Blood sprayed and spurted, and he punched and punched again with all of his remaining strength, wanting to butcher the boy.

Then Ittai's vision was shot through with white streaks as something solid struck his skull from behind, and all was black, and he was swimming in the sea again, the figure of Dagon lurking below him in the darkness, circling him like a predator. He heard the throbbing waves overhead and the raging storm. He beseeched the god with every incantation he knew. He was losing sight of the scales in the water as the black and green colors of the raging sea swirled.

He reached out to the god for help, but none came. He saw the sneer on the hideous face. His heart lurched in despair as he watched the god slowly sink farther beneath the murky waves; then it all faded.

When David reached him, Eleazar was crumpled in a heap in the center of the field. He feared that Eleazar was dead, killed by the Philistine. Hebrew soldiers were about to impale the Philistine with a spear when Eleazar raised his arm and shouted, "Stop! He is their commander!"

They were going to ignore him and kill the Philistine anyway when David shouted, "Don't kill him! I want information from him."

"Lord, he just killed our men—"

David raised his sling up. Terrified, they relented.

David collapsed next to his friend in relief. "Thought you were gone," he said, panting.

"Should be."

"Who was that with you?"

Eleazar looked at him questioningly. "There was someone with me?"

David looked at the sky. "Bless you for your covering, Lord." Then he grinned at Eleazar. "Yahweh protects us this day, my friend."

Eleazar closed his eyes.

Praise your name. You held the ground.

David turned to two of the Hebrew soldiers. "Bring the Philistine back to the cave. If anything happens to him, you will greet the two commanders I killed earlier in Sheol."

FORTY-ONE

David pulled Eleazar along the side of the mountain. Men stepped forward to give assistance, but he shook them off. He would personally carry this warrior all the way back to Hebron if he had to, but he first wanted to get farther down the valley to be ready to engage the Philistines again. They would need to be chased out of the valley entirely and their idols destroyed.

"Where is the runner?" he called out to no one in particular.

"He was sent half an hour ago, lord king," said one of the bodyguards who had just arrived from the caves.

"Keep sending them. I need to know what is happening on the Bethlehem road."

Eleazar buckled next to him. Despite his own weariness, David caught him, but they fell together. He saw that Eleazar was in no condition to reengage anything at all; the last of his strength had been used in the field.

"My friend, these men will help you back to the cave."

"I will kill any man who drags me there," Eleazar rasped.

David shook his head, torn between frustration and gratitude for the courage of his warriors. He whispered thanks to Yahweh for these stubborn fools. "What if I ordered you?"

"I will go if you take a drink of water."

"Yahweh spare me from this." David tried to stand up straight. Exhaustion suddenly struck him like the midday sun and he could not do it. His bodyguards reached for him but he slapped them away. "Help Eleazar; I am fine. Take him back to the cave."

The Gittite mercenary pulled back and eyed Eleazar warily.

Eleazar held up the broken sword clenched in his wrist. "Touch me, and I will cut off both your hands and hang them around my neck."

The Gittite glanced back at David.

"He is not your king. I am. Obey my word," David said.

"Drink water and I will go back to Adullam," Eleazar muttered.

As if on cue, three mercenaries of the bodyguard ripped open their own paltry water bags and thrust them toward him, offering the last of their rations. David stared at them. Even the Philistine mercenaries were willing to sacrifice their last ration for him. For what? What had he done to deserve any of this? Besides cowering behind palace walls and filling his bed with women? He spat, disgusted with himself. He shook his head.

"You slept after we did, you ate after we did, and you drank after we did," Eleazar said, discerning his thoughts.

"Not in many years, my friend."

Eleazar shrugged. "That does not matter. We will never forget it."

"Lord king, please!" the Gittites urged.

David shook his head again. He wanted to weep; he was so unworthy of such an offer.

Someone called out and they looked up. Around the bend in the valley, the remnants of the Thirty appeared. The Hebrew soldiers cheered when they saw them. David picked out Benaiah, Josheb, and the other familiar faces that were so dear to him.

Somehow, his brave and loyal soldiers had held off the Sword of Dagon, and he gave thanks to Yahweh for it.

But when they got closer, there was no triumph on their faces. Josheb, Benaiah, Keth, and Gareb were the first to reach him.

"How many lost?" David asked.

"Four."

Josheb quietly gave the report of the battle. When he was finished, David walked to a tree and leaned against it, his back to the other warriors. *Lord God, thank you for the victory. The cost is great, but so is the victory.*

He let his head sag for a while. Then he turned and looked at his men. "We will mourn them later. The day is not over yet."

No one moved.

"I promise, I won't stand in the back of any battle, and I will never send men to their deaths without reason."

"What reason was there to attack that force on the road?" The question came from one of the quiet warriors of the Thirty, a man named Zalmon the Ahohite. David knew him to be a brave fighter. David had just learned that his friend, Eliphelet, was one of the Thirty who had died in the forest.

"They cannot take Jebus from us," David answered gently.

Zalmon kept his tone respectful, but there was deep hurt in his eyes. "There are other cities, lord."

"There are. But we need to stop them from taking that one."

Zalmon bowed his head in acquiescence, but he did not look at David.

David walked over to and lifted his head up. "Did he have a wife and children?"

Zalmon nodded.

"Then I will take care of them myself. Any who falls among the Thirty will have his family provided for until they are dead. My vow." David raised his sword over his head. "This place will be called Baal-perazim, because Yahweh has burst through our enemies like a flood!"

Then, to everyone's shock, he collapsed.

Eleazar shrugged off the assistance and stumbled to where Benaiah, Keth, and Gareb were standing over David. Pain stabbed under his arm. Must have been a stray blade swipe, he thought. Would need to get it treated.

The king was limp—flecks of white saliva covering his beard—but conscious.

"Don't frighten us like that," Benaiah said.

David squeezed his eyes shut and shook his head. "Oh, what I would give for a drink of the cool Bethlehem water."

Benaiah placed the tip of a water satchel into the king's mouth, and David almost took it before realizing what it was and spitting it out. The soldiers gathered around gasped.

"You have to drink this!" Benaiah said, exasperated.

"How ... many water pouches ... were recovered?" David said between gasps.

"A few dozen. The Philistines slit most of their bags open when they were dying to make sure we didn't get any. Only enough for one or two sips for each man until we can find water."

"Then give it to the injured," David said, gesturing toward the rows of wounded soldiers who were screaming ever louder.

"You are one of those injured, lord," Gareb said.

David waved his hand to end further discussion. Benaiah tossed the water pouch to a soldier who then carried it to the rows of wounded.

"Why has Yahweh cursed us with no water anywhere?" Benaiah complained loudly.

"Yahweh has given us a mighty victory today! Be grateful!" The strength in David's voice surprised everyone. "You four help get everyone moving back to the cave. We need to prepare for their next attack. It could come any day. There are still other regiments on the plains and more soldiers at the garrison in Bethlehem. That might not have been all of the Sword of Dagon soldiers."

When David said the word "Bethlehem," his voice cracked with longing, and Eleazar imagined that if he could have produced it, a tear would have fallen. Such was the power of the memory of his hometown.

The four of them bowed, and Benaiah, Gareb, and Keth helped Eleazar toward the center of the field as several troops obeyed David's orders to help him up. They watched as the king staggered to where Josheb and other members of the Thirty were discussing their withdrawal.

"I know what the men need to see to rally them," Eleazar said.

"What?" asked Benaiah.

Eleazar looked at David again.

Then he told them.

FORTY-TWO

Benaiah, Gareb, and Keth crept through the forest, following old game trails and secret evasion routes that their ancestors had forged centuries before. Gareb knew this land better than Benaiah, who was from the south, so he led. Generations of Israelite men knew these hills and woods, the central hill country bordering the Forest of Hereth, their knowledge passed down from father to son.

Only Eleazar had known of their departure, and since it had been his own idea, he had vowed not to mention it to the king.

After hours of jogging, they reached the ridge overlooking the town of Bethlehem, and as they arrived they noticed the deep blue wall of a storm in the east. They had heard about storms popping up on the borderlands, only to rain themselves out before reaching Israelite country. Still, the sight of it filled them with hope.

Benaiah held up his arm. Exhausted, the men all leaned against trees to rest. Leagues of running after a full day of fighting had put them at their limit.

"We can hold here until we figure out our plan. There is a cave just over there," Gareb said.

Benaiah knelt, then rolled to his side. He inspected the wrapping on his chest that covered the arrow wound, his tunic damp from the oil soaking the entry point. The cut had reopened an old scar.

"Always seem to start these missions hurt," Benaiah mumbled. Keth, lying next to him, chuckled.

"You should have been injured by a lion; it makes a better story," Gareb said, probing at the dagger wound in his own mouth.

"He got a Philistine arrow before we arrived at the cave, and it has not slowed him. He should not be complaining as much as he is," said Keth.

"Avoid arrows, Benaiah, unless you are shooting them."

"We need to make a plan," Benaiah said. He cleared away some of the leafy soil and sketched a map. For the next few minutes, they discussed the best strategy.

They reached an agreement, then crept into the cave Gareb had mentioned. It faced the town. As they waited for darkness to fall, Benaiah asked Gareb how he knew about it.

"We used it when we were hunting David years ago," he answered simply.

They huddled together in the entrance as the last rays of the sun behind them dimmed. They would wait inside the cave until nightfall.

Gareb picked up his sword and scraped the blade across a stone. "I wonder why David did not drink that water today," Gareb said.

"You know why," said Benaiah.

Gareb nodded. He drew a breath. "I was Jonathan's armor bearer."

They stared at him.

"We know," Benaiah said after a few seconds. "David told us not long after you arrived in our camp after Gilboa. He recognized you. He told us not to bother you about it, and that you would tell us in time."

"I thought he had abandoned us years ago," Gareb continued. "I was there, on Gilboa, when Jonathan fell. He sent me to David. Hardest moment of my life. I hated David. Thought he should have died on Gilboa and not Jonathan."

Gareb looked away from them and outside the cave. The breeze picked up, suddenly chilly. Benaiah pulled his cloak over his knees.

"Yahweh uses broken men. I don't know why he uses David, why he uses any of us." Benaiah said quietly.

They listened as the wind increased.

FORTY-THREE

Ittai did his best to lift his face off the ground. His vision cleared, and he could smell the wood smoke from campfires nearby. A deep cut on his lip throbbed. Wincing, he let his face rest on the sharp pebbles once more.

It was still light out, but evening was closing in. He lay on his chest with his hands tied behind his back. Every area of his body was wracked with pounding, driving pain. His smashed jaw throbbed, his broken nose was swollen and tender. The Hebrews had beaten him mercilessly, and he was surprised to still be alive. Not only that, but he realized that his wounds had been treated with oil and bandages.

He tried to lift his head again, but a voice spoke out of his line of sight.

"You ought to rest."

Ittai turned his stiff neck until he could see the form of a man sitting next to him, leaning against a boulder. He recognized him as the Hebrew demon warrior.

Ittai hesitated, unsure how to respond. Had this man spared his life again?

"I expected to be dead," he mumbled at last. The movement of his lips forced the cut on his lip to reopen, and he tasted blood as it trickled into his mouth.

"You fought well," the Hebrew replied in the Philistine tongue. His breath was labored.

Ittai watched him. The Hebrew looked equally bad. His face was covered in cuts, and his clothing hung in tatters. His exposed thigh displayed a wicked-looking gash that had been closed up with bronze clamps to staunch the bleeding. They protruded through the bandage wrapped around the leg, dark stains seeping through the wool.

More interesting, though, was the bandage wrapped around his right hand. It bulged to a girth much larger than a fist, and out of the top of it jutted a broken sword blade. The Hebrew was resting his hand in a bowl of heated oil. Ittai could see slight wisps of steam rising from the bowl.

Noticing his gaze, the Hebrew said, "Physician says it will loosen the hand by heating it."

"I thought your people hated physicians."

"Hmm."

Ittai moved his head to see where he was. He lay at the edge of a large clearing at the top of a hill, with several ravines and rocky draws breaking away from the summit. On one end of the clearing was a large stone pile that looked as though it guarded a cave entrance leading into the depths of the mountain. The forest surrounded the clearing and stretched beyond the cave until it ended abruptly at the foot of a bluff, the highest point on the mountain. As a commander, he could not help but admire the tactical genius of such a spot and was amazed that the place had not been discovered by his own people.

"You would need water access if you were here a long time," he thought aloud.

"Normally not a problem, but the springs have dried up. Yahweh has not provided rain."

"I saw storm clouds over the eastern sky today."

"It goes no farther than Bethlehem. The rest of the kingdom is dry until the plains. Yahweh has withheld the rain," the Hebrew repeated.

"Your god is powerful."

"He is the only God."

Ittai said nothing. Before this day, he would have answered quickly and defended his patron until death. "Tell me about him."

The Hebrew shook his head. "Perhaps later."

"Why did you spare me?"

"Yahweh wanted you to live. I felt it in the covering."

"The covering?"

"Perhaps later," the Hebrew said again. He coughed, hard. Then he leaned his head back against the stone and closed his eyes.

Ittai asked the question that had been nagging at him all day. "Why is Keth of the Hittites in your ranks?"

If the Hebrew was surprised at this knowledge, he did not let on. "He came several years ago when many others did. You would have to ask Benaiah."

"So the rumors of Benaiah are true?"

"They are. Many of your countrymen probably fell by his club today."

Ittai nodded. "It must have been him I saw earlier. He and Keth."

"He has a Hebrew name now as well. Uriah."

"What does it mean?"

"Yahweh is fire."

Ittai had to agree. On this day, in these fields, their god had shown that he was fire. If a man like Keth had thrown in his lot with these Hebrews and their god, perhaps ...

Ittai shook his head, too tired to think. "Give me the honor of knowing your name, warrior," he said.

"Eleazar ... the son of Dodai." He took a labored breath. "Tribe of ... Benjamin. Yours?"

"Ittai. Of Gath. I suppose you are part of David's Thirty."

"Yes."

Ittai watched him for a bit, as though looking for the sign of the Hebrew god's favor carved somewhere on his body, for no man could battle the way this man did without his god's favor. He blinked and closed his eyes himself. He was too tired and too hurt to puzzle on it further.

But he could not sleep. The mighty warrior who fought next to Eleazar in the field and then vanished would terrorize his dreams.

FORTY-FOUR

In the cave overlooking Bethlehem, the three of them dozed in and out of restless sleep.

"Benaiah?" Keth whispered, his voice muffled by his cloak.

"What is it?"

"Do you think this will matter?"

Benaiah did not answer at first. Then, after a while: "It has to." He shifted in his position. "I still cannot believe Abner is dead. I will kill Joab myself."

"We need every man right now, including Joab," Gareb said.

Benaiah turned and stared out into the blinding storm, then laid his head back down.

"This is the best time to hit them. Philistine sentries are lazy."

"These might not be regular Philistine sentries. It's possible that not all of the Sword troops marched out against us," Keth said.

"I'm getting weary of dealing with them. Perhaps we should just pay them to fight for us," Gareb said.

Keth smiled. His sickle sword was clutched against his chest and his bow was on his lap. A layer of mist covered the iron blade, and he wiped it clear every few seconds to keep his mind off the impossible task they were about to attempt.

Benaiah leaned forward once more and stared at the sheets of gray rainfall. He was the only one who could see down the slope from the cave.

"Now!"

In one motion, all three of them shifted forward and rolled out of the cave. Benaiah was on his feet first and immediately sprinted down the mountainside, leaping between the rocks, Gareb close behind him and to the right. Keth felt his sandals sink into the mud between the stones, but he forced himself forward. Blinded by the drenching rain, he angled himself to the left toward a cropping of trees he had seen earlier.

The sentries were lazy, as Benaiah had suspected, and were not watching the tree line as they should have been, lulled by the sound of the rain into staring at the ground, snugly wrapped in their cloaks. Benaiah and Gareb split apart just before they reached the line, and Keth watched as Benaiah's blade slit the first man's neck. The soldier slumped forward. Gareb cut the throat of the second sentry.

Keth threw his short sword into the mud at the foot of a boulder and then climbed the stone. His bow was in his hand, an arrow notched, and he sent the shaft whistling through the storm toward the third sentry, who had just seen the attack and was rising to sound the alarm. The arrow thudded into his thigh.

Keth cursed the rain for distorting the flight path, then drew again and sent another one. The sentry was screaming a warning toward the distant city wall, but before he could finish his sentence, the arrow struck him in the side of his face. Gagging, the soldier went to his knees, the arrow slicing through one cheek and out the other.

Frustrated, Keth jumped down from the boulder and snatched his sword out of the mud. Benaiah and Gareb were moving toward the gate and about to disappear from sight, so he ran after them as fast as he safely could. A peal of thunder, and the rain suddenly increased again. Lightning flashed for the first time.

A glance told him the sentry was too wounded to rejoin the fight. Keth wasted no time finishing him off. He reached the path at last and pressed toward the city wall. The plan was holding for now. The city was ahead of them, but Benaiah and Gareb had darted into the forest off the road.

The city was not their objective.

A dense stand of trees just outside the city walls made the road narrow, and Benaiah and Gareb took positions there, Gareb facing the town and Benaiah facing the direction they had just come. Keth raced past Benaiah, slipping on the muddy road but maintaining his footing.

Gareb nodded as Keth ran past his position. "We'll guard the road! Speed!"

On his right as he ran into the trees, even through the noise of the storm, Keth could hear the growing clamor of troops emerging from the town. The three of them had broken through the line, but the town had heard the screaming soldier, and now there would be officers organizing a counterattack. He needed to hurry!

He arrived at the small clearing in the forest with a small limestone cliff overhead, thick vines and forest plants growing down the side of it. The saturated trees were dumping rain water into the clearing, filling the wells to overflowing. Normally there were three holes in the ground in the center of this clearing, but the massive amount of runoff made the clearing appear to be a single lake. He hesitated, panting, afraid of emerging into the open where archers would cut him down. It would have been so easy to simply dip the water pouch into the puddles by his feet. It would not matter—water was water. But it had to be the well!

Pulling a small leather pouch from his waist, Keth dove forward toward the pool just as the first arrow from the city gate reached him. There was a gap in the trees that led to the archer's tower, cut many years previously to guard the well from intruders and bandits. The arrow hit a rock and splintered next to his foot. His head plunged into the mud, his body sliding through the shallow water.

Reaching the rim of the first well, Keth dipped the satchel down into the deep hole and let the water fill it. Pulling it out, he hurriedly tied the top off. Another arrow, then another splashed into the water nearby. Lightning was now flashing so frequently that he knew the Philistines could see every move he was making. He checked to make sure he still had his weapons, the bow and the short sword, then rushed out of the clearing back to the road.

Soldiers from the garrison at the town had reached Gareb. Their officer had sent them into battle without any plan, assuming that his men would be able to handle the lone warrior stationed on the road.

Keth watched as Gareb swung his sword left and right, killing the first three men to reach him. Dark blood filled the water at his feet.

"I have it!" Keth shouted hoarsely.

Gareb turned instantly. The two of them sprinted up the muddy tracks of the road toward Benaiah. Keth slapped him on the back as they passed, and the three of them charged forward into the first ranks of soldiers coming from the forest counterattack. They now had Philistines on all sides of them.

Unlike the commander in the garrison, the officer in charge of the forest perimeter was sending a more concentrated and disciplined force against the warriors.

"Wedge!" Benaiah shouted.

He went to the front, Keth dropped back to his right, and Gareb covered his rear left. They ran through the rain, their sandals slopping through the puddles. The dark trees overhead acted as waterfalls, dousing them. Keth felt a sharp pebble slide between his toes, and he winced in annoyance. He wiped his forehead clear of rain, then held his sword out to catch the first soldier.

The troops in the woods were assaulting in a mass formation, which meant that the three of them would need to stay tight in order to rupture back through the lines into the safety of the deep woods. Long pikes were aimed at them, troops behind shields in a frontal line bracing for their attack. It was a barricade that no fighting team should ever attempt to penetrate and expect to survive.

As Benaiah reached the first pike, he ducked low, reached up, and pulled the long shaft out of the soldier's hand while swiping his sword low across the man's shins. The blade bit deep and the soldier screamed. Keth and Gareb repeated the same move. The three troops who had formed the front of the column coming toward them on the road staggered forward, their legs crippled.

Fifty men suddenly lined the road ahead of them, and Keth realized that they would never be able to penetrate the concentrated ranks.

Benaiah saw it as well.

"Tight!" he yelled, giving the preparatory command for a change in their fighting formation. Keth lowered his shoulder and slammed into Gareb, and the two of them closed on Benaiah from behind until they pressed against his back as a huddled mass.

"Disperse and rally!" Benaiah yelled again, his voice piercing the storm.

Keth wrenched his legs to the right as he jumped over the bushes lining the road and rolled into the forest. Gareb and Benaiah did the same to the left, drawing the Philistine troops after them and away from the precious bag Keth was carrying. Keth heard the clash of metal as the soldiers took the bait.

He raced through the forest, water everywhere, the thunder

increasing in power and ferocity, lightning ripping through the clouds. He glanced up and felt his eyes fill with the liquid cascading down the tree branches, certain that this was the worst storm to ever confront these lands.

They were going to die; he was sure of it. His courage failed him, alarmingly fast. Despair bore into his heart. They would never get out of this alive.

Then fire roared over him in a torrent, searing into his scalp and fingers as though he had been struck by a bolt of the lighting terrorizing the sky above. He cried aloud as a man about to die, but the power was vicious, and before he could take his next breath, he felt his feet pushing through the undergrowth and surging runoff back to the line of Philistine troops leaving the road to pursue Benaiah and Gareb.

Keth's sword appeared in his fist, the bow across his back. Somewhere deep in his thoughts came the notion that he needed to escape, the desire for self-preservation commanding his limbs to cease their foolish errand, but he realized that the fury of the covering was not going to release him but drive him into the ranks of the enemies of Yahweh.

He burst out of the wood line next to the road and could no longer hold his arm in check. His sword lashed out and severed the first head it touched. His body tensed; then he twisted into a spin and cut down the next four soldiers in the ranks.

He was beyond comprehension of events, his spirit raging like the burning fire that refused to leave him, but he was suddenly aware of Benaiah and Gareb a short distance away, making their stand.

Blood and rain covered Keth's face; he could taste the copper flavor. The fire flared hotter and many more soldiers fell in front of him before he realized that he was facing Benaiah and Gareb, their own torsos covered with blood.

He jerked his head to the right and yelled in release at the sight of the Philistines fleeing away from them back into the woods toward the road.

Benaiah, panting, looked as though he were about to shout something at him, but Keth saw the light of recognition in his eyes. He knew what was happening.

That moment was all the covering allowed, because then Keth felt himself running forward again, pursuing the troops once more, cutting and slashing at them as he scrambled up the slope of the hill.

The pouch of water slapped against his waist, the precious liquid securely tied to his belt, and he hoped that if it fell the others would notice it. Benaiah and Gareb, gasping for breath, followed him back onto the road.

Keth killed Philistine after Philistine down the length of the road, turning to attack back toward the city from which more Philistines would come. Several turned to face him and fell before they could swing a sword. Then his bow appeared in his hands, and arrows flew and killed men, but he did not know what he was doing. The sword came back into his grip, slick with rain; he screamed and screamed and screamed. Philistines pleaded for their lives before he slaughtered them.

More ranks of soldiers appeared around a bend. Keth fought them. He never stopped running and leaping. He jumped off a boulder and dove over the heads of the first rank and tackled the officer commanding them. He slit the officer's neck with a dagger that appeared in his hand, then he threw the dagger at another man's face. It slipped through his teeth and into his throat, knocking him backward.

A spear hit Keth's skull from behind, but he felt it glance away harmlessly, miraculously. He turned, pulled the spear out of the man's hand, and killed him with it, then used it to kill more men.

More kept coming, and he kept killing them. The fire seared and drowned his senses like the fury of the storm.

Keth charged forward one final time, then realized that there were no more Philistines in front of him, no more blood to spill this day. Roaring, the fire slipped out of his head and chest and dissipated as quickly as it had come.

Keth fell sideways on top of a body. His lungs burned. Muscles suddenly ached, his head pounded, and he had no more energy, nothing left. He let the rain flow into his open mouth and allowed it to saturate his eyes and ears. He swallowed several gulps in a row before he realized what he was doing.

He shoved his finger down his throat and wretched all of the water back up. His gut clenched in aguish. White shocks of light appeared in his vision. He cursed himself for giving in to his flesh; the three of them had made their own water vow with David's.

Benaiah knelt down next to him, wary. "Did it leave? The covering?"

Keth, too exhausted to say anything, only nodded. He hoped Benaiah had not seen him drinking the water. Gareb arrived and knelt on the other side.

Benaiah nodded in return and wiped his face. Lighting flashed again. "Let's move, more may come," he said.

The two of them helped Keth up. He walked hunched over like an old man, his muscles and bones weary from the power that had assailed him. Helping him take the first few steps, Benaiah and Gareb pulled their friend through the trees along the side of the road.

They stumbled on through the forest, the shouts of pursuing Philistines dying away in the torrential rain. Gareb led them up the side of a mountain, following a washed-out crevice slick with rain. At the top, they collapsed into the cave they had left earlier.

Keth leaned against the cold walls and began checking himself for hidden wounds. A man could be mortally injured in the midst of battle and not know it. After looking over his midsection and legs, he decided that he was unscathed. He checked Gareb, who was doing the same with Benaiah.

When each man was satisfied that no one was unwittingly bleeding to death, they took off their cloaks and tunics to wring them out. The three of them shivered violently and eventually huddled together, skin to skin, while their cloaks dried out.

"Not a word of this to anyone," Gareb said.

"We would probably be stoned if I said something anyway," Benaiah said as his teeth chattered.

Keth, whose native culture did not have such prohibitions on male contact, grinned weakly. "I promise I won't say a word."

They listened as the rain picked up outside the cave entrance.

"Well done, foreigner," Gareb said.

"The ... covering," Keth replied, trying to steady his breathing. "Never felt it like that before. Must ... be what David has ..."

"I have never known it," Gareb said.

"He gave it ..."

"Wonder if it will show up that same way the next time you see that new wife of yours. Her beauty is already legendary."

Moments passed. The sound of the storm and their panting breaths were the only noises in the cave.

"Do you think this is reaching Adullam?" Benaiah wondered aloud.

"I pray to Yahweh that it is. They can send runners, but that won't be enough to take care of thousands of troops. The Philistines won't wait around for them to refill the army's supply," Gareb answered.

Benaiah watched as Keth stared at the puddles of cool water filling at the entrance. His eyes were glazed, his lips scaly despite being drenched.

"Our vow," Benaiah reminded him, whispering so Gareb could not hear.

Keth nodded wearily. He closed his eyes. No one could ever know his shame. Breaking the vow was unthinkable.

They listened to the life-giving rain fall outside the cave, praying that it would make its way to the west and their brothers.

FORTY-FIVE

The deep forest stilled as the sea breeze faded and the sun disappeared in the west, passing silently behind the distant hills. At the entrance to the cave, the troops who had fled from the Philistines and abandoned Eleazar organized supplies and stacked the remaining water pouches taken from the dead Philistines in the valley. There were enough to give each man a few more rations, but they took no hope in such promise. Their eyes darted warily to the cave as they worked dividing them up, careful not to raise the further ire of the king.

Eleazar opened his eyes. The pain worsened steadily. Every breath was labor. He had to fight off sleep. The Philistine commander lay quietly next to him, watching the troops stack supplies.

Eleazar listened to what the men were saying to one another when they thought they could not be overheard by officers, especially the veterans now streaming in from the south, the advance units of the rest of David's army being sent by Joab. The hollow of rocks Eleazar sat among enhanced the sound of nearby voices.

"He'll drink when we aren't watching," said a young soldier as he hoisted another pouch.

The veteran he was working alongside, a section leader who had been ordered to supervise, sighed. "You don't know this king. He isn't Ishbosheth."

"He won't keep the vow," the young soldier said, but Eleazar could hear the awe in his voice. The two of them resumed their work in silence.

Eleazar glanced down at the bandages covering his arms and legs. There were wounds of every type on his body: burns, scrapes, gouges. All were packed with hyssop and oil. Aides came every few hours to change the bandages, and Eleazar was too weak to resist. He was still covered in ash, a remnant of the purification ritual the priest had performed when he arrived in the camp. Eleazar had touched many unclean corpses this day.

"The sword is still in Eleazar's hand," came the quiet voice of the young soldier, who had stopped working again to look at him.

The sword was, indeed, still frozen in his hand. He looked at the shattered blade that now felt like it was part of his body. The muscles in his grip were locked into place. The physician had directed that it be heated in oil so the muscles could relax, though everyone was certain he had never treated a wound like it.

"They said that he killed so many pagans that Yahweh molded the hilt to his hand as a challenge to lesser men."

Eleazar heard the veteran chuckle. "Stop listening to third squad."

"Well, *have* you ever seen a man do that?"

The veteran arranged several pouches on the stack so that they would not fall over. "No," he said, "I have not. But he's one of the Three, and that's what they do."

Eleazar let his head roll to the side so he could see the working men. All had stopped and were staring at him in the growing dark, unaware that he was looking back at them.

"Well, I will never run again, not after seeing that. Praise to our God," the young soldier said.

"Arrows to our enemies," came the murmured reply of the group.

Satisfied, Eleazar allowed his eyes to close a moment, trying to ignore the thirst that gnawed away at him. The still night wrapped itself around him like a gentle blanket from his bed. He was rarely cold; his body would produce so much warmth that his wife was always complaining that he was going to burn her alive in their bed.

The pain in his chest sharpened. He inhaled slowly before holding his breath. Air leaked out of his ribs. There was nothing that could be done.

But he had held the ground. That was all that mattered.

He shook his head. His last thoughts would be of her, not war.

She was probably making a meal now. Children were crowding her while she worked, frustrating her so much that she would order them out. Then they would fight about who was not obeying her, and she would pull her hair in anxiety, sometimes tearing up in spite of herself. She cried too easily. He smiled at the scene in his head, and felt the despair, for the fourth time that hour, that he would never see them again.

He looked back down at the parchment on the rock next to him.

He had written the letter to his wife while he'd waited in the valley. He picked it up with bloody, trembling fingers. The script was shaky and hardly legible since his writing hand was still wrapped with bandages around the sword hilt, and he did not believe for a moment that the letter would make it through to her, nor was she even able to read, but he'd needed to write it:

Love,

This will come to you by David's hand. It means I am gone, and I trusted no other to deliver it. He owes me this favor. Honor him as king. Yahweh's spirit rests upon him.

Marry a good man. Make certain Josheb does not choose him for you, or else he will have a beak nose and refuse to bathe. Love him, wife. He will need it living with you, for you are as unruly as a mule.

Hold my children close. Tell them Yahweh will be with them even on the dark nights. Make certain my sons are warriors first and poets second. David's influence is only so healthy for a boy. But make sure they are there when he sings. Life has few moments of happiness. A good day of fighting, a good woman's love, good wine and food, and David's singing.

It looks grim for us. Many will fall. My life was lost holding the ground that no other could hold. I am grateful that Yahweh let me finish well.

Never doubt how much I have adored you. I want your memory to stay with me even into Sheol. You are Yahweh's blessing to me, and I have been only yours since we were young.

Eleazar had signed it with the secret name that only she knew. Tears were now splashed across the page. He lowered his face so the men could not see him.

Out of the corner of his eye, he saw the Philistine commander watching him.

Ittai finished working the knots loose when it looked as though Eleazar had fallen asleep. Before crawling away into the forest, he glanced one more time at the Hebrew warrior who had fought like a god and by himself had stopped the invasion.

The arm was propped up. Ittai assumed it would help with the swelling. He shook his head. There was much to ponder after what he had witnessed on this day. Never had there been courage and bravery like this Hebrew had shown. He tilted his head, acknowledging the warrior in his own way.

Then he slipped away into the night.

Eleazar watched him go through the barely open slits in his eyes. Apprehension flared up in him; it violated every principle of warfare. *Never* let your enemy escape to kill another day.

But the covering had spoken, and Eleazar obeyed.

He felt the deep, burning pain in his chest again. It was stronger this time than before.

There had been a blade strike that slipped through. He hadn't noticed it until they were back at the caves, assuming it was just more enemy blood. But his head was getting lighter, and his breathing more labored.

They would wonder why he had said nothing about the wound. But nothing could have been done anyway. Better to remember him as he was. Better for the men.

So it was done, then. It was his time. Sheol awaited. His path was run.

Yahweh, hold them close.

He gazed at the sky above. Blood was filling his mouth, but he didn't care. Only noticed the stars, and the distant storm …

… the army is out of the city now. Need to hurry, Rizpah, my love. Need to get to the Rephaim and stop the Philistines. Need to protect my home. Only a few more moments together.

"I see them," I say.

"Who?" she asks.

"Hebrews I have killed. I see them."

Her breathing is shallow. She listens a moment longer, but I cannot say anything else about it. I hope that she does not ask me further, that she just . . . knows.

"After the slaughter at Gibeon, I went to the Ammonite pleasure tents."

She goes still. Waits for what I will say. Anguish in her spirit now.

"But I fled. Came back to you. Forgive me, love. I did not go to her, but I wanted to."

She breathes again. Love her breathing, love her warm neck. Hope she forgives me for my wicked heart. Yahweh, forgive me.

"We have another one coming," she says.

"Another what?"

She tilts her head back and smiles. It has been forgiven. Undeserved mercy, God of my salvation.

"But we just had one!" I say.

"It isn't my fault!" she teases, "I am not the son of the mighty Dodai."

I look in her eyes as she stares up at me. They are the color of dark honey. My lips press against her forehead. Another child. I must be strong for them. Yahweh help me, I must be strong for them.

"I believe in you," she says.

"Why do you say that?"

"Because I know you need to hear it." She looks up at me. "I believe in you," she repeats.

She goes quiet again.

Praise you, Yahweh. You know what I need when I need it.

If your courage holds in the small battles, it will hold in the great ones.

For her. I pull her close . . .

FORTY-SIX

David was grateful to see fresh platoons streaming in throughout the night. A soldier would appear out of the gloom and report to the chief of the watch about the size and other necessary details of an incoming unit. There were fast-strike teams of twenty, special detachments of slingers and archers, platoons that were proficient with heavy pikes and axes. Men from all over the known world had come to David in the previous years, some out of loyalty to his legend, others looking for the ample wealth he was bestowing upon those who fought with him. He was happy to see them now, answering his summons as fast as they could.

Word came that Shammah was sending companies as soon as they mustered, choosing to rush warriors to their aide as they became available rather than marching a large, cumbersome force fully assembled. There would be more men available for the next battle because it would likely take several days for Philistine commanders to recover and begin another orderly advance.

The arriving men had only their own water rations, not enough to be sufficient for the whole army. Josheb organized platoons of runners to go back and forth to surrounding villages to see if any extra water could be strained out of the town's supply. David had decided that they could not abandon Adullam, since doing so would open the valley once more to the Philistines, so they had no choice but to rely on water that could be rationed or feebly gathered. Soldiers who had been injured during the day's fighting were being treated in the corner of the clearing near the cave. The archers had been struck the hardest by the enemy, and the remorseful glances of the foot soldiers did little to ease the wounds they suffered.

The Philistine arrows were barbed and impossible to extract neatly. When the first of the army physicians had arrived, he was put to work removing these arrows. Despite the victory, dozens of men had been killed or wounded in the day's fighting, and in the hours since the end of the battle, four had died of blood loss. With each death, a designated soldier called out an anguished cry to the camp, singing the song taught to them by their king to mourn the loss of comrades. Other men joined in the song, echoing it back and forth, singing both grief and praise to Yahweh for choosing them as his people.

The physician did his best, but by the late hours of the night, the last of the wounded archers was lost. When the herald sang the news that all of them were dead, he was greeted by silence. Many of the soldiers who had fled the day's fighting laid on their bellies in grief. They dropped the ash on their head from the sacrificed heifer, hoping that it would cleanse them of their guilt.

David wandered among them, too tired and too wary to sleep. His feet and legs quivered with exhaustion, so he stepped carefully among the rows of encamped Israelites, occasionally pausing to kneel next to younger troops huddled together near small fires for warmth against the night chill. He searched for things to praise them for, such as the skill with which they created their cooking fire pit, or the manner in which they had maintained their weapons. Terrified eyes greeted him wherever he went, the memory of him killing the failed Hebrew commanders still vivid in everyone's minds.

David walked into the forest and felt the cold night deepen. The bodyguard of Pelethite mercenaries, taking a shift while his Gittites slept, paused, afraid of evil spirits in the Israelite woods.

"Stay here," he said, doing his best to look disapproving. They nodded with relief and took up positions behind trees, vanishing from sight to anyone who might have been following them. David continued walking.

His throat rasped with every breath. Dry air coursed along his tongue and through his nose, aggravating the bloody cuts formed when the flesh inside of his throat split from lack of water and the constant breathing of dust. He found that inhaling through his nose kept the agony of the throat at bay but knew eventually the same would happen to that flesh as well.

David reached the edge of the woods and stepped out onto the moonlit stone. He gazed gratefully on the dark ridges stretching to the horizon, happy that he could see the view of his land that he so loved. In the distance, to the east, large thunderheads towered toward the heavens, occasionally flashing with lightning inside the clouds.

"Yahweh, forgive me for the sin that consumes me."

His voice cracked painfully. His eyes were too dry for the tears he yearned for, the cleansing tears of forgiveness that he knew would come when he confessed himself to his God. David hummed through broken and bloody lips the melodies of the music of praise. He knelt onto the stone near the edge of the cliff and raised his aching arms heavenward, swaying gently as he began to mouth the words of worship.

David watched the clouds and thanked God for the rain in that part of the land. Grass would grow, cattle would feed, cisterns would be filled. Far over the ridges to his right, he knew that his hometown was nestled in for the night. The people were probably terrified to be surrounded by Philistines, but they would be joyful at the coming of more rain.

"Send it to the whole kingdom, Lord of my people. To all but that cursed spot on Gilboa where Jonathan and Saul fell, send your rain of mercy. Find the wickedness in me and purge me of it. Cover my people in the day of war, Yahweh."

Leaning against the stone, he listened to the quiet sounds of night in the forest. A heavy weight descended on his eyelids. David blinked several times to clear his sight. The landscape was pale and marvelous as it spread before him and lulled him with its beauty. His heart ached for his land.

"The Lord your God is pleased with you."

David inhaled sharply. The skin on his neck quivered. Slowly he turned his head.

A large, powerful-looking man was standing with his arms crossed at the edge of the forest behind David. He had noble but hard features. His stare was severe, and David looked at the ground. The flicker of warmth that accompanied these messengers rose up in his heart.

"I am wicked. He should not be pleased with me."

"He knows of your repentance."

David let himself meet the warrior's eyes. He had to fight the urge to kneel, but the last time he had done that, he had received a reprimand. *Only kneel before Yahweh.*

"You have come to me before."

The warrior nodded. "Do you remember when?"

David said, "You were there when the bear attacked when I was young. And the lion. And the giant. You were the old man today. The one who stopped me from killing Korah."

The warrior nodded again. "You have many years of battle ahead of you."

David took a deep breath. "I had hoped for peace."

"You are not a man of peace. Rest will come to this land eventually, but not until you have poured yourself out as an offering to Yahweh."

David exhaled. His sorrow was almost overwhelming. But he nodded. It was as it should be. The warrior's stare burned into David. The figure was a cubit taller than himself, his eyes and hair a terrifying black. His voice was not harsh, but it rumbled as deep as the roar of an ancient river. He wore a cloak and armor. Battle-worn armor, not gleaming and perfect as David might have expected. David tried his best to examine him, although he could not hold the stare. What wars had he fought since time began? What untold magnificence at the right hand of Yahweh had he seen?

"Will you be there again? When I need the covering?" he asked the warrior.

"The Lord your God never abandons you, even when you abandon him."

David choked up and could not speak anymore. He saw the lecherous palace life he had been living. He had to close his eyes to avoid the stare.

"He knows of your repentance," the warrior said again.

David was so overjoyed that he leaned forward and placed his face in the dirt. The taste of the earth was dry and stale, how he felt in his soul, but that was changing now. New days would come. New chances. He had a scroll of the Law to copy. He would write out the Law and carry it with him all of his days, just as Yahweh had commanded.

"Will he send the waters again? My men need water. My people need water," David managed. "I need water."

He heard footsteps next to his head. The warrior's massive hand then covered David's bent neck. The hands were calloused and felt like the sanding tools of carpenters, a hand that had held a weapon through the eons of time and fought wars that David could never grasp. Then there was a feeling of warmth and oil that streamed through his hair and into his eyes, and he thought suddenly of the old days when he was a boy, and how the old prophet had poured the oil over his head, and the fire of the covering had ripped into his body and burned ferociously throughout his chest. And he saw his father glaring at him, and his brothers would never sing songs about him, and then, through darkness, the Lion roaring.

"The Lord your God is sufficient for you," rumbled the voice of the warrior. "Remember this in the dark days ahead, when you will be tested. You will lose many dear to you. But the Lord your God will be sufficient."

Then all was quiet.

David felt the chilly night air drift back over him. He was too exultant to move, too eager to stay in this place of joy and life to return. Yahweh had not abandoned him, even when he deserved it. But who else would he lose? He lost Jonathan. Was that not enough?

"Reveal my faults to me, Yahweh. Show me where I am weak, where I am vulnerable."

His vision became dizzy. Suddenly overcome, he lay on his side and closed his eyes. Sleep overtook him ...

She has been returned to me, brought by Abner, but Michal's head is bent. Everyone leaves, we are alone. She does not look up at me. I do not know what to say. It has been long, she has been defiled by another man, there are other women in my chamber.

"You were my prize. I loved you from when we first met."

She does not answer, looks at the ground.

"I want you back."

Her eyes flash bitterness and anger. "My family is destroyed because of you. My father, brothers, all of them."

"What happened? Between us? Why did you betray me to your father?"

"You left me, and then you took others."

I could give her reasons. Alliances. Maneuvering. My heart is heavy. Those were not the reasons. You were my first love, Michal. You must know my grief.

"Is the king finished with me?" she asks.

"Yes."

She leaves, hates me still. Go then. Go back to the harem, nothing more than a concubine to me now. Yahweh, why ...

Saul and Jonathan slain on the heights. I hold his crown. My brother gone. So much death, so much sorrow in our lands. I see him now, lying in a pile of dead Philistines. I hope he killed many of them. I hope he slew hundreds upon hundreds and tasted their blood before going to Sheol ...

And now I stand in a wave of corpses rising from the earth, their bodies fastened together by my blades. They are ghostly white, limbs stretching out to me, their black eyes screaming. Men I have killed, men I have known who are now slain. They all scream and reach for me, and the wave rises ever higher on the slopes of Mount Gilboa.

But it parts when it reaches the crest, where the body of Jonathan rises up to touch me on the wave. The valiant prince's body impaled by arrows, his ribs torn apart by lances, his eyes lifeless. He does not scream, but his dead eyes are crying, tears are flowing down his face and pooling on his chest.

I try to push my way through the corpses to him, to hug him one more time ... but the darkness, and flame, and the roar of a lion, terrifying and powerful ...

When David awoke, the moon was out, crowning the distant thunderstorms with a burnished silver gleam. His heart was racing. He took several deep breaths through his burning throat to steady the wild pounding in his chest.

I'm in the forest, near Adullam, battling the Philistines.

He breathed again.

Not on the slopes of Gilboa. It was a vision. A dream. Yahweh has shown me where I am weak.

He looked around, trying to think of something other than the wretched vision. He would think on it later.

The storms were no closer to them, but instead stood atop the mountains where the Jebusite city lay. The sight of them gathering in strength and reaching to the heavens calmed him.

Yahweh was bringing rain.

Not where we are right now, he thought, but where we need to be. There will be enough when we need it. *You have never abandoned us, oh God. Give us rest from our enemies.*

David got to his feet, his mind functioning again. The Philistine army would counterattack soon, and it would be larger, reinforced by more troops from the Bethlehem garrison, and bent on avenging the day's defeat. Yahweh had promised victory. But they were low on supplies; strict rationing would continue.

He trod carefully back into the forest, his body protesting the lack of water, quietly humming his songs through a painful throat, hoping the men would hold out, and hoping he had what it took to lead them.

FORTY-SEVEN

The storm poured itself out over the eastern mountains, drenching the town of Bethlehem and the surrounding valleys, stopping short of Adullam. But it had come, and there would be life again in the Hebrew lands. Word spread that the Jebusite city was their next destination, and it gave the men hope, because the rumors were that water would now be overflowing in that country. The Philistines had been routed and would not come again until they could regroup.

In the morning, three men, haggard, bloody, and caked in dried mud, stumbled to the entrance of the cave. As they passed, a voice challenged them.

"Tell my lord that we have retrieved his refreshing drink," Benaiah rasped heavily.

There was commotion, and men appeared in the early morning light outside the dark entrance. One of them came forward on uneasy steps, refusing the assistance offered to him.

"What did you do?" David asked, trying to keep his back as straight as possible so that the troops did not see how sick he was.

Several hundred soldiers had gathered around, emerging from caves in the ravine nearby. Benaiah repeated himself. "Delivering your drink of Bethlehem water. From the well."

"When did you leave?"

"When it was decided yesterday."

Angry, David said, "You had no right to leave, we might still have been engaged."

"Yahweh's armies fought yesterday, great king. And you never use me anyway," Benaiah said. David's features softened in the fading light.

"We saw the clouds in the distance yesterday evening. I was going to send men to retrieve water."

"Yes, lord. We knew you were thirsty."

"All of the men are thirsty," David said.

"Not like you. We vowed not to take a drink until you got this water."

"You went through the Philistine garrison, alone, in the storm?"

"Not alone. Uriah lived up to his name. Yahweh was his fire," Gareb said, then glanced, smiling, at Keth. Benaiah was supporting him by holding him around the waist. Keth reached for the pouch tied to his belt and untied the cords. He handed it to their king.

The king gazed at the bag a moment.

"You could have filled it with water from any source. You could have simply held it open in the rain last night."

"Yes, we could have."

David hesitated, then reached for the bag as though it were a small child and clutched it to his chest. "I am unworthy of this act," he whispered.

Benaiah said, "We are all unworthy."

Gratitude overwhelmed David, and he could say nothing further. The troops all gazed in wonder, believing that surely he would drink *this* water.

One of the men called out, "Lord, we know you are willing to suffer with us, so please, quench your thirst!" Others echoed him until it rose to a loud chorus of encouraging shouts.

David walked away from them toward the cave. When he reached the entrance, he turned to face them again. He looked around at the army. The regular troops were pleading with him to drink and end his suffering.

The Thirty, however, said nothing. They knew what he needed to do.

David stared at each of his Mighty Men: Josheb. Benaiah. Gareb. Uriah. He thought of Shammah doing his duty humbly back at Hebron, not complaining when he was ordered to stay; Eleazar still up on the hillside, his sword frozen in his hand from hard battle.

Their faces were covered with grime, blood, and dried sweat. Each man of the Thirty, knowing what he was silently asking them, silently answered by shaking his head. David looked at Benaiah, Gareb, and Uriah again. They shook their heads as well. David understood: *You drink when we drink, you eat when we eat. Show the men. We are with you until Sheol takes us.*

David opened the pouch of water filled from the well of his youth, more valuable to him than any of the treasures he had ever won.

"I will not drink what was purchased with the blood of brave men," he said to the group, his voice strengthening. "Only one is worthy of such a sacrifice."

David lifted it up to the heavens. He whispered something, a prayer of offering to Yahweh, his heart aching with love for these men.

Then he poured it out.

EPILOGUE

David knelt by Eleazar. He ran his fingers over his warrior's wrapped sword hand.

Benaiah, Gareb, Josheb, and Uriah knelt next to him. Eleazar's breathing was very light; the movement in his chest was only perceptible when David laid his ear on it.

David looked up and searched for the face of the army physician who had come into the camp earlier. "What was it?"

"It looked like a sword slipped through his ribs. It went deep."

"Will he live?"

"I do not know, lord. It went deep," he repeated.

"Do everything you can! Don't let him die!" David shouted at the man.

The physician, startled, backed away and bowed low to the earth. "Lord king, by Yahweh's strength I will do everything I can, but Sheol reaches out for him."

"He has a wife and small children. A Philistine force ten times as large as the one we fought today is coming. *I need this man.*"

"Yahweh gives and takes," Benaiah said. There was no anger in his voice, though. Only sorrow.

"Where is the Philistine commander?" Gareb asked.

"Must have escaped. He will know where we are and bring troops here. Probably more Sword of Dagon troops," Benaiah answered.

David fought the feeling of hopelessness swelling up. The thirst was still there. Terrible, terrible thirst.

They could not grieve, could not rest until the pagans were gone. Yahweh, strengthen us, he thought. For Eleazar. For your land. The cost is too great. *Be with him in Sheol, great God of my people.* He reached over and put his hand on Eleazar's shoulder.

They all sat together for a long time, until the land grew quiet and cold, and the stars dimmed with the coming of the morning sun.

NOTE TO THE READER

The identity of the three Mighty Men who broke through the Philistine lines to retrieve the Bethlehem well water is not known for certain. The Bible gives us only tantalizingly vague information and phrasing such as "three of the thirty chief men" (the typical English translation). Some scholars say it was Josheb-basshebeth, Shammah, and Eleazar, who are mentioned in the immediately preceding paragraph. More likely it was another group of Mighty Men that was later inserted into the story to mention yet another amazing feat that displayed the love the troops had for their commander and king. So, as always, I tried to give an answer that is consistent with the Bible and fit within the Lion of War story parameters.

As for the rest of the book, I took a long series of complicated guesses and arranged things chronologically in a way that (1) fit within the biblical narrative and (2) fit the story in my head. I based my sequences and timelines on historical research but ultimately had to adhere to the story when making crucial decisions about events that are not clear in Scripture.

Of all the periods of David's life that I intend to fictionalize, this was easily the most difficult to arrange, and the one I beg the reader to allow the most leeway with.

Portrayed here is the theory that seems to work best about whether David attacked Jerusalem immediately after being crowned king. As John Bright wrote in *A History of Israel*, it's not likely that he would take such a risk when he knew the Philistines would be coming for him. I think Bright is right on this. More likely is the account in 2 Samuel about the Philistines invading the Rephaim "when they heard of David being crowned king" and that being his most pressing concern, not the capture of an impregnable fortress.

The impact of a single great warrior on the tide of battle has rarely been in dispute, Eleazar being the focus in this instance. Wars are won or lost based on the combined efforts of a large group of men working together, but the actions of the individual elite are always instrumental in a given engagement, especially as inspirational material for other, less stouthearted troops. Eleazar's magnificent stand was recorded in the histories precisely because it was magnificent, and would have poured courage into the hearts of lesser troops timidly awaiting the next nightmare of battle. There likely developed around David and the Giborrim a cult of personality that drove weary, outnumbered men onward through impossibly desperate situations.

I benefitted greatly in my studies of the psychology of warriors by looking at Dr. Jonathan Shay's books *Odysseus in America* and *Achilles in Vietnam*, as well as *On Killing* by Lt. Col. Dave Grossman. Also, the volume *The Military History of Ancient Israel* by Richard A. Gabriel is an outstanding resource for many of the nuts and bolts of biblical battlefields—even though it appears we disagree on the supernatural nature of the Bible.

As always, this is fiction. Please regard it as such. The errors within are entirely my own.

ACKNOWLEDGMENTS

Thanks to my friends Todd Hillard, Nic Ewing, Mike Altstiel, Lee Rempel, Jerry Smith, Jeremy Banik, Adam Haggerty, Jesse Ewing, and Bryan Yost for being essential to this project from the start. Thanks to Katie Doerksen for helping me keep my sanity and schedule. Thanks to Keith Scheffler and Larry Watkins for locking shields.

Thanks to my agent, Joel Kneedler at Alive Communications Literary Agency, who goes above and beyond the call, steps up to the plate every time he's needed, and gives me steady and firm career advice. You were the missing link in the team, and I am excited to have you in our corner.

Thanks to David L. Cunningham, Grant Curtis, and John Fusco for their vision as they bring the Lion of War series to the big screen, as well as Nicole Nietz, Alden Dobbins, Uli Kimmich, Matt Finley, Jeremy Wheeler, Mitch and Amy Wheeler, and all of the team members at Global Virtual Studio and GiantKiller Pictures for their work on the movie front. It has been a blessing to get to know each of you.

My heartfelt gratitude to Chaplain (Col.) Gordon Groseclose for taking me under his wing for a few weeks at Fort Sam Houston;

the chaplains at the U.S. Army Chaplain Center and School at Fort Jackson, South Carolina, who trained me; Col. (ret.) Jim O'Neal, for his poignant insight into combat thoughts and behavior; Dr. Heath Sommer of Idaho State University, who gave invaluable support to the combat stress theory as a psychological trauma expert; and a host of other experts in battlefield psychological trauma. My gratitude to Dr. Scott Carroll with the Green Scholars Initiative/Museum of the Bible for expert assistance. To Faith Beckloff for all the top-notch design work.

The team at Zondervan: Cindy Lambert, Sue Brower, Alicia Mey, Don Gates, and Jackie Aldridge. Special thanks to Dave Lambert for applying healthy and hard pressure to me to make this as good as it can be, and to Bob Hudson for batting "cleanup" with his deft touch.

My church families at Rimrock E. Free, Alamo City Christian Fellowship in San Antonio, and Alpine Church in Utah, for all being instrumental in the season I was with them. Special thanks to David Walker, Jerry Smith, Bryan Dwyer, Steve Bennetsen, Bill Schorr, and Scott Creps.

Thanks to my dad for always being my first reader and biggest champion.

As always, the biggest thanks is for my wife, Cassandra, for putting up with me. Joshua, Levi, and Evan, I love you and am always proud of you.

I wish to finally thank the wounded troops at Brooke Army Medical Center, Fort Sam Houston, Texas, for letting me hang around them for a couple of hours. No one knows your story but you, but we are as grateful as we know how to be. Those who have experienced the hell of battle walk a lonely road, much like a group of men three thousand years ago, desperately trying to establish a homeland, and following a leader who alone understood them.

ABOUT THE AUTHOR

Cliff Graham lives in the mountains of Utah with his wife and children. He is a military veteran and currently serves in the Army National Guard Chaplain Corps. He travels around the country, speaking and writing about David and his Mighty Men.

You can follow him on Twitter @cliffgraham or on Facebook.

For the author's blog, updates about the Lion of War books and upcoming movie series, author speaking requests, and other general information, please visit http://www.lionofwar.com.

The Lion of War Series
by Cliff Graham

Book 1: *Day of War*

Book 2: *Covenant of War*

Book 3: *Song of War*

Book 4: *Fires of War*

Book 5: *Twilight of War*

Lion of War Series

Day of War

Cliff Graham

Day of War, author Cliff Graham's first novel, has earned him a film option for the entire book series—Lion of War—from director David L. Cunningham (*Path to 9/11*) and producer Grant Curtis (Spider-Man films).

In ancient Israel, at the crossroads of the great trading routes, a man named Benaiah is searching for a fresh start in life. He has joined a band of soldiers led by a warlord named David, seeking to bury the past that refuses to leave him. Their ragged army is disgruntled and full of reckless men. Some are loyal to David, but others are only with him for the promise of captured wealth.

While the ruthless and increasingly mad King Saul marches hopelessly against the powerful Philistines, loyal son Jonathan in tow, the land of the Hebrew tribes has never been more despondent—and more in need of rescue.

Over the course of ten days, from snowy mountain passes to sword-wracked battlefields, Benaiah and his fellow mercenaries must call upon every skill they have to survive and establish the throne for David—if they don't kill each other first.

Available in stores and online!

Share Your Thoughts

With the Author: Your comments will be forwarded to the author when you send them to *zauthor@zondervan.com.*

With Zondervan: Submit your review of this book by writing to *zreview@zondervan.com.*

Free Online Resources at

www.zondervan.com

Zondervan AuthorTracker: Be notified whenever your favorite authors publish new books, go on tour, or post an update about what's happening in their lives at www.zondervan.com/authortracker.

Daily Bible Verses and Devotions: Enrich your life with daily Bible verses or devotions that help you start every morning focused on God. Visit www.zondervan.com/newsletters.

Free Email Publications: Sign up for newsletters on Christian living, academic resources, church ministry, fiction, children's resources, and more. Visit www.zondervan.com/newsletters.

Zondervan Bible Search: Find and compare Bible passages in a variety of translations at www.zondervanbiblesearch.com.

Other Benefits: Register to receive online benefits like coupons and special offers, or to participate in research.

CPSIA information can be obtained
at www.ICGtesting.com
Printed in the USA
LVOW08s1912070717
540616LV00009B/46/P